SUBVERSIVE DISCOURSE

SUBVERSIVE DISCOURSE

The Cultural Production of Late Victorian Feminist Novels

Rita S. Kranidis

ST. MARTIN'S PRESS
NEW YORK

© Rita S. Kranidis 1995

All rights reserved. For information, write:

Scholarly and Reference Division,
St. Martin's Press, Inc., 175 Fifth Avenue,
New York, N.Y. 10010

First published in the United States of America in 1995

Printed in the United States of America

ISBN 0-312-10739-0

Library of Congress Cataloging-in-Publication Data

Kranidis, Rita S.
　Subversive discourse : the cultural production of late Victorian feminist novels / Rita S. Kranidis.
　　　　p.　　cm.
　Includes bibliographical references and index.
　ISBN 0-312-10739-0
　1. English fiction—Women authors—History and criticism.
　2. Literature and society—Great Britain—History—19th century.
　3. Feminism and literature—Great Britain—History—19th century.
　4. Women and literature—Great Britain—History—19th century.
　5. English fiction—19th century—History and Criticism.　6. Women's rights in literature.　7. Discourse analysis, Literary.　I. Title.
PR878.F45K73　1995
823'.8099287—dc20　　　　　　　　　　　　　　　　　　　　94-29336
　　　　　　　　　　　　　　　　　　　　　　　　　　　　　　CIP

Interior Design by Digital Type & Design

*I dedicate this book to my mother,
Sevasti Doulou Kranidi, who always said
there ought to be more to women's lives
than men and children, and encouraged me
to accomplish all she could not.
I know she would have been pleased.*

TABLE OF CONTENTS

ACKNOWLEDGMENTS viii

INTRODUCTION: SOME PRELIMINARY CONSIDERATIONS ix

1. IDENTITY CRISES AND PROTEST:
   THE LATE VICTORIAN CULTURAL SUBJECTIVITY 1

2. "THE IDEA IS THE FACT":
   ART'S INTERIORITY AND LITERARY PRODUCTION 23

3. THE POLITICS OF PUBLICATION:
   WOMEN IN THE LITERARY MARKETPLACE 47

4. LATE VICTORIAN FEMINIST DISCURSIVE AESTHETICS 71

5. DEFINING THE POLITICAL:
   THE "REALISTIC" APPROPRIATION 107

ENDNOTES 129

WORKS CITED 135

INDEX 141

Acknowledgments

I am grateful to Helen Cooper and E. Ann Kaplan for their suggestions, criticisms, and enormously helpful input. Very special thanks go to Michael Sprinker, who has guided and shaped my interest in class issues over several years. All three have been instrumental in the book's strengths, which I am sure would still be some sort of a draft if not for their help.

Thank you to Mara Kranidis for responding to the earliest drafts with insight and enthusiasm. I would also like to thank Donesse Champeau and Mita Datta for their invaluable responses to early drafts.

At Radford University, my thanks go to Steven Pontius for his support, to Carolyn Sutphin for her typing and goodwill, and to Vickie for countless small favors. I am grateful to Gail Cunningham, Elaine Showalter, and Patricia Stubbs for bringing the feminist novels to my attention; they piqued my curiosity not only about the feminists, but about the cultures that produced and then rendered them invisible, also.

Finally, I thank my family for their unconditional love and constant encouragement, and Sandy for reading and marveling at these novels with me, and for making it all worthwhile.

INTRODUCTION

Some Preliminary Considerations

When I began this project I had two very simple questions: first, what constitutes oppositional literature, specifically in the context of late Victorian England? and second, how can progressive, feminist literature successfully insert itself into mainstream discourse and maintain its political purpose, that is, without compromising its message in the process? I wanted to read some late Victorian feminist novels in order to address these questions, because I knew that the last two decades of the nineteenth century were a time of social unrest, featuring extensive socialist and feminist agitation. It was interesting to me that such political activity appeared alongside the aesthetic and decadent movements, especially since in literary history it was better represented. One heard more about the latter in discussions of the 1890s, than about revolts and the challenges to normative ideologies. It remains one of the main features of the period that feminist discourse is often contradicted and overshadowed if not altogether negated by aestheticism. This period is also interesting to investigate because it features a quite inclusive reading public resulting from the Education Acts of the 1870s. It has been noted that "by 1898 *no* county's literacy fell below ninety per cent for either sex" (Lee 1976, 33). As such, the 1890s also introduce the element of feminists' really appealing to a diverse public through their writings. That 1890s progressive writing and the question of the function of political writing relates not only to literary readers but to a *mass* readership is especially apt, because it is precisely the *generally* social function of progressive literature that I want to explore.

Holbrook Jackson, author of *The Nineties* and a contemporary of the period he describes, notes that in the 1890s "social conscience overtook the terrain of interest in metaphysical consciousness," and argues that this is evidenced by the volatile social activism of the period ([1913] 1950, 17). This description stands out as a central one in accounts of the decade, in that it points to the importance of the social and political contexts to the cultural discourse of the nineties, all of which I concern myself with here. The shifts in focus and values experienced during the period may explain why the issues that characterized the 1890s have traditionally been treated as particular to the period exclusively and hence not appropriate for other humanistic inquiries. It may be, as the theorist Walter Benjamin has said of Proust, that "much of the greatness [of this body of literature] will remain inaccessible or undiscovered until [our own] class has revealed its most pronounced features"—that is, until we account for the prejudices of our own age, not least among which are prejudices concerning history, gender, and power relations, which have informed how the nineties have been read as a culture and as a literary period (1968, 210).

Women's scholars have long found and revealed in their works the invisibility of women as social and political subjects. Works by Elaine Showalter (1977), Patricia Stubbs (1979), and Gail Cunningham (1978) proved invaluable to my appreciation of feminist authors of the 1890s. In some instances, they served as bibliographic guides through whom I could rediscover women authors, virtually all of whom were once widely read but are now out of print. In other cases, they served as companions as I sorted through various accounts of the period, many of which treated women as marginal figures. However, helpful as these sources have proven to be, my questions and priorities took my examination of the feminist writers and their texts in a direction different from theirs. While I do not stop to document my deviation from their conclusion during the course of my discussion, I felt and feel that there was not enough attention paid to the specifics of late Victorian cultural subjectivity, notions of aesthetics, and cultural production as systems relevant to all genders and across class lines.

My research does in fact reveal a sinister relationship between public discourse and history, and shows that historical accounts of the 1890s (and, by definition, history as a discipline) are permeated by inaccuracy and confusion, depending on whose account is being considered.[1] Some of the confusion is created by that lag in time that Benjamin has shed much light on: the lag between events, their immediate reception, and their subsequent perceived meaning in retrospective accounts such as Jackson's. Consequently, in establishing my approach to the historical accounts of the nineties and attempting to rectify some misrepresentations, I found that thinking about the art of any age needs to be a threefold project, and that it needs to include 1) the period's view of itself, that is, the widely shared cultural self-definition that, in the process of asserting itself, projects fantasies of itself; 2) current interpretations that work to shape the general understanding of the period and to rewrite its dynamics; and 3) finally, a critical perspective that will enable a view of the period that would incorporate cultural imaginings as well as historical events into the final analysis.

Apart from the enormous amount of research this approach would require, it further proves to be a difficult task, since, as Louis Althusser has argued, "while there is *one* (Repressive) State Apparatus, there is a *plurality* of Ideological State Apparatuses . . . [and] [e]ven presupposing it exists, the unity that constitutes this plurality of ISAs as a body is not immediately visible" (1971, 144). This last point is by far the most significant—and problematic—part of my approach, because it calls for a historically specific reading of the 1890s, including that culture's internal contradictions. As a first step, arriving at a revisionary formulation of the events encompassed by the nineties makes it possible to transcend the many contradictions in the discourse of the age by reading that discourse in its original, multifaceted contexts. By the same token, since "there is no such thing as a purely ideological state apparatus," discourse itself becomes only one of many instrumental "sites of struggle" in reconstructing the contexts of nineties' literature, since texts respond not only to established discourses but also to unarticulated and misrepresented realities (Barrett 1986, 95). In short, neither the discourse (whether literary or extraliterary) nor the contexts to which it makes explicit reference can be accepted unconditionally. Given the kinds of questions and problems that cropped up during my preliminary exploration of the period, my two initial questions eventually led me to examine the settings of these novels, including: the literary marketplace of the nineties and the status of the novel within it; the cultural and political climate of the 1890s, including the British imperialist project; late Victorian definitions of normative cultural subjectivity; and subversive narrative strategies. Therefore, while this study concentrates on late Victorian novels written by women's rights advocates and on other novels that take issue with the women's rights movement, it also works to recharacterize late Victorian culture in order to provide the appropriate context for thinking about these works, that including aesthetic ideology and notions of legitimated subjectivity. Nineties' feminist novels keep pointing to their social, political, and ideological contexts, and these contexts invariably focused on a changed public forum, a different "culture" amid which feminists wrote. An examination of the "new" public reveals some important relationships between feminism and other progressive movements, but also a suspect, superficial identification between women and the "masses," which I discuss in the first chapter.

The analytic model I found most useful for contextualizing 1890s feminist novels, and that got me doing far more research than I had anticipated, is a model outlined by both Terry Eagleton and Michele Barrett, who stress both the ideological and material bases of literary texts. Specifically, in *Women's Oppression Today*, Barrett proposes for feminist theory and criticism a "theoretical framework in which broader questions are built into the method" of literary analysis. These questions include: 1) The General Mode of Production, which seeks to account for the effects of economy and labor;

2) The Literary Mode of Production, i.e., the production of texts and literary categories; 3) General Ideology, including culture's self-definitions and national politics; 4) Authorial Ideology, concerning individual authors' beliefs and prejudices; 5) Aesthetic Ideology, which examines the ramifications of evaluations of texts and their contexts; 6) The Text itself, which manifests the culmination of the relations between the above categories (101-102).

These categories are not always so distinctly or clearly illustrated in the texts themselves, nor do they all manifest an equally important influence. But it is important to isolate as many of them as possible, especially those that appear to have acted as censoring forces against progressive and other nonmainstream texts. By extension, one cannot assume an essential subjectivity for the feminists, nor for the Realists or the antifeminists. None of the authors lends herself to that kind of understanding or treatment, since all of their relationships to the issues at hand, namely gender and literary aesthetics, were fairly temporal and inconstant. It is feasible and important, however, to name their apparent political positions and agendas as they figured in the dynamics of various moments during the period. Finally, with these considerations built into literary analysis, the text is no longer privileged as an "object of art" but can be viewed as a product of economic/material circumstances and, in terms of cultural analysis, of ideological determinants. As an example of the uses to which Barrett's theoretical framework can be put, the conceptual lags I alluded to earlier necessitate an exploration of the space that exists between belief and practice, ideology and its enactments, but also of the ways in which their relationships are often obscured. The need for historical research once again becomes apparent, but a historically based analysis of this kind needs to also be an exploration of the *mediations* between these relationships, defined by Fredric Jameson as "the establishment of symbolic identities between the various levels [of culture and society], as a process whereby each level is folded into the next, thereby losing its constitutive autonomy and functioning as an expression of its homologues" (1981, 39). An exploration of the socially symbolic relationships among late Victorian politics, culture, and art, and the subordination of women's autonomy as writers and social beings, makes it possible to "allow general matters and specific events [to] recover their original urgency . . . [by telling them] within the unity of a single collective story" (19). An acknowledgment of the cultural and political "mediations" accompanying literary texts in the 1890s makes it possible to construct such a "story," a narrative that includes not only events as they were perceived and represented generally, but also includes the marginalized discourses that commented on such events as they sought to change them.

Introduction

At the center of this investigation, as in other feminist literary and critical projects, is the presumption that in considering "literary production, distribution, consumption, and reception, we should attend to the different ways in which men and women have historically been situated as authors," and, I would add, as cultural subjects (Barrett, 17). Therefore, my analysis considers that while in the 1890s both men and women became significantly repositioned in relation to their work and their readers, it was male writers such as George Moore, George Meredith, and George Gissing who acquired cultural recognition for producing revolutionary representations of female subjectivity, while feminist novelists such as Mona Caird, Sarah Grand, Olive Schreiner, and Mary Cholmondeley were generally dismissed as sensational or overly subjective. Feminists were granted only secondary status as authors and as cultural commentators, both by the publishing world and the social agents defining literary aesthetics. The political mission of feminist novels, as well as their marginalized place in the establishment of late Victorian aesthetics, compromised feminist writers' status as literary figures and compelled them to engage in some interesting, albeit often compromising, negotiations with their novels' subjects through a series of remarkable experiments with literary form.

Insofar as the feminist novel served as a political tool for the women's rights cause, it is noteworthy that its positioning in relation to audience and its relative value as "art" were determined by other cultural developments and by the novel's own fluctuating status as commodity in a constantly changing aesthetic, political, and moral climate. One of the censoring forces with which the feminists had to contend was the late Victorian cultural climate, as I illustrate in Chapter 1. When Salisbury took office in 1895, a conservative and elitist cultural climate set in, and progressive writers found that they had to do battle with a newly legitimated traditionalism and reactionary rhetoric. Hence, part of the problem I encountered in attempting to delineate the "late Victorian feminist literary aesthetic" was the extent to which feminist writers were forced to address some of these censoring voices through their works: In fact, this argumentation with conservatism proves to be a key component of the feminist novels I analyze. The 1890s feminist literary aesthetic foregrounds narrative attempts to intrude on social discourse and to engage in a series of discussions attempting to either appease or discredit the conservatives and reactionaries of the period. One of the many ways in which feminist novelists attempted to counter High Culture's aesthetic proscriptions was to address the exclusivist implications of its discourse in their novels: Invariably, criticism of the aesthetic status quo is woven into the formal construction of feminist novels. In working to define the political objectives of women's rights activism and the feminist agenda for themselves and their readers, feminist novelists engage in social and literary criticism as well. One strategy feminists employ in characterizing the feminist heroine and advocating transformations in gender definitions is to construct a revision of the traditional literary female heroine. They accomplish this by combining the conventional, tradition-bound figure of womanhood with the enlightened New Woman, whose object is to liberate herself and other women completely from patriarchal repression. And yet for the feminists, this new type of heroine is more a literary and political attempt than an actualized, accomplished fact or an established type. The New Woman one encounters in feminist novels remains an unknown in many ways, because she has not yet materialized socially. For the feminists, then, the New Woman serves as a theoretical concept and as a dynamic social projection, and as such is continually revised and refigured. Nonetheless, feminists use her as a model of political and social independence, and contrast less liberated women to her, in formulating their critiques of patriarchy.

In addition to their understandable preoccupation with conservative rhetoric, feminist novels of the 1890s also testify to the multidimensional character of late Victorian feminism and hence to the various relationships between feminists and mainstream culture and politics. Always, at the very outset, feminist novels' own internal politics stand in a polemical and oppositional relation to the dominant cultural and literary ideologies. Thinking about feminist texts of this period is further complicated by the fact that the last two decades of the nineteenth century were a time of transformation in the publication, circulation, and reception of novels. As I discuss in Chapters 2 and 3, primary among these changes was the advent of "new journalism," a mode of publication through inexpensive newspapers and journals that capitalized on social problems as sensational subject matter while it also, inadvertently, provided a forum for radical social commentary. While feminists made ample use of this new medium, they were often commodified and sensationalized by it, so that they had to remain actively engaged in experimenting with literary form and courting an audience among novel readers. Prior to "new journalism," the production of the novel was controlled by the circulating library system headed by Charles Mudie, who imposed the "young girl standard," according to which novels had to be appropriate reading for a general and presumably naive audience, including young girls whose morals had to be sheltered from potentially corrupting influence. Authors' protests against Mudie's moralistic censorship would benefit feminist writers enormously, since its elimination provided them with various other means of publication such as independent presses and alternative journals, mediums that enabled them to initiate more frank discussions concerning women's compromised status in society. Nonetheless, none of the publication alternatives available to the feminists was free of external censorship and ideological proscriptions, so feminists initiated a series of narrative strategies that would enable them to write faithful to their political objectives.

Concerned more specifically with aesthetic ideologies, Chapter 2, entitled "The Idea Is the Fact: Art's Interiority and Literary Production," also examines the impact of aesthetic theory as it evolved from the earlier Carlyle and Ruskin to Arnold and Pater, and notes the conservative and reactionary features of late Victorian aesthetics. A consistent movement toward a separation of the social from the "aesthetic" (or High Culture) spheres, and the exclusion of social reality from aesthetic discussions, reached its climax with the aesthetic movement of the 1890s. The deliberate and forced exclusion of social "fact" from the realm defined as "aesthetic" is important to any discussion of late Victorian oppositional literature, because it served to negate an important component of the feminist novelists' project: namely, enhancing social activism with supporting narrative accounts of the need for female emancipation. Mainstream, nonpartisan aesthetics served either to "privatize" feminist concerns and themes, or to exclude them from High Culture and to group them with Low Culture and issues concerning the "masses." As a result, the potentially empowering referentiality between the feminists' novels and their social activism was compromised; negating any connection between life and literature, the dominant aesthetic ideology opposed feminists' attempts to make public, and to theorize and politicize, women's "private" lives. In these and other similar ways, feminist issues were not considered appropriate "cultural" material, and feminist novels were ideologically distanced from the social and material contexts upon which they relied for their legitimation. Paradoxically, feminist novels were in this singular, sweeping gesture remanded to the vaguely "cultural" realm, so long as they were disqualified as *literary* texts. When they could be said to have some cultural value, feminist novels were not seen to possess it as "fine literature"—their value was always subliterary. Chapter 3 illustrates some of the practical ramifications of this kind of censorship and evaluation of women's texts.

My study of late Victorian feminist novels reveals that their authors resisted mainstream appropriations and proscriptions of women. Progressive women writers such as "George Egerton" made it very clear that they would not presume to stereotype woman, or to create a literary or cultural metaphor of her, but would basically allow her to remain an unknown—an "enigma." Unfortunately, this strategy also presented some complications, since Egerton's act of resistance would be interpreted as a manifestation of her "aestheticism," insofar as she presumably refrained from acknowledging the "externals" of women's lives, as I elaborate in Chapter 4. Hence, in addition to the dangers of marginalization, feminist authors also faced the danger of appropriation.

In the case of the "feminist-related" novels I discuss in Chapter 5, novels that have unconventional women as their subjects, the New Woman appears as an interesting contrast to the heroine constructed by the feminists. In novels by the Realists, the social phenomenon of the unconventional woman is co-opted and utilized in order to serve the Realist literary agenda. She is either apolitical in not defining herself as a member of a repressed gender class, is represented as elemental, or is neutralized politically by being combined with a more traditional model of womanhood. The Realists, then, used the same strategy as the feminists, but to very different ends. In these novels, duality serves to eliminate the possibility of the enlightened New Woman's existence and her authenticity. The Realist model of womanhood that encompasses traditional and radical characteristics disallows the possibility and the validity of the feminist conception of the New Woman, who, according to the feminists' formulations, embodies both tradition *and* acts of rebellion against it. Unlike feminist models of womanhood, Realists' representations of women accept and utilize normative cultural female types and do not attempt to redefine them. Certainly, they do not appear to be politically committed to constructing an effective characterization of the New Woman, and they appear to see and make literary use of her as challenging subject matter. In short, Realists simply utilized and re-presented a problematized female subjectivity already constructed by the feminists, both in their novels and through their social activism. The late Victorian cultural appropriation of feminists and feminist oppositional activity was effective enough so that both their texts and social presence are now encountered as a hidden subtext in the most forcefully promoted late Victorian aesthetic theories.

1

IDENTITY CRISES AND PROTEST: THE LATE VICTORIAN CULTURAL SUBJECTIVITY

Despite the decline of national religious sentiment and the increase in suffrage, and despite all the agitation of socialists, Irish Home Rulers, and feminists in that decade, it may well be the most striking fact of the 1880s that a revolution did not visibly take place.
Donald Stone, *Novelists in a Changing World* (1972), 16.[1]

♦ ♦ ♦

In the last two decades of the nineteenth century, feminists wrote novels that furthered the women's cause. Given the political nature of that project, and the ways in which the gender hierarchy maintains other social and political hierarchies, it would not make much sense to consider feminist novels of the 1890s as *oppositional* political literature without first establishing the politics of the culture in which feminist literature was situated and to which it responded. Here I want to consider how both feminist texts and the women's movement were situated, culturally and politically. These contexts are especially important since they determined the forms the feminist novel would take, as they shaped the women's movement itself. A quick glance at late Victorian literature, whether fiction or newspaper articles, makes clear that the prevalence of specific concerns, including "the woman question," national identity, and the "masses," are issues that appear beside one another consistently enough to merit an investigation of the relations between them. The dynamics of these relationships reveal nineties' culture as something other than monolithic or unified in any way. Rather, the decade appears as a series of crises and dissonances, and elicits the question, "Why did a revolution not take place?" In this chapter I outline both the ideological and material contexts of 1890s literature in order to consider its relationship to the social questions it foregrounds. To the extent that literature serves as a reflection of culture, the circumstances that contributed to the cultural character of the 1890s often find their expression in its literature, itself transformed through the displacement of "High Art." As Hobsbawm has pointed out, the tone of *fin-de-siècle* literature "can hardly be understood without knowing the general economic and consequently social malaise" out of which it grew (1987, 35-36).

The 1890s in England have been summed up by Holbrook Jackson, one of its contemporaries, as featuring three main—if contradictory—characteristics: "1) Decadence 2) Introduction of the sense of fact into literature and art (i.e., a heightened appreciation of "truth," defined as being distinct from subjective apprehension) 3) Development of transcendental view of life" (Jackson [1913] 1950, 17).[2] In *fin-de-siècle* England, art came under public and intellectual scrutiny as it exhibited a problematic relationship to the formation of a new national identity. Nineties' literature has traditionally been typified as an embodiment of art's vulnerability to external influence and compromise and has, as a result of this characterization, long been slighted as the subject of serious critical inquiry. Therefore, studies of the 1890s such as those by Holbrook Jackson, Richard Altick, and Ernest Baker have traditionally tended to focus on either the aesthetes or the Realists, both of whom have been considered suitable subjects for study since they had pronounced aesthetic and, it would seem, more "literary" agendas. Other kinds of turn-of-the-century literature, such as the then-popular women's and sentimental novels, have been compromised because of their close association with forces that destabilized literary standards during the nineties; namely, the prominence of the popular press and the arts catering to the "masses." For it did happen that "the traditional status of high culture would be undermined by the arts appealing to the common people" and that art itself would undergo what Hobsbawm calls an "identity crisis" such as the middle classes were also experiencing (220). Against this historical context, I will examine in this chapter the impact of social and political change on late Victorian culture In chapter 2, I will then proceed to examine its aesthetics.

In examining late Victorian politics and culture, it becomes apparent that we are dealing with at least a dual reality: one, of material conditions, and the other, of England's projected self-image, or of the fantasies it promoted of itself. The general transformations of the period that are important to situating feminists and feminist literature in context included various understandings of oppression, repression, and difference, accompanied by the predominance of directed questions concerning art and aesthetics. Underlying cultural change, fluctuations in the economy and in political leadership were important in contributing to the character of the period and to its redefinitions of art and literature. Between expressed ideas and their enactments lie ideological and material mediations, and so the interdependence of the spheres of art, culture, and politics is extremely important. English imperialism, women's concerns, labor, and capital present themselves in problematic relations in the 1890s, relations in which self-representations constitute responses to an often unacknowledged but instrumental cultural and political subtext. First, a conservative government was reinstated in 1895, while in that decade Britain's expansionist efforts were challenged by competition from Germany, France, and the United States. Furthermore, amid economic and political fluctuations, domestic unrest challenged England's activities both at home and abroad. Late Victorian cultural hegemony struggled to both conceal and accommodate the economic insufficiencies that it promised belonged to the past, while it promoted fantasies of affluence and omnipotence. The available facts suggest that "the trade cycle, which forms the basic rhythm of a capitalist economy, generated some acute depressions from 1873 to the mid-1890s" (Hobsbawm 35). As Hobsbawm argues, by the 1890s the British economy was operating not according to "the wisdom or practicability of production, but its overall profitability," a practice that enhanced fantasies of prosperity while it failed to meet the real needs of the majority of English people (53).

The severe consequences of these economic developments had an impact on late Victorian society and thought, so that by the nineties, cultural discourse took on a decidedly practical tone: "intellectual, imaginative and spiritual activities were concerned mainly with the ideas of social life, culture, [all of which] endeavored to answer the question 'how to live'" (Jackson 26). Jackson thus pointed to a prevailing concern with social and economic problems, one that became increasingly pragmatic and activism-oriented. It was during the late Victorian period that the middle classes, including women, "learned about the situation of [the working classes] and came to see them not as passive objects of pity but as people who had to organize. In many cases, this experience radicalized the middle-class observers"

(Rowbotham 1985, 63). Part of this "radicalization" consisted of thinking about the poor as a social class and was instigated by literature itself: Potter's *Pages from a Girl's Diary* was published in 1888, while Charles Booth's *Life and Labour of the People of London* began appearing in 1889. Although the appearance of such socially enlightening literature was not unprecedented, Booth's work "told a much more serious and documented story than Mayhew's" had earlier and revealed that one-third of London's people were living in poverty, a statistic that in effect established the poor as a population and as a class (Cole 1961, 15). Given the new awareness of class as a social problem, and the easy access that the public had to this information, the most innovative among artists and writers began to address the problem of the common people's material existence with a sense of urgency that was tantamount to politicizing late Victorian society, giving second place to earlier preoccupations with morality. Due to the new awareness just described and the internal unrest and dissonance this social-ism generated, the 1890s in England feature a culture that increasingly lost its previously rigid hierarchical social structure and gained a far more disorienting scope. The cultural margins of 1890s England were perpetually extended to include yet another previously unacknowledged irregularity, yet one more Other, both in terms of domestic politics and in relation to colonialism.

In addition to this informational and sensational literature concerning the lower class, the political activities if not the writings of Marx and Engels had a remarkable impact on late nineteenth-century English thought by addressing the problems of the day, just as Macaulay, Carlyle, and Ruskin had spoken to an earlier generation. Yet more important than any question of intellectual influence was England's domestic politics, which proved conducive to scrutiny and harsh criticism. That social problems needed to be addressed immediately became increasingly apparent with the installation of Salisbury's Conservative government, which managed to highlight class and social inequities:

> The Imperialist initiative was bound to be unofficial and entrepreneurial, because Victorian England was always an expanding society, and because in late Victorian England the divorce between politics and society as a whole was widening. Government remained in the hands of an aristocratic class whose social influence was being whittled away, and whose responses to changes in that society were bound to be defensive and disapproving. (Tuchman 1962, 357)

It is precisely this ideological divorce of politics and society that needs to be mended so that the dynamics of late Victorian culture and society can be addressed. The condition of the working classes, for example, would deteriorate as colonial ventures had tremendous consequences for domestic labor and class politics. Reflecting a trend that had begun much earlier, more than half of all British savings were invested abroad after 1900 (Hobsbawm 220). Both economically and socially, governmental emphasis was not on domestic issues but on foreign interests; this system of priorities took its toll on the working classes after 1895, and Salisbury's government proved far less "populist" than that of his predecessor, his elitist values standing out as eccentric if not altogether anachronistic. Salisbury's notorious antidemocratic stances toward enfranchisement and labor legislation for the "masses" effected a decidedly conservative turn in late Victorian society. Barbara Tuchman's description of "The Patricians" notes that Salisbury was not interested in "the people" and that his influence restored old class antagonisms; "He did not believe in political equality. There was the multitude, he said, and there were 'natural' leaders" (11). The elitism that Salisbury enabled and facilitated during the period is important since it informed the literature and aesthetic discourse of the decade, while it also prompted a more concerted effort on the part of progressive activists to promote their social and political agendas. It is also important insofar as it complemented the promotion of the fantasy of British omnipotence, which required that domestic dissention be negated. For while Victorian foreign policies engendered visions or "fantasies" of an England that produced extensions of itself wherever it turned its figurehead until it finally encompassed nearly half the globe, within England itself the 1890s were a battleground for the "masses," including both middle-class women activists and the working classes, against the established order.

At this point, Judith Williamson's analysis (1986) of the negation of cultural diversity or difference within capitalist patriarchy is useful, because it foregrounds the problematic relations among economy, politics, and culture and provides us with a configuration of their interdependence:

> The daily grind appears meaningful only because of the life outside it. The social structure is justified not only in social but in personal and individual terms. This shows how separations of difference, the opposition between terms, produce a meaning not just in theory but everyday life. . . . (110)

> It is difference that makes meaning possible, and though in reality [certain] spheres are not separate, it is their separation into sorts of ideological pairs that gives them meaning. (103)

Williamson's point, that the cultural Other is simultaneously exploited and eradicated, puts emphasis on the ways in which Others and Otherness are variously used toward repressive ideological ends such as the promotion of the sense of cultural unity. Others are denied recognition, inclusion, and multiplicity of purpose, so that cultural dissention is subordinated to a higher purpose, that of enforcing the fantasy of the dominant culture as self-sufficient. Hence, as Williamson concludes, "[e]conomically we need the Other, even as politically we seek to eliminate it" (113). This concept of ideological impositions and mediations also helps account for antagonisms between progressive movements of the 1890s when there was no real political claim at stake. For example, feminists were as much inspired by socialists as vice versa, but the two rarely allude to one another as a source of influence, nor, given their common goals, did the two movements collaborate as much as one would expect, which may help account for why there *was no* "revolution" as such during the period, as Donald Stone observed (16). In the last two decades of the nineteenth century, politically grounded ideologies promoting "difference" between social and economic classes discouraged class and gender-group identifications and created distortions in what must now be perceived as a network of influences that constituted the complex late Victorian cultural economy. Not coincidentally, it is during this time that Social Darwinism experienced its height in popularity as social analysis, the ramifications of which were not favorable to women and to the working-class "masses." As Raymond Williams has observed, the tenets of Social Darwinism were "consciously in opposition to liberal egalitarian tendencies, to measures of social welfare and reform, and classically to ideas of socialism" (1980, 90-91).

Among the most visible and socially active agents of political and ideological mediation of the 1890s were the philanthropic and otherwise liberal organizations prominent during the period, groups that sought to provide redress to social problems in a variety of ways. Social consciousness, or the awareness concerning the lower classes and women, had by the 1890s become a category in itself, one that elicited concern not only among labor unions and women's rights activists, but also among middle-class idealistic organizations that did not align themselves with existing political movements and that resisted forming coalitions with other groups. Nonpartisan groups and the even less political philanthropic societies often served to displace and subvert the specific political agendas of more legitimately formal progressive movements such as labor and feminism. Starting in the early nineteenth century and extending into the 1890s, such independent organizations grew very popular, but came to have primarily a social rather than political mission. These organizations included The National Association for the Promotion of Social Science, the Society for Promoting the Employment of Women, the Women to the Workhouse Visiting Society, the Women's Co-Operative Guild, Ladies of the Prison Committee, and the Board for Poor Law Guardians. These philanthropic societies made no large political claims and insisted on remaining "neutral" through a policy of nonaffiliation, at least in theory. Philippa Levine, Martha Vicinus, and other feminist historians of Victorian women agree that philanthropic societies were a positive force in shaping the women's movement because they enabled women to enter the public realm and to break free of domesticity, starting in the mid-1900s.[3] While this is a valid and important observation, philanthropy cannot be seen as entirely helpful in terms of the political aims of the feminist movement later in the century, since it never asked that women band together as a class with self-serving causes. Compared to 1890s women's activism and political philosophy, philanthropy appears rather as institutionalized and politically circumscribed activity that once again asked women to be self-sacrificing and self-negating. The best organized among such liberal organizations, the Fabian Society, founded in 1883, listed "permeation" of the political apparatus as its top priority and saw the equality of the classes as predestined and inevitable. The society's political agenda stated that "their aims could be realized most easily, they believed, by a policy of winning over the leaders of the established political groups," and much of its particular brand of reform was directed toward this goal (Adelman 1986, 8).[4] This objective of "infiltration" was contrary to those of the labor movement and, in retrospect, may have done more harm than good where specific issues were at stake and in terms of the more radical movements' general impact. Lacking a concrete alliance with the classes it represented, and situating itself centrally in debates on class and other social inequities, the Fabian Society and similar idealistic reform movements masked the presence and importance of more overtly political groups, and obscured the role women activists and the working classes played in challenging the general social and political climate. Such organizations ultimately operated as "reconciling" agents in that they served to buffer the visibility and impact of the more radical movements' narrower, explicitly stated, and more radical objectives. Margaret Cole points out that the Fabian Society, even as one of the more progressive among such organizations, adopted a number of dubious positions concerning some of the most important issues of the time:

> On all these three [the South African War, the Education Acts, and the Tariff Reform Campaign], the Society ... took up ... a line

> so widely at variance with the general consensus of radical and Socialist feeling that, had political groupings been as sharply defined as they were fifty or even thirty years later, it would certainly have been expelled from the organized Labour movement or forced into resignation or resolution. (95)

In contrast, the labor unions seem to have been aware that seemingly separate issues concerning governance were closely related. Women's rights activists recognized that political and social change had to be instigated on various grounds, had to be demanded, possibly even forced. And they recognized that each of their actions challenging the extant political structures would have far-reaching implications and consequences.

Insofar as the labor and women's movements worked to undermine the legitimacy of extant political structures and "reconciling" organizations sought to work within them, they often worked at cross-purposes, (although both sects shared the common egalitarian goal of social progress). Hence, the two prominent radical movements that stood in direct opposition to late Victorian elitism and oppression are the middle-class women and the working classes, both of which constitute two of England's "internal contradictions." They generated a series of by-movements exemplifying oppositional and antagonistic resistance to the Victorian status quo and were to prove all too volatile and decisive in determining the tone of the decade. Middle-class women and the laboring classes had long been instrumental in the economy's essential workings, but their inclusion had thus far been so exploitative in nature that it effectively guaranteed their marginalization and exclusion from power. Long eluded by governments in power, the women's and labor movements had by the 1890s consolidated their agendas on several issues concerning women and labor, and had become powerful oppositional voices. One instance of this coalition is the Match Workers' Strike of 1888, which was organized, led, and carried out by women, but became a victory that encouraged the work of union organizers in other fields (Hobsbawm 220). Despite their nonidentification with one other, both the labor and women's movements used similar strategies in establishing themselves as networks focusing on a series of related projects opposing established rule. Most important, their agendas consisted not only of separate immediate objectives but of unifying themes encompassing the concerns of workers' various demands and needs, as my overview of the women's activists' multiple agendas will illustrate. Gradually "more male trade unionists were beginning to see the need to work with the women and sens[ed] the wider implications of female industrial militancy," as Rowbotham observes, so that feminists and labor activists often supported each other's actions in different parts of the country, endorsing issues included under their own umbrellas (62). Both feminists and labor leaders sought to effect change through campaigning, mass strikes, sanctions against industries, and publicity and mass propaganda, all multifaceted strategies that enabled them to persevere in the face of powerful resistance.

It would not do, at this point, to assume that women's activists were so unified and effective that they "mentored" the labor movement, since complications often arose between the two because the majority of women's rights activists were middle class; feminists' commitment to labor reforms was complicated by this, and their self-definition as progressives in the area of labor was daunted by their class identity. Hence, working-class women, who by and large did not identify with the women's movement (although the movement acted on their behalf on many occasions) aligned themselves most closely with the working-class movement. Still, the general impression of the "masses" excluded both women's rights activists and women in general as a culturally recognizable political body. Much of the skepticism on the part of working-class women was well founded, since feminists active in labor reform were often quite "philanthropic" in their approach to the problem of female workers' exploitation. At the same time, feminists were becoming increasingly aware of classism among their ranks. As early as 1876, Frances Power Cobbe noted, in an essay entitled "The Two Classes of Women," a great disparity between the "affluent" women "lapped in every luxury which the hands of loving fathers and husbands can give them" and the majority of women, pointing out that affluent women were a minority in the population of women in England. Cobbe elaborated that at the other end of the class spectrum are "several hundred thousand women—perhaps there are a million or so—who are very poor, struggling sorrowfully, painfully, often failing under pressure of want of employment, or of grinding oppression and cruelty from those whose duty it is to protect and cherish them."[5] However, given that women's rights activists were taking steps toward a primary gender identification that would encompass class differences, it makes the most sense to treat women as a single class here and to make this category inclusive of the dissention and distrust it encompassed.

Apart from the ideological coercions political movements encountered in late Victorian culture, some of the conflicts that existed among them were founded on significant differences in constituency, objectives, and philosophies. But there are other sources of dissention as well, less easy to define. The 1890s can be viewed as representing a critical moment in capitalism's and nationalism's evolution in England despite dramatic increases in production, according to Hobsbawm's analysis. Hence, it is helpful to consider that capitalism "need[s] some imbalance, something other than itself: riddled with contradictions, it is not internally sufficient," and thus needs to create excessive and materially unfounded relations of difference that act as metaphors for its material, economic inequities and insufficiencies (Williamson 112). The cultural production of "difference" is always difficult to look past in cultures in transition because ongoing negotiations in self-definition are understood to constitute social expressions of that culture. Middle-class women and the working classes had historically been subjected to the coercion and oppression of bourgeois standards that imposed from above the facade of a homogeneous national and cultural identity. Revolutionary feminists and socialists, speaking as radical self-defined subjects in the midst of that tradition, demanded not only acknowledgment and occasional victories but permanent empowerment toward self-representation and self-determination. Significantly, Britain's power to define *any* national identity in the 1890s, especially those of the peoples it colonized, was contingent on domestic English culture's ongoing ability and authority to define itself. In the face of protest and agitation coming from within its own national and cultural boundaries, "exclusivism" and an elitist hierarchy served to appropriate and contain threats posed by England's own internal "Others," the disgruntled "masses." At the height of empire in the late nineteenth century, England's self-representations were constructed along class and cultural lines, to highlight English culture's distinctness from and superiority to both foreign cultures and its own disenfranchised subjects. The structures English culture and politics relied on for legitimation were both geographic and chronological: English culture of the 1890s contrasted itself to cultures of the past and to the foreign, deliberately excluded cultures of the colonized. Colonized Others were used toward the dominant culture's maintenance of its self-image of omnipotence and domestic uniformity. In this respect, foreign Others constituted an important if often unacknowledged part of England's national and cultural identity. Much like women, they figured as variable signifiers to serve the ideological needs of the present moment in the dominant English culture's attempts at self-aggrandizement.

Quite significantly, along these lines, the main link between the various progressive social movements in late nineteenth-century England appears to have been their not always conscious opposition to nationalist ideology, the one "fantasy" that was promoted and popularized to all alike, regardless of sex or class. Nineties' writings and activism came out of, and responded to, a context of nationalist and colonialist ideology, a social education in imperialist thought that was, paradoxically, quite insular in its attempts to safeguard its tenuous hold on Others. For British nationalism, the problem eventually became that "an Englishness centered exclusively on such [repressive] institutions could hardly hope to mobilize the people in its defence. What about the others?" (Dodd 1986, 7).[6] Hence, while English culture relied on "Otherness" and "Others" for its self-definition, it was also not able to entice its own alienated subjects to act in the interests of the desired national unity. Such support had to be actively recruited. H. G. Wells, a critical if overly subjective historian of the nineteenth century, provides one account of the zeal with which social education in nationalism was promoted:

> Throughout the nineteenth century, and particularly throughout its latter half, there [was] a great working up of . . . nationalism in the world. . . . Nationalism was taught in schools, emphasized by newspapers, preached and mocked and sung into men. Men were brought to feel that they were as improper without a nationality as without their clothes in a crowded assembly. . . . ([1920] 1961, 782)

According to late Victorian imperialist ideology, people held a place of cultural privilege as long as they were native English, regardless of sex or class; that is, as long as they were the products of English normative institutions and socialization. The assumption underlying such vast generalizations relies very heavily on an already enforced "sameness" and its parallel negated "difference." This polarization of the self and the Other was problematic, because the move toward a single, unified national identity conflicted with the 1890s' self-conception as a "popular" age at the same time that it witnessed a remarkable rift between conceptions of High and Low Culture. The rift between a presumed homogeneous subjectivity and the enduring dichotomization between High and Low Culture resulted in a "breakdown of certainty [which led to] a growing alienation of intellectuals from society" (Gilbert and Gubar 1986, 949). The outcome was also the alienation of the privileged classes and the reinforcement of the masses as a distinct class.

Louis Althusser has argued that all "ideology hails or interpellates concrete individuals as concrete subjects, by the functioning of the category of the subject" (1971, 173). In terms of English nationalist ideology, then, it is significant that English "subjects" obtained at least part of their identity from the larger, tenuous trade market and the extended British national boundaries that effectively repositioned them in relation to their work and their value as labor power. The production of the late Victorian national and cultural identity was economically, politically, and socially implemented, propelled by a dominant bourgeois culture that sought stability and affirmation of its status as certain governing reality, that is, as "authorized" governing body. In the 1890s, the meaning of "subject" required redefinition since it could also include other nationalities and cultural identities. Hence, at the very height of empire, the English citizen experienced an identity crisis of her own, one that required that she be afforded her due as *primary* English subject. Demarcations between the self and "Others" became more distinct, serving both practical and ideological functions. Notions of difference became radically important as applied to the common English citizen, especially as the "subjects" being produced as a laboring class were increasingly unpredictable in their viewpoints and political positions. Contradicting and implicitly challenging the English nationalist stance of cultural superiority, common English subjects, the underprivileged "masses," and women of both classes emphasized a need for assured and adequate wages, education, and political representation. During the economic crises of the 1870s and onward, "the skilled worker in industry was as usual the first to be sacrificed by the employers," as she was in times of national instability (Adelman 14). Challenging the ruling ideology that promoted and at the same time controlled notions of cultural difference through nationalist and imperialist ideologies, 1890s' mass movements worked on establishing a mass identity and promoting sameness and identification with the Other. In practical terms, the working classes and women's rights activists began to define themselves as repressed Others, as having been colonized and exploited by England, in relation to the established and complacent middle classes. The difference between earlier women's activism and that in the late Victorian period lies mainly in the fact that during the 1890s, the women's movement intersected with the labor movement in some critical ways. Their culturally aberrant process of self-definition may be accounted for by the fact that "mass culture depends on (and participates in the making of) technologies of mass production" and therefore reinforces the "homogenization of difference," as Huyssen argues (1986, 9). Thus, the working-class advocates' agenda, especially as it was stated by the delegates at the Second International, challenged the nationalist ruling ideology of the period when it concluded that "if class was not . . . the primary loyalty of the worker, then it followed that his interests like those of any citizen were bound up by the national interests of his country," which was most clearly not the case (Tuchman 502).[7] Identification with national interests was clearly perceived as an undesirable alternative by the working class, since for them, difference was delineated along class and not national lines. National and imperial interests were all too clearly not those of the "masses," especially as "the terrible riddle posed by the nineteenth century" became obvious: "the greater the material progress, the deeper the resulting poverty," as Marx had already argued (Hobsbawm 35).[8] By the late nineteenth century, large-scale manufacture overtook other industry, resulting in "sweated industries" of an enormous underpaid class.

Because of these complexities in defining social subjectivity in relation to the national status quo, unity among the various oppositional groups was hindered by the fact that each occupied a position of materially and ideologically imposed and internalized understandings of "difference" in relation to the political apparatus but also to one another. Unfortunately, the central obstacle to forming a solid coalition on shared issues was the extent to which these groups were ideologically and politically complicitous with Victorian gender ideology. As Rowbotham illustrates, "cultural and sexual attitudes about female inferiority continued and contributed to women's economic compliance," so that labor leaders felt justified in keeping women out of skilled, better-paid jobs, and forced women into lower-paid, undervalued work by keeping an almost exclusive focus on male laborers (59). Given their displacement in labor, in conceptualizing the character of the women's rights movement in the 1890s, it helps to see women as having been compromised both materially and culturally. The material constraints imposed by gender ideology were starkly revealed by the women's movement, which addressed women's economic needs. As a result of their double marginalization, both in the dominant culture and in the labor movement, women's activism was much too slow and gradual, whereas working-class activism was at once more unified and forceful. And while references to an apparently singular "New Woman" and her supporters abound in late Victorian publications, the feminist movement was in actuality not quite so unilateral nor so cohesive, when we take a close look at its history. The heading of "New Woman" appears to have concealed a fairly complex series of events and relations, even within the women's movement itself. During the nineties, moral issues such as sexuality were grounds for serious disagreement and dissention among the feminists, based on what were perceived as irreconcilable and nonnegotiable differences. Philippa Levine points to the many conflicts and antagonisms within the feminist movement as resulting from the different political and moral positions held by feminists. She categorizes the diversity of women's rights activists as: (1) activists who did not subscribe to the feminist credo but nonetheless worked toward promoting legislative change affecting women; (2) those who embraced visions of women as primal and more natural than men; and (3) those who were strictly concerned with sexual matters and the sexual liberation of women. In the case of suffrage alone, the movement became depoliticized in certain ways because of internal dissent after 1881, when it was decided that the London Central Committee should become the focal political force of the suffrage movement. Later, political and ideological dissention within the suffrage movement became evident when the membership and political orientation of the suffrage movement were scrutinized:

> In 1888, the umbrella organization debated the proposal to open its doors to the new women's sections of the political parties who would enter the feminist organization with the same power and authority as the suffrage societies. The older generation of feminists were unanimously hostile to this suggestion, regardless of their personal political views. (Levine 1987, 66)

This particular debate led to the resignation of many of the older feminists and the assignation of feminists who were new to the movement. By 1897 the National Central Committee for Women's Suffrage was replaced by the National Union of Women for Suffrage Societies, claiming a victory for new feminists. The primary source of these antagonisms appears to have been the concern among the younger feminists that, in the midst of an assortment of different approaches to "the woman question," they would be associated in the public's mind with the earlier feminists whose efforts concentrated mainly on prostitution regulations and on sexuality control and who were identified in the popular imagination almost exclusively with sexuality. In short, the later feminists of the 1890s recognized that they had a political history with which to contend. Disagreements in policy and approach remained unresolved, and even after 1892 unity was provisional and dependent on oversimplifications of objectives. Feminists would work together on only one issue, the vote, and had to put other collective concerns aside in order to do so. Clearly, differences were given more credence than were similarities, to such a great extent that the meaningful fact that the same signatures appeared on vastly different petitions on women's concerns escaped the notice and appreciation of many.[9] Furthermore, problems arose when feminists attempted to address working-class issues, namely the "thorny question of protective legislation," which was argued extensively and which served to divide the movement for some time (Levine 118).

Feminism's relation to the specific social and political features of the nineties had much to do with its progress as a movement and with its eventual impact—and with the fact that it became divested from other political groups on the grounds of gender. However, the late Victorian suffrage movement did not by any means mark the advent of women's rights activism, and feminism's history is once again important in understanding the particulars of activism in the 1890s. A brief listing of some of the accomplishments of the women's movement during the Victorian era illustrates most clearly the difficulty with which women's rights were ultimately recognized and granted:

- The Factory Acts of 1844, controlling working hours for women and children, did not extend to protect women's wages despite the foundation and many efforts of the Women's Provident and Protective League in 1874; this struggle continued until 1888, the time of the Match Workers' Strike.

- The Married Women's Property Act was first presented in 1857 and defeated until a fairly comprehensive Act was passed in 1882, which granted women only limited rights; it was not until 1891 that the bulk of the Act's demands were met.

- The Contagious Diseases Act, first introduced in Parliament in 1869, was not passed until 1886, after nearly two decades of unrelenting agitation.

By the time it had become a fully organized and "many-sided movement," as Millicent Garret Fawcett was to describe it, the women's rights agenda included "political status" or suffrage, labor (trade unions and Factory Acts), Contagious Diseases (later to branch off to the Property Committee), Matrimonial Causes (and violence against women), and education (Spender 1982, 486). The women's activism of the late nineteenth century, extensive and promising as it was, simply did not yield the kinds of results in policy that earlier activism promised because it met with conservative resistance. This caused feminists to lose faith in the political process and to rely instead on social agitation and a more aggressive public visibility. Historians of late Victorian feminism generally agree that lurking beneath the surface of this forcefulness, by the 1890s there seemed to be a sense of discouragement and frustration about feminist activity compounded by a feeling on the part of women's activists that they were running out of time.[10]

As is evident in this brief summary, by the nineties many strides had already been made toward higher education, marriage and divorce reforms, and political enfranchisement. In light of this, the New Woman is clearly not so very "new," unless it was in that she now possessed a greater awareness and cynicism toward legislative process. Strachey also breaks the women's movement down to two periods, and her description is useful in thinking about late Victorian feminism in relation to feminist activism during the century as a whole. She names 1870 to 1900 "The Deceitfulness of Politics" period, starting with the block of the Suffrage Bill in 1870, and names 1897 to 1906 "The Beginning of the Militant Movement" (1978, 286). Part of the radicalness and "militancy" of the women's movement at the close of the century, Strachey observes, centered on the necessary production of "systematic propaganda" in the form of various kinds of literature (264). Most clearly, then, by the 1890s, at least, feminists had come to see and treat literature as a political tool. Part of women's sense of historic injustice was based on the fact that even in the earlier and more effective years of activism, "the 1830s and the 1840s, Englishwomen active in politics joined other movements rather than organizing to win rights for themselves," and gained very little in the process (Anderson and Zinsser 1988, 358). Emmeline Pankhurst recalled in 1894 that "our leaders in the Liberal Party had advised the women to move their fitness for the parliamentary franchise by serving in municipal offices, especially the unsalaried offices" (Murray 1982, 289). She discovered that the experience of philanthropy with the Board of Poor Law Guardians resulted in reinforcing her determination to gain women the vote and she came to see "the vote in women's hands not only as a right but as a desperate necessity" (289-290).

Lessons learned through time told feminists that women's true independence could be gained only through self-representation and self-empowerment, not through alliances. This history would serve to motivate and direct women's activism later in the century, so that the women's movement became more militant and focused almost exclusively on female suffrage. Most important, late nineteenth-century feminists differed from their predecessors in claiming for women a right they believed had once been theirs and of which they had come to be deprived, as Roger Fulford has also argued (1958). In fact, feminists' emphasis on history was an important component of the women's movement during the nineties:

> The existence of ancient rights, some of which still survived, was known and accepted by many in Britain. It was relatively easy to establish that under these ancient rights women had enjoyed many extensive powers . . . many as recently as the seventeenth and eighteenth centuries, and that it was custom and not law which prevented women from exercising such rights in the Nineteenth Century. (Spender 387)

The critical perspective of 1890s feminism called for constructing an inclusive history that would speak more accurately of women's actual, as well as their potential, status in society. Women's belief in a history presumably unmitigated by censoring "customs" and hence granting them access to *truly* independent women enabled women's advocates to speak with some authority of the injustices women were suffering during their own time. Among the most impressive feminist historians of her time, Olive Schreiner wrote in *Woman and Labour*, "the truth is, we are not new. We who lead in this movement today are of that old, Teutonic womanhood [of] twenty centuries ago" (1911, 107). Despite their separate, distinct causes, the majority of women's rights activists, such as Frances Power Cobbe (a Matrimonial Causes activist) saw ideological or "customary" oppression as being implemented through material means. In addressing the problem of domestic violence in her article "Wife Torture in England" (1878), Cobbe's general analysis of patriarchal oppression is applied to specific social problems and stresses the importance of challenging "custom" as well as law. Diagnosing the oppression of women as systematic on the part of patriarchal tradition, feminist activists sought to eradicate its injustice by redefining and reshaping power relations, specifically their own domestication, which they saw as exemplary of the oppression of woman's "nature." In an 1870 tract protesting against the Contagious Diseases Act and signed by 251 women, Josephine Butler's sophisticated analysis of existing inequities in power accuses oppressive power relations of having caused the spread of venereal disease. Arguing that "the conditions of this disease, in the first instance, are moral, not physical," the petition also calls into question the legislative establishment itself, which women's advocates considered to be synonymous with patriarchal oppression: "The general depreciation of women as a sex is bad enough, but in the matter we are considering, the special depreciation of wives is more directly responsible for the outrages they endure—the notion that a man's wife is his PROPERTY . . . is the fatal root of incalculable evil and misery" (cited in Murray 121). Angrily challenging law to administer equal justice and daring it to "define clearly an offense which it punishes," the petition places the burden of moral responsibility on the legal system rather than on prostitutes and the guilt to men (Murray 430-431).

The late Victorian women's movement continued to be primarily middle-class in its constituency, but it featured some important differences from the women's movement of the past. The most important aspects of the late Victorian feminists were their activism, that is, their ambitions and goals as they were translated into public action, and their striving for effective social change. It is distinguished from the earlier phases of the movement by a sophisticated critical understanding of their culture's oppressive ideologies, comparable to the earlier feminists' astute criticisms of patriarchal institutions. It is also distinguished, as I discuss later, by its new identification with the "masses." Primary among these feminists' immediate goals was to cross social and political boundaries by inserting themselves into the national, political, and social sectors that affected them, and their success in this rendered them truly multidimensional: The movement now worked actively on accounting for and improving factory women's lives at the same time that it worked to liberate middle-class women's political consciousness. Through the movement's many chapters and sects, women's rights advocates worked on a vast number of issues pertaining to women in general, encompassing a range of problems from labor to education, from health to civil liberties. Despite its internal conflicts, then, the women's movement still can be viewed as having posed a broad-based challenge to Victorian conceptions of women's role in society and culture by undermining Victorian society's moral pretensions, exposing its exclusivist cultural underpinnings, and by proclaiming the social, economic, and national status of women a problem. By the 1890s, the women's movement had developed into a force that could quite conceivably displace patriarchal domesticity, challenge ideological gender polarities, and incorporate vast numbers of women into the forefront of society and culture.

The impact of the women's movement was compounded by the many parallels between feminism and the representatives of the laboring "masses," who served to criticize middle-class and conservative complacency and to problematize notions of power and representation. In fact, the terms in which women's protests were couched paralleled the socialists' political working model of the oppressor versus the oppressed. The socialist-minded labor movement forced England's imperialist and nationalist ideologies to reflect, unfavorably, back on domestic issues and away from projected, distant "Others." Engels notes as much when he contrasted England in the 1890s to the earlier 1860s he had studied closely. In the 1892 Preface to *The Condition of the Working Class in England*, he writes that "today there is socialism in England: conscious and unconscious, prosaic and poetic. Socialism has become respectable and has actually pervaded the 'society' world" ([1892] 1968, 18). Whether socialism had in fact become "respectable" is debatable; given that it had at least become "fashionable," however, we can be certain that it had by the 1890s secured a place for itself in the cultural consciousness. Class was now widely acknowledged as an important factor in the makeup of cultural identity, and the politics of class were being investigated by the working classes. Hence, socialism's specific makeup as manifested in the political activism of the labor movement is just as telling as Engels's acknowledgment: "Socialists" at this time were "based on factory, mill and mine, and [were] fundamentally working-class in origin, aims and outlook"; that is to say, different brands of socialism were equally centered on the working-class subject (Adelman 1986, 19).[11] The working-class objective of self-command took precedence over the desirability of incorporation into the political mainstream. More often than not, appeasing self-defined socialists would not be accomplished through legislative change alone, since much like women's advocates, the poor in England had suffered enough disillusionments concerning the efficacy of parliamentary law. The "Poor Laws" of the previous decades had effected few real changes or improvements, and it was clear that the means toward resolving class conflict lay in the public as opposed to the legislative domain. Having come to the same realization as the feminists—that they had to act in their own interests and be leery of alliances—the socialists' role as conscientious objectors was complemented by their unanimous goal to remain politically autonomous in order to effect lasting change.

Representing the progress made by working-class advocates, the labor movement offers a record of the workers' struggle to achieve self-determination by gaining basic rights over their wages and standard of living. The many transformations that were eventually necessitated within the labor movement serve as indications of the kinds of adjustments that needed to be made in defining both the working class and the other vast and growing populace, the middle class. And, although the labor movement was not by any means inclusive of all ranks of the working class, changes in the movement point to the revised characterization of the "masses" as politically disenfranchised subjects. Attempts by the organized working classes to gain autonomy were often confronted by economic and eventually political rebuttals that rendered their oppositional acts ineffectual. Each labor victory, usually gained through direct confrontation and violence, was eventually renegotiated and neutralized, both economically and politically. Following the labor union activism of the late 1880s, with the Great Dock Strike at its apex, 1891 marked "the beginning of a counter-attack organized by the employers, and [the unskilled workers'] link with trade unions, tenuous at best of times, could hardly survive a prolonged period of unemployment" (Adelman 14). That labor advocates strove for a restructured culture and politics became increasingly obvious when "the service industry" experienced a boost that brought it to the forefront of political concerns. During the 1880s and 1890s, conspicuous consumerism was promoted in order to accommodate excess goods procured through colonial exploitation and foreign trade. This development produced a new "service class" of clerks, retailers, and domestics that would include women into the workforce in large numbers. Women's inclusion into the workforce threatened to diffuse the social and political identity of the more traditionally laboring "masses." Evidently, while the oppression of women had traditionally been an ideological product of Victorian society's need for a class emblem, by the nineties women also met a strictly economic need for a "tertiary" class of workers, as Hobsbawm has called it (172). Predominately female, this "tertiary" class served social and ideological as well as material purposes in the wider context of labor activism and a troubled economy, insofar as it was relatively cheap labor and was not socially or economically aligned with the working-class "masses." Although working-class women had long held posts in occupations traditionally viewed as masculine, the new "service industry" recruited in vast numbers middle-class and educated women into the ranks of clerical and luxury-item workers. Labor thus became a more pressing issue for feminists than it had been before, now that gender cut so obviously across class lines.

The new class of workers emerging in the late Victorian period consisted of semieducated white-collar workers and succeeded in undermining the construction of a working-class "mass" cultural and political identity; they saw themselves as distinct from the larger body of laborers. The interests of this "tertiary" class and those of the general laborers conflicted: The service industry workers ranged higher on the social if not the economic hierarchy, which often left the "masses" without sufficient labor representation (Hobsbawm 202). Unskilled laborers had already been hard put to claim their specific case, since semiskilled workers had long had almost exclusive rights to union membership; now they also had to contend with the elite among workers—the clerks and other white-collar semiprofessionals. Inadvertently, women found themselves in an antagonistic relationship to the working classes when they were actively recruited to fill men's positions in the work field in order to diffuse labor's challenges to employers. Since women as a gender class were newly placed in the labor market and were thus especially suited for tertiary, semiskilled labor, their presence in the labor market caused even more division between women's and labor advocates, while it problematized women's social and political identity:

> The trend of industry between 1870 and 1900 was such that the conflict between men and women was apparent. In spite of the

traditional customs, in spite of the hostility of the men and the obedient apathy of the women workers, "encroachments" were constantly taking place, and in all the light metal trades . . . , as well as in tobacco and a dozen other industries, unskilled women were being taken in place of skilled men, at half or less than half their rates of wages. (Strachey 238-239)

Women were further marginalized within the labor sector because the labor market was so competitive; men allowed women into their ranks only when the demand for labor was so great that it outweighed their personal and political prejudices (Rowbotham 57). Such conflicts and disputes in the labor sector were instrumental in highlighting demarcations of difference between women and the "masses" in the public domain. The diffusion of class identity and political identification I have described here made its way to the middle classes as well although less directly, for they then sought new means of defining and distinguishing themselves from the "masses." The new mobile middle class's desire to differentiate itself "as sharply as possible from the working-classes inclined [it] to the radical right in politics," in opposition to both labor and the women's rights movement" (Hobsbawm 181). In this way, reactionary elements not already inculcated by Salisbury's government were to stem from the economic sector, over class issues.

As I have illustrated, it is not at all accurate to group feminists with the labor activists or vice versa, since the differences between them establish them as separate political entities. Similarly, it is inaccurate to align women with the "masses," although as has been argued, this was in fact the case during the nineteenth century. The consequences and implications of this identification remain ominous, as observed by Huyssen:

> during the Nineteenth Century . . . mass culture is somehow associated with woman while real, authentic culture remains the prerogative of men. In the age of nascent socialism and the first major women's movement in Europe, the masses knocking at the gate were also women. . . . It is indeed striking to observe how the political, psychological, and aesthetic discourse around the turn of the century consistently and obsessively genders mass culture and the masses as feminine. (47)

The ways in which women's activists and labor activists were pitted against one another and at the same time conflated into one general category along with the "masses" made them more easily dismissible. That their similarities were distorted through the co-optation and manipulation of women by the economy and politics, and given their manifestation in the cultural imagination, all point to the discrepancies between late Victorian ideologies and the specific events that gave rise to the rhetoric one encounters in late Victorian publications. These discrepancies are reflected in women's political writings and in their social and political efforts to redefine an economically and politically compromised class of women. By the 1890s, for women, the notion of a solid subjectivity needed to be based primarily on gender although it included class issues, all other factors being uncertain and evidently subject to constant political negotiation. Consideration of the context within which women's rights activists operated serves to clarify what feminists understood the "political" to signify, since this understanding emerged from their experiences with political process and their desire to divest themselves of any privileged social status by aligning themselves with the other dominant self-defined oppositional group of their age, the working class. The factors just outlined that contributed to the destabilization of the working-class and women's rights movements served also to marginalize them socially and to compromise them through the cultural and aesthetic ideologies dominant during the 1890s. Therefore, in addition to the challenges posed to the movement by late Victorian economics and politics, women's rights activists had to battle gender assumptions entrenched in elitist notions of art and culture, ideologies that once again aligned women with the "masses." This proved a most difficult challenge, since late Victorian culture's hierarchical structures were of such long standing in capitalizing on classism and exclusivism that by the 1890s they pervaded all facets of culture and would often be essentialized as "natural." It was especially during the nineties, Raymond Williams reminds us, that notions of "natural" and "unnatural" were used in political ways and as a means of social control: Eugenics and Social Darwinism got to decide the acceptability of certain social characteristics and roles while rejecting others, and both women and the masses were compromised in the process (1980, 90-91).[12] The same end was accomplished more subtly by theories of culture and art.

2

"THE IDEA IS THE FACT": ART'S INTERIORITY AND LITERARY PRODUCTION

> [A]fter the world has starved its soul long enough in the contemplation and the rearrangement of material things, comes the turn of the soul, and with it comes ... a literature in which the visible world is no longer a reality, and the unseen world is no longer a dream.
>
> Arthur Symons, *The Symbolist Movement in Literature*
> ([1908], 1971, 4)

♦ ♦ ♦

The vast body of late Victorian literature by and about feminists testifies that progressives such as the feminists relied not only on political agitation but also on cultural command to promote their positions. As a result, we are compelled to regard what comprised "culture" during the last two decades of the century, to whom the dominant voices belonged, and how politically progressive agendas were translated by and within mainstream culture. It would appear that late Victorian culture's deliberations concerning the art it produced and patronized significantly translated the new social and political identity of women and of the working classes. Artistic and literary representations of both women and working-class subjects were informed by the dominant culture's own more specific deliberations concerning art and its function. It becomes important, then, to examine the dominant aesthetic ideology of the period so that feminist novels' own aesthetics can be appreciated in their social and cultural contexts. A consideration of 1890s' politics makes apparent the negotiations into which feminist authors entered in order to speak to the period's literary standards and expectations. This chapter addresses the exclusivism of nineties' aesthetic ideology, and assesses the politics of publication practices in relation to the dominant aesthetic ideology.

As I suggested in Chapter 1, the social unrest that comprised an intricate network of political, economic, and cultural determinations was in the 1890s construed as mysteriously or naturally cropping out of the times. The prominence and relevance of protest to cultural and political conditions was obscured in late Victorian rhetoric, especially as "individualist, pro-imperialist and conservative politics was strong" (Colls 1986, 49). The sources of agitation most pronounced during the 1890s, socialism and feminism, demonstrate the kinds of negotiations for prominence that occurred between seemingly separate areas of life in the nineties, both conservative and potentially revolutionary. Exploring the notions of aesthetics prevalent during the late Victorian period is particularly central to detecting the dynamics of oppression and protest; this is especially so in this case, because during the nineties aesthetics were deliberately dissociated from their social foundations at the same time that they were informed by them and commented on them, as a rule. During the 1890s, especially, the aesthetes and decadents insisted on the separation of art and society, and promulgated a theory that justified and augmented that desired separation. If we understand the term "aesthetics" to refer to discourse relevant to the production and reception of art, then an analysis of late Victorian "aesthetics" must take into account literary market practices but also the general cultural and political climates as forces relevant to literary production. Indeed, here it becomes vital to understand aesthetic ideology as being inclusive of cultural ideology and vice versa, insofar as "an 'ideology of the aesthetic' [pertains to] a signification of the function, meaning and value of the aesthetic itself within a particular social formation, which is in turn part of an 'ideology of culture'" (Eagleton 1978, 60).

The High/Low paradigm consigned to evaluations of art and culture during the Victorian age concurred with class polarities, with Low (or "mass") Culture alluding to the leisure activities of the working classes, women, and other marginalized subjects. The collective classification of women, the working classes, and foreign subjects as indistinct "masses" identified none of these groups with privilege, High Culture, and society. While the material conditions of the working-classes and disenfranchised women were detailed in several texts produced by feminists and socialists criticizing and foregrounding the differences between themselves and bourgeois patriarchy, High Culture saw to the dissociation of literature and culture from all that was mundane, practical, and materially defined. This dissociation rendered High Culture and art virtually antisocial, as it lent aesthetic philosophies such as aestheticism an ethereal supremacy, a prominence and authority that had previously been reserved for religious and moral speculations. Holbrook Jackson's retrospective observations on the 1890s support this view since they suggest that late Victorian culture en large sought to slight its social problems; aestheticism mirrors the wider culture in his description, in viewing itself primarily as a self-sufficient, "self-culture . . . with little or no reference to the rest of humanity" (1913, 26). As a tool for understanding the ideological underpinnings and political ramifications of late Victorian aesthetic ideology, nineties' treatises on art's nature and function provide us with a model of the various cultural determinations in notions of aesthetic value, aesthetic judgment, and, finally, artistic expression. Late Victorian cultural ideology as a whole had much to do with how nineties' aesthetics was defined as being purportedly exclusive of practical social reality and with the kinds of fantasies and idealized images of social reality the period's aesthetics projected onto that culture. Ultimately, late Victorian conceptions of "good" art would do away with art that explicitly acknowledged and reflected cultural diversity or social conflict. Late Victorian aesthetic discourse would establish the chasm between literature's traditionally imagined audiences and subjects, the middle classes, and the newly visible "masses." Included in this separation would be women and their concerns.

HIGH AND LOW CULTURE: DICHOTOMIZING ART

G. M. Young points to the disparity between late Victorian aesthetics and the High Victorian cultural status quo when he observes that "the mind of 1890 would have startled the mind of 1860 by its frank secularism, not less by its aesthetic and socialistic tone" (1954, 248). That such extreme advancements as the 1890s exhibit should have been accompanied by aestheticism and secularism is "startling" only if we fail to remember that strides made on the cultural and ideological levels were paralleled by changes in economics and national politics, as I argue in Chapter 1. Within the broader domain of art and "aesthetics," which the bourgeoisie saw as their exclusive territory, there are the earlier cultural theorists such as Arnold, Pater, Carlyle, and Ruskin to consider, who, despite their individual beliefs and discrete approaches, articulated a recurring set of problems concerning art's relation to society. They are essential to this discussion because their philosophies informed the thinking about art's nature and function. Mainly, late Victorian aesthetic theorists served to desocialize art and to fortify the conservatism dominant during the 1890s. At the same time, they inadvertently incited the opposition to that conservatism, as feminist writers, for one, found that they had to challenge these imposing figures' definitions of art and its relation to society.

Central among the dominant cultural figures is Matthew Arnold, whose main arguments late in the century serve to illustrate the conflict between the dominant aesthetic ideology and the political foundations of oppositional discourse. A statement made by Arnold in 1880 typifies late Victorian culture's preoccupations with the nature of art and its function in relation to social reality. In "The Study of Poetry," which advocates favoring the humanities over the natural and social sciences, Arnold advocates a "positive" criticism to be accomplished through an idealized unity of knowledge and "sense." His proposal was a response to what he saw as excessive "materialization" and a trend toward pragmatism in art and in culture:

> Our religion has materialized itself in the fact, in the supposed fact; it has attached its emotion to the fact and now the fact is failing it. But for poetry the idea is everything; the rest is a world of illusion. Poetry attaches its emotion to the idea; the idea is the fact. The strongest part of our religion today is its unconscious poetry. (1947, 62)

Substituting the word "art" for "religion" to reflect late Victorian culture's high regard for art, this definition of poetry suggests that art could invent its own categories and independently determine its relation to society and material conditions. Arnold's "the idea is the fact" formulation paradoxically preserves the ideological dichotomy of real and ideal and displaces art's relation to social reality. Here, also, "ideas" are aligned with "unconscious poetry" and signify creativity that is not socially reproducible, while "knowledge" refers to information that is in essence generally accessible and hence of less intrinsic value to the individual.

Arnold's deliberate division of ideas from knowledge grants art an ideological autonomy not substantiated by late Victorian economic realities and practices, nor by the conditions of art's or literature's production and consumption. However, this nostalgic fantasy of an autonomous art was ideologically maintained in late nineteenth-century England through the High/Low paradigm. The conception of a pure and disinterested art served as a model for the distinctions between morality and fact, faith and reason, privileged and popular cultures. The dichotomy is endorsed by Arnold, for one, as a means of restoring art to an idealized former place of greatness. He implies that since much of the discourse of the age was founded on "illusion," poetry needed to, and could, speak to the individual more truthfully and more personally than it was doing; by extension, only poetry could nullify social mediations, apparently also encompassing national politics and its contestants. Informing late-century attitudes toward art, Arnold's thesis speaks of the period's estimation of its art, which it viewed as fallen and compromised. In particular, harsh criticisms of "Moderns" such as George Meredith and George Moore for their "brutal virility," Realists who were said to have been "merely reproducing photographically, scenes commonly known and best forgotten," suggest that there was considerable consternation over the function and nature of art (Jackson 221). This anxiety was exacerbated by the fact that the traditional ideological separation of art and life was increasingly blurred by "intellectual, imaginative and spiritual activities . . . concerned mainly with the ideas of social life" as "culture," threatening High Art's desired insularity (27). Arnold's position on the function of art in the 1880s needs also to be considered in relation to his earlier proclamations concerning high art in relation to knowledge and to general audiences, including the "masses." His argument in *The Function of Criticism* ([1865] 1932), that "the mass of mankind will never have any ardent zeal for seeing things as they are, and that very inadequate ideas will always satisfy them," expresses most explicitly the kind of classism and general elitism underlying his censure of socialized aesthetics, and reveals his motivation for supporting the High/Low art distinction (25). Similarly, his call for a "disinterested" criticism suggests that he prefers a dissociated and decontextualized response to texts (35).

The literary market exhibited a similar classism to the extent that the emerging substantial working-class readership during the latter part of the nineteenth century was "served mostly outside the system within which the middle-class novel was produced and distributed" (Lovell 1987, 50). The double standard of "literary works" versus other kinds of writings was established along class lines, so that the working classes had access either to the "bare facts" they already knew through their lived experiences or to the sentimentalized distortions provided by the popular press. All this while the middle class were served "nobler truths" closely aligned with morality and critical evaluations of culture and society. As Arnold would emphasize in "Literature and Science" (1882), "civilization" consisted of a select few main ingredients or "powers": "conduct, intellect, knowledge, beauty, social life and manners," all characteristics that the working classes were not considered to possess but that were educated into the middle classes. Moreover, the absence of these characteristics was assumed to define the character of the working classes. And, whereas the middle classes are considered "educatable" by Arnold and are seen to possess the potential "capacity to enjoy works of art and literature," he attributes to the working classes an essential and apparently innate deficiency (1947, 104). The working classes are, in short, represented as lacking what would later be called "interiority" — "masses make movements, individualities explode them," he makes clear (97). Finally, according to Arnold's distinctions, bare "knowledge" is relevant to the "masses" who lack the ability to appreciate finer truths, while profound, innovative, and critical ideas are more appropriate to the "cultured elite." Knowledge and ideas, therefore, are juxtaposed as inherently incompatible, as are, by extension, the subjects to whom each is ascribed.

At this juncture, "Aesthetic Art," or art that occupied a privileged position according to definitions subscribed to by aesthetic theories maintaining the High/Low distinctions, is best understood as the site of forced assimilation and homogenization of extant differences in the social realm. According to the distinctions outlined thus far, High Art's late Victorian corollary, "aestheticism," proclaims the domain of value judgment exclusively its own. Aestheticism serves a symbolic function in my analysis of oppositional texts because of its relationship to social reality, a relationship of immediate dependence but also of influence, and as a mediator between itself and the cultural imagination. The High/Low art distinctions prevalent in the 1890s served to both resist and accommodate perceptions of art as "fallen" and to reform art. Art's perceived deterioration was evidenced by its reliance on "bare facts," a trend that pointed to "the destruction of [its] 'aura' [and] of seemingly natural and organic beauty."[1] By the last two decades of the nineteenth century, much of the aesthetic question was informed by the most practical aspects of art's production, on its accommodation of mass audiences, and on the practical uses to which art could be put. Hence, according to the High/Low model of aesthetics, by the 1890s art had indeed "fallen." Whatever may be said of the aesthetic frame of mind or of the social aesthetics of certain prominent figures such as Oscar Wilde and Aubrey Beardsley, elitist notions of aesthetics were significantly challenged by a booming mass culture movement exemplified by entertainment industry forms such as the music hall and the popular press, and by technological advances such as photography and film, which made art accessible to general audiences. Because of its easy and indiscriminate reproducibility, to a great extent art lost its presumed ability to transcend social reality. It had compromised its "aura" as it became immersed in its audiences' everyday lives and assimilated with other elements of daily life. Artists active in redefining aesthetics, such as the Realists and artists with social and literary agendas, consciously sought to incorporate art into everyday life interactions and vice versa, to bridge the gap between life and artistic representation.

By the 1890s, Arnold's allusions to the growing materialism in art would have been most applicable to the commercialization of art and the accurate general sense that, as Ellen Moers claims, "literature and personality [were] thrown open on the marketplace," featuring an alarming emphasis on "publicity, showmanship, [and] selling talent" (1960, 4). Perhaps the most prominent example of this commercialism is Oscar Wilde, who commodified himself and his problematic status as author and social figure for public consumption, by forcing deviation from the gender norm into the forefront of the *fin-de-siècle* imagination. Recent critics have viewed Wilde and the aesthetes as serving a function apart from their relationship to the politics and cultural elitism of the period. Eve Sedgwick, for example, sees the controversy surrounding homosexual practice and Wilde's part in it as having "divorced the sexual, and even the imaginative, from the political" (1985, 217). It is not constructive to view Wilde as so very instrumental, however, since to do so is to discount the fact that gender had already been politically problematized by women's rights activists. The feminists' frank treatment of sex and sexuality was paramount in the late Victorian imagination; its intrusive presence had been established during the previous three decades, with the prominence of the Contagious Diseases activism.[2] In light of this, Wilde's position on gender was emblematic of the preexisting relationship between the literary marketplace and sex and gender, although his public visibility was distinctly a product of late Victorian commercialism. Wilde's self-promotion can be viewed most precisely as an act of resistance against the literary market's modes of operation: He resisted them by caricaturing and exposing their self-interest toward both writers and the reading public and by co-opting its modes of exploitation for his own benefit. Thus, in addition to reflecting late nineteenth-century attitudes toward the status of art, Moers's statement about the literary marketplace is accurately descriptive of the art scene of the time, when new production and circulation practices created a more heterogeneous context for art than ever before.

"NEW JOURNALISM" AND THE NOVEL

The primary source of heterogeneity in art's consumption was initiated in the 1880s with the advent of "new journalism," which promoted mass-produced publications designed specifically to appeal to mass audiences. New journalism's contribution to the mass production of visual art and literature served to broaden and problematize the term "art" itself, its contents, and the classification of its audiences. Alan Lee's *Origins of the Popular Press* offers the most comprehensive analysis of new journalism's impact on late Victorian aesthetics, defining new journalism as a more accessible kind of writing and as a potentially more egalitarian means of disseminating particular kinds of information. In Lee's account, new journalism grew so rapidly that by 1881 there were 514 newspapers, weeklies, and magazine-like monthlies in London alone, publications whose "most conspicuous feature . . . was typographical innovation aimed at making the paper more readable" (1976, 33). New journalism's main justification for tampering with literary standards and for the sensationalism and gross oversimplification of issues in its publications was the educational benefit their lower-class readership would derive from them. Yet publishers' many proclamations concerning new journalism's social usefulness was merely a socially amenable smokescreen for sheer profit motive. Ultimately, new journalism set a low baseline for the mass readers' perceived intelligence and risked very little. As much as the new journalism sought to embrace its new desired readers, and while it had everything to gain from having an accurate sense of its readers' needs and preferences, its entrepreneurs were unfamiliar with all that pertained to the "masses" most directly. In the process of appealing to their "popular" audiences, the publishers redefined them and created a cultural stereotype of the "mass" reader, and then resorted to "creating" such news and information as they supposed would appeal to her. Subsequently, because new journalism's publishers could not agree on or set their own exact standards of their medium's literary and public function, and because their single motivation in publishing was not so much to educate as it was to create a profitable business enterprise, an important feature of new journalism was that, "having failed to establish, or to manufacture a consensus from above," it sought to create "the illusion of a greater contribution from the 'public'" (181). The purpose of this illusion was both to give the impression of close links between new journalism and its readers and to effect that connection. In eliciting readers' responses, the handful of businessmen who owned vast numbers of new journalistic publications made it their business to exploit existing social events and conflicts.

Alongside its repeated conservative depictions of socialism and feminism, new journalism served primarily to inculcate in its readers imperialist sympathies in an attempt to create a single, unified "mass" readership with set political views. Ultimately, no subject was quite as profitable, and none captured the popular imagination, better than imperial ventures. Hence, new journalism served a political as well as a "cultural" function. Sensational stories about distant lands and imagined national victories were depicted replete with illustrations that reified Britain's imperial glory.[3] This new kind of "art" permeated the public realm, amid general "knowledge," social agitation, the problems of poverty and unrest, and other pressing realities. The desire for escape seems to have been great, however, since by 1887 sensational novels in serial form exceeded 2 million copies per week in sales (Altick 1957, 308).[4] Despite the fact that new journalism often capitalized on events by distorting them into more marketable items, it derived much of its popularity and social power from the fact that it was commonly thought to bear a closer connection to "real" life than other kinds of literature. New journalism was thus able to profit from its nonassociation with High Culture while, as John Stokes argues, the rift between "culture" and literature was undermined by the production of "mass" literature in the form of newspapers and journals of various kinds (1989, xxi). Writers for new journalistic publications were compelled to produce writings that had sensation as their main ingredient and immediate end. This making of literature "commonplace" caused much discomfort to those who stood to lose social and class privileges, as the case of "Ouida" (Marie Louise de la Ranee) would suggest. In her reaction to new journalism's offensiveness, Ouida illustrates the extent to which changes in modes of literary production in the 1890s also unsettled assumptions concerning the identity of the average reader. Ouida's complaint further reveals that the literary market's accommodation of the "masses" was seen to debase literary standards. In an essay titled "Unwritten Literary Laws" she protests that:

> The vulgar, insatiable curiosity of the general world breeds such traitors as these makers of post-mortem recollections; breeds them, nourishes them, recompenses them. There would be no supply if there were no demand. The general world has a great appetite for diseased food (1899, 813).

Ouida's criticism of the literary marketplace ultimately extends to her criticism of the "mass" public, revealing that the masses themselves were held responsible for the demise of literary standards. It follows quite logically, then, that she should proceed to object to "new journalism" on the grounds that, in its "intrusiveness," it fails to respect and sustain distinctions between "public"/"mass" and "private"/elite spheres: "the scheming intrusion into private life which now disgraces journalism must, to any temper of refinement and reserve, be an offence irritating beyond endurance" (813).

The general audience's response to art, mostly figured by circulation numbers and copies sold, became a significant factor in the production of certain types of literature and in the forms literature would take. However unfavorable it was judged by aesthetic standards seeking to sustain exclusivism in art, popular literature such as newspapers, magazines, and abridged novels was indeed important; it was the main source of reading and cultural education for the majority of 1890s readers who were really the consumers at the core of the new literary market. Culturally, journals carrying both human-interest and national-interest material were to the 1890s "masses" what museum- and privately owned art and literature had been to the middle classes. Moreover, the Education Acts enacted and revised over decades resulted in a greater number of readers during the latter half of the century, and a vast number of publications catered not only to this audience's desire for entertainment but also to their vast curiosity, their desire to gain access to the knowledge and ideas that had previously been the sole property of the middle classes. An unprecedented number of new readers were now interested in gaining access to the discourse that generally commented on matters that affected and determined their daily existences:

> The 1870 Education Act provided much of the framework for subsequent expansion of elementary education.... By the 1890s at the latest it had become a cliche to link the large circulation of the popular press with the efforts of Board School education.... There were many ... who noted the potential readership created by the Act, but there were also many who noted it only to deplore what they considered to have been the production of more readers, unable to concentrate upon more than a few lines at a time, and lacking entirely any critical faculty. (Alan Lee 1976, 21)

The issue of a "mass" readership is problematic in itself, as Lee has argued, since the high literacy rates were found primarily in cities, and even then the figures pertained mostly to males. The need for subsequent expansion of elementary education was addressed indirectly by the creation of a "myth concerning literacy in nineteenth century Britain," rather than with the necessary additional legislation (23). In fact, as Levine notes, such necessary changes in legislation were not forthcoming (1987, 39). Despite their strength in numbers, the literature these new readers had access to was a modified literature that included themes that reinforced imposed and real social and cultural differences and promoted the dominant cultural ideology. Hence, novelists documenting social change and those seeking to instigate it through literature were addressing an audience whose interests and sympathies had already been claimed by mainstream and conservative profiteers.

Nonetheless, "new journalism" was relatively autonomous, compared to the production of novels, which was effected under numerous constraints. The potential power of novels to reflect social turmoil was mediated by the interests of both the marketplace and aesthetic ideology. The circulating libraries exercised enormous control over their production. This no doubt has had much to do with the survival of some texts and the loss of others and also with what we consider stylistically and ideologically worthy of study among late Victorian novels today. Most instrumental among the standards novels had to meet was Mudie's unwritten rule as the key figure in circulating libraries, that novels promoted by him abide by the "young girl standard," a criterion he enforced which was meant to ensure that all novels in his circulating library were appropriate reading for even the most impressionable "young girls." Under this mandate novels had to meet certain moral standards, which tended to limit their scope. Mudie's moral standard, as well as the circulating libraries' expectation of the three-volume novel, determined the success or failure of most novels, since the bulk of fiction was published with the monetary and aesthetic consensus of circulating libraries and publishers. Mudie's patronizing moral stance toward women as readers and authors, as well as his moralistic censorship of novels' contents, were not contested until it began to seem possible to circumvent the entire circulating library system by creating a different literary market altogether. The three-volume format to which novels were expected to adhere limited authors' choices as to length, plot development, and even content. Novels that violated this standard did not qualify for publication and had to seek different venues for promotion. Writers of these novels, such as the Realists, authorized their own literary schools and eventually their own markets. As Feltes has argued, the serialization and hence the popularization of novels was to prove as problematic to authors as had Mudie's three-volume format requirement, since too many of a novel's essential components, ranging from characterization to theme and plot resolution, were subject to editorial censorship.[5]

Such restrictions on the creative literary process produced a number of novels that, while not very innovative or controversial, are interesting in that they point to the kinds of negotiations and compromises that occur between literature as a cultural product and as social critique and the repressive forces of ideological reproduction. Within the domain of traditional literary forms and specifically the novel (historically, a form catering mainly to the middle classes), writers whose works proposed radical social change embarked on territory that had remained unchallenged for a long time. Thanks to Mudie's control of the novel market, it would remain inviolable until the mid-1890s, even past the point where social and cultural circumstances such as changes in the visibility of the working-class and middle-class women called for modifications in literary form. For the most part, novels coming out of the Mudie period, prior to 1894, adhered to bourgeois social and moral norms. But some novels produced during this repressive time and afterward also answered to the more pressing demand among mass audiences for sensationalism and entertainment while challenging publication controls and offering sharp social criticism. Authors of such works used the novel as a discursive vehicle and, at the same time, assured themselves publication and readership. Among them are the feminist novelists, who had very pressing reasons for wanting to circumvent these limitations. As I illustrate in Chapter 4, their argument with the literary establishment was complex, just as it was quite sophisticated in pointing to the power politics implicit in these standards. The prominence of satires and other subgenres during the last two decades of the nineteenth century also attests to literature's attempts to defy restrictive demarcations, as do parodies that express critical views of the dominant aesthetic ideology and that render these norms *doubly* susceptible to mass scrutiny. Satires such as Max Beerbohm's *Zuleika Dobson* and Robert S. Hitchens's *The Green Carnation* appeared either shortly after or during the events and trends they satirize, the 1890s. Beerbohm's novel mocks the New Woman and depicts her as a mindless flirt; Hitchens's book is a parody of aesthetes' texts and personas, focusing on Wilde and Alfred Douglas as his targets of ridicule—most of the dialogue in this novel is actually a monologue, and an "epigram" at that. Different genres include horror stories and utopian fiction, and similar critiques of aestheticism published as "fiction" included H. G. Wells's *The Time Machine* (1895), which depicts aesthetes as atrophied, spoiled children incapable of sustaining themselves and who are totally and quite literally reliant on an underground working class. Texts like these were light, entertaining reading, and as they express an intolerance toward aesthetic trends not openly challenged in society, they serve to undermine the secularism and elitism of those trends.[6]

As these features of the period indicate, late Victorian art still catered mostly to the interests of those who stood to gain by it both financially and politically, namely publishers and advertisers. But this assured control was beginning to diminish by the nineties, mostly because of the changes already taking place on the social and political levels: The move of the working-class masses toward political enfranchisement made great strides in establishing previously slighted multitudes as cultural subjects. Even the new artistic phenomenon of advertising posters, which optimistically encouraged indulgent consumerism and excessive spending, was shaped by the "masses" as an audience because commercial artists, too, were forced to respond to that mass audience's understandings of reality if they were to claim them as an audience. That the masses were given any consideration at all is remarkable, and publishers' concerns serve to illustrate the critical new presence of the "masses" and its eventual influence on the ongoing redefinitions of art: "Arguments about the appreciations of the visual arts . . . involved the relationship of minority to mass, popular to 'advanced.' How could an artist paint what many denied was there to be seen? What was the relationship of 'subject' to 'treatment?'" (Stokes xx). Mass audience has great implications for aesthetic theory in general, apparently, as the politics of perception gained as much significance as its objects. At the same time that the "masses" were a definite presence and had to be catered to, exclusivist tendencies on the part of the dominant aesthetic ideology argued against their instrumental existence. Authors had to negotiate this contradiction, as is evidenced in literary/aesthetic ideology of the eighties and nineties. Most explicit among them, Henry James's "The Aspern Papers" illustrates the concern toward literature's blatant commodification and sees it as intrusive and violent toward the sacred spaces of the past, emotion as opposed to reason, and privacy. James seems to argue that there are "private" and inviolable texts such as the love letters in the story, which must not be used for didactic or any other social purpose. A common feature of texts commenting on literary production generally is the sense of privacy being violated by agents of the literary marketplace and the threat of popular demand for privileged information.

Outside literary representations, there are stark indications that authors did literally struggle to gain control of their texts. Feltes points to a number of court cases over authorial autonomy starting in 1881, noting that "what was being fought over was . . . not only control of the product, of the book, but also control of the labor process and of the surplus value produced in the new, fully capitalistic mode of production of the modern magazine and newspaper" (59). As an alternative to the controls imposed on the novel and as a means of circumventing Mudie's monopoly, new journalism's publications provided politically progressive writers with a forum for voicing their views, even though content was often compromised. Exercising controls of its own, new journalism did not prove a very attractive alternative. In the case of feminist authors, the price exacted for reaching a mass audience was often too high, as I argue in Chapter 3. Hence, forms traditionally geared toward a narrower readership, such as the novel, enabled authors to intrude on their culture's privileged domain, respectability and conventional morality.

Progressives were able to intercept and challenge rhetoric maintaining the disparity between themselves and their "mass" reading public, even during Mudie's reign. This oppositional activity was facilitated by the opening up of the literary market following 1894, which induced the liberation not only of the novel, but of literature at large. When copyright laws were amended to give both authors and independent publishers greater autonomy, the chasm between the novel and popular literature seemed to diminish. The novel became even more favored as a literary medium when its status as a privileged middle-class art form was threatened by inexpensive printing and binding, reprints, and single-volume "yellow-back" editions affordable to nearly anyone. With the fall of Mudie's circulating library and the declining popularity of circulating libraries in general, many of the restrictions imposed on the novel, such as the "young girl standard," were removed, and the novel as an art form became subject to its readers' preferences. However, the debate did not cease, and the stakes for literary authority remained quite high.

PATER'S REVISION OF HIGH CULTURE: 1890s' AESTHETIC IDEOLOGY

The aesthetic ideology promoted by the "aesthetes" late in the century stood diametrically opposed to progressive literature's aims and would have effectively barred it from consideration as "art" or as a product of "culture." The late Victorian subject and function of art were questioned, as was its treatment of certain themes. This questioning stemmed primarily from the presence of a mass audience as consumers of art. Similarly, definitions of "reality" and "fact," as opposed to "sense" and subjective impressions, were being contested, as was their place in the expanding and increasingly diverse art market. As Stokes has argued, this was an age that could no longer take for granted and "was preoccupied by the relations between high and popular culture, one medium and another, art and life" (xx). It had to account for the prevalence of social issues that complicated the relationship between artistic form and content, depictions and their contexts. Questions of art's relation to society were not new concerns, although they centered on the mass public for the first time. Serving as a precursor to the arguments on the value and nature of art late in the century, the earlier debate between Ruskin and Whistler in 1878 had already brought questions of intentionality and artistic responsibility to the forefront of late Victorian aesthetic ideology. Ruskin's contention that Whistler's impressionistic approach to painting, with its disregard for "natural" laws or for imitating natural reality with any accuracy, was a violation of all that art ought to be, initiated a necessary discussion on the nature and social function of art. A very important moment in the aesthetic history of late Victorian England because it publicized the previously underplayed significance of art's profound relation to social life, the Ruskin-Whistler argument is important in articulating the rift between normative Victorian aesthetic ideology and the "new" school of aesthetics shaped by late-century redefinitions of the status of art and the artist. This debate exposed the shift of aesthetic values from High Victorianism's emphasis on art's inherent moral and social beneficence, to the more subjectivist late nineteenth century. Significantly, by 1896 the Arts and Crafts Exhibition would argue in no uncertain terms that art could no longer serve as its own end, by proclaiming that "the spirit of a great age is found in its art: cleanliness, order, virtue" (Jackson 256). At this point the relationship between society and culture was posed as being as much of a pressing aesthetic and cultural problem as High Art itself already was.

Parallel to socially minded redefinitions and in contrast to Carlyle's earlier reprimands in *Sartor Resartus* against catering to privileged audiences' expectations, we find in the works of Arnold and Pater gestures toward high elusive ideals and values for art, much as we do in the 1840s in Macaulay, whose object was clearly to embrace and affirm the values of his chosen audience, the rising middle class. The unspecified and elusive ideal that Matthew Arnold and Walter Pater see the finer literature as transmitting to receptive audiences, and which they contrast to apparently intrusive "facts," parallels the deeply entrenched myths of culture's "organic unity" characterizing nineteenth-century cultural ideology in whole, including the premises of industrial advancement and colonial expansionism. Such idealist notions of organic wholeness served to affirm High Culture's idealized self definitions and to exclude as inappropriate other types of literature that could not be said to be inspiring any high ideals.

Truth and beauty, when they are said to be one and the same, as they are in Pater, must be regarded with suspicion, for they are represented as being separate from—and in many ways antithetical to—the modes of art's production. By extension, questions of "beauty" and "truth" are not as concerned with the contents and essence of art as they are with its projected "aesthetic" value. In *Appreciations* (1889), Pater echoes Arnold when he argues in favor of art's promotion of the "one indispensable beauty," truth, and contrasts it to "bare fact" in "low literature"—that is, literature that does not correspond to aesthetic ideology's "eclectic" parameters:

> ... [T]ruth to the bare fact in the [lowest literature], as to some personal sense of fact, diverted somewhat from men's ordinary

sense of it, in the [highest literature]; truth there as accuracy, truth here as an expression, that finest and most intimate form of truth, the *vraie verite*. And what an eclectic principle this really is! employing for its sole purpose—that absolute accordance of expression to idea—all other literary beauties and excellences whatever: how many kinds of style it covers, explains, justifies, and at the same time safeguards! ([1887] 1908, 32)

The distinction Pater makes between the "personal" and "ordinary" sense of "fact" illustrates the underlying late Victorian notion that the "masses" lacked interiority, as Andreas Huyssen has observed. In Pater's analysis High Culture and the "masses" are defined as contradictory and possibly oppositional realms; whereas High Art, and later Modernism, is "self-referential" and "self-conscious," and the "masses" represent a collective "threat" (Huyssen 53). Within the parameters of this ideology, the highest form of art must be that which does not make reference to social reality. As I have already indicated, by the time Arnold and Pater wrote about art's ideals, which they posit against "fact" and the harshness of social reality, the novel and other privileged art forms such as poetry had become significantly repositioned in relation to popular culture. Art was being redefined primarily in terms of how it was being produced and consumed, but also in terms of the projected effects of its contents. Aesthetic theorists' notions of "truth" were informed by these developments, so that when Pater acknowledges that "different classes of persons . . . make . . . various demands upon literature," he also maintains that literature is best served in the hands of "disinterested lovers of books" who seek in it "a sort of cloistral refuge from a *certain vulgarity* in the actual world" (1908, 14; emphasis added). Taken to its logical conclusion, this argument promotes a kind of art that serves as a vehicle of escape from the world of "fact" while it commands High Art forms' social inconsequence. In doing so, it effectively restores the previous gap between society and "culture."

For Pater, as for Arnold, "truth" as an aesthetic "quality" is not to be found in "fact" as common people would know it, but in the transformation of "bare fact" to ideal "expression."[7] "Truthful" artistic expression, then, appears to modify the real or "facts," by making it more suitable for perusal. Implicitly working to reinstate "High Art," the ideology of aestheticism in the 1890s speaks of the work of art as if it were, or ought to be, independent of the conditions of its production and the realities it may address. Aesthetic ideology of this kind is based on the presumed difference between art and its social contexts, and accepts this relational and perceptual difference as fundamental. In it, the "characteristics of social difference are appropriated . . . to provide the trappings of individual difference," so that real differences and their ensuing plurality are appropriated for the purpose of promoting exclusivism (Williamson 1986, 116). Aestheticism's definition of difference serves to privilege the interests of a specific segment of society and not the "mass" public. In this respect, the premises of Pater's aestheticism and its earlier ramification, "High Art," are similar to those of decadent art, insofar as they purport to be

> . . . contained by nothing. Although [aestheticism] employs existing conventions, it usually negates them at the same time, denying the normal grounds of interpretation and reception. Its subject matter often concerns the violation of codes. It utilizes systems or mythologies [of legend, the occult, aestheticism] to oppose what is, without accepting those systems and mythologies. Decadence drives toward noncontainment and disconnectedness through the paradoxical act of self-imposed restraint. (Reed 1985, 15)

Always posing as the purest "truth" and striving toward an independence from the dissonances embodied in social reality, the ideology of High Art appropriates and incorporates into its workings the same social reality from which it seeks to dissociate itself, much as the philosophy of decadence disowned its origins and contexts: namely, it defines itself primarily in its difference from or opposition to what it sees as "mass" culture. The high tone of aestheticism, compared to that of decadence, is directly relevant to its degree of disconnectedness from its contexts and the extent to which it both appropriates and negates existing conditions that influence art and literary production. When the differences between aestheticism and decadence were articulated by aesthetes such as Oscar Wilde, Max Beerbohm, Aubrey Beardsley, and Arthur Symons, aestheticism's own reactionary elements, its deliberate detachment from its setting, and its attempts to mask the terms of its composition were explicitly revealed to be self-serving, its own sole object.

Aestheticist perceptions of art and its function, dominant during the 1890s, were articulated best by Arthur Symons, who maintained the separation of the real/material from the ideal, the internal from the external:

> [Symbolism] is . . . an attempt to spiritualize literature, to evade the old bondage of rhetoric, the old bondage of exteriority. Description is banished that beautiful things may be evoked, magically; the regular beat of verse is broken that words may fly, upon subtler wings. Mystery is no longer feared. . . . As we brush aside the accidents of daily life, in which men and women imagine that they are alone touching reality, we come closer to humanity. . . .

> Here, then, is this revolt against exteriority, against rhetoric, against a materialistic tradition . . . in this dutiful waiting upon every symbol by which *the soul of things* can be made visible; literature, bowed down by so many burdens, may at last attain liberty, and its *authentic* speech. (Symons 8-9; emphasis added)

It is striking that Symons succeeded in marking the similarities between symbolism's cultural aesthetics and those of the earlier theorists Carlyle and Arnold. Like them, he acknowledges the tensions between "culture" and perceptions of the "masses"—unlike them, he makes most clear and blunt the terms of the debate, placing art at the core of cultural meaning, the masses at its most outer periphery. According to Pater, the highest goal, or the ideal of literature, is to escape exterior reality and to look for superior truths within the individual consciousness. Already, by definition, the "masses" cannot and do not possess such an individual consciousness. Social reality cannot be a reliable source of inspiration or subject matter; it is corrupting to the artistic endeavor, whose legitimacy and value lie in its ability to reveal the essence, the "soul of things." This aesthetic ideology (and its translation in Pater's *Appreciations*) is founded on the Platonic premise that "the end of life is not action but contemplation—*being* as distinct from *doing*—a certain disposition of the mind: is, in some shape or other, the principle of all the higher morality" (Buckler 218). In turn, "contemplation," or specific "dispositions of the mind," are "sterile" and immutable, according to Pater, but these are positive terms in his analysis, since it is this immutability or resistance to change that lends them authenticity and truth. The very essence of art and life, along these lines, is not so much "duty," as Carlyle and Ruskin argued earlier, but the subjective impulse motivating artistic expression. Pater was to refigure this principle as the external subserving the internal when he referred to art as "the finer accommodation of speech to that vision within" (219).

MARGINAL INTERVENTIONS: THE SOCIAL MEANING OF ARTISTIC DISSONANCE

The apparent exclusion of the social from the aesthetic illustrated here was partly a response to changing audiences, audiences that, as I have argued, late-century ideologues, artists, and publishers could not profess to know well enough and yet needed to be able to make reference to. In the 1880s and 1890s aesthetic attention was focused almost exclusively on the artistic product itself, and in this way aesthetic ideology filtered out real-life intrusions and determinations. The forced exclusion of an intrusive new audience and of social unrest from anything aesthetic or vaguely High

Cultural was similar to the kind of censorship one can detect in mainstream late Victorian narratives exhibiting a kind of sterile classism. This separation of spheres was an important ingredient in progressive literature as well, in which aesthetic and ideological exclusivism was important primarily as it needed to be circumvented or negated. As Fredric Jameson suggests, narratives "systematically . . . satisfy the objections of the nascent 'reality principle' of capitalist society and of the bourgeois superego of censorship" (1981, 183). In the literature of the 1890s, an age that was perpetually reinventing its desired cultural image, filtering the masses out of High literature appears to function as a kind of censorship.

The aesthetic censorship illustrated in texts functioned through coercive social or "cultural" influence, and there was often little common acknowledgment or recognition of specific repressive agents. For example, it was not until Moore's one-man crusade against Mudie that the circulating library system came to be spoken of as institutionalized repression of artistic expression. In reaction to such subtle and not so subtle literary constraints, the naturalistic literature imported by George Moore from France endeavored to offer the most accurate and precise representation of "mass culture," excluding authorial judgments and intrusions. This project necessitated a direct confrontation of the literary marketplace and the mandates of the circulating library system in particular. In a pamphlet entitled *Literature at Nurse: Or, Circulating Morals* (1885), Moore declared that late Victorian authors wrote under unprecedented circumstances that imposed far too many limitations on their creative endeavors and did not grant them enough autonomy or authority over their texts:

> . . . [N]ever in any age or country have writers been asked to write under such restricted conditions. . . . [O]f the value of conventional innocence I don't pretend to judge, but I cannot help thinking that the cultivation of this curiosity is likely to run the nation into literary losses of some magnitude. (19)

Moore elaborates that Mudie's aesthetic practices threatened the "bond of sympathy that should exist between reader and writer" and that it had become virtually impossible for authors to create such relations, since formal experimentation and frankness of presentation were curtailed by Mudie's monopoly (20). Given that, as Lovell has emphasized, "it was the libraries rather than individuals who purchased the novels" and that "[n]ovel-readers wished to read not to own," Moore's anger aimed at Mudie is astute (51). Implicit in Moore's protest against Mudie's authority and control is his belief that a new means of socializing and reforming fiction was necessary if he was to serve a significant social function as a novelist, a role that required a more direct communication between authors and readers. However, Moore is quite explicit in revealing the power attributed to texts by society, thus making clear that the debate over literary autonomy was understood to have enormous social and cultural consequences: "The 19th century alas! believes as implicitly in the power of a book to corrupt as the 15th century believed in the power of old women to fly through the air on broomsticks." (1890, 362). Hence, not only had the "masses" been monopolized as a new market for literature, but Mudie's insistence on privileging the tastes of bourgeois readers alienated writers even further from general readers and censored their communication, as Moore noticed.

If, as I suggest in Chapter 1, the late Victorian national fantasy promised a wide incorporation of cultures and nationalities into its workings without threatening its own internal cultural economy or the coherent national identity of English subjects, the aesthetic theories I have discussed in this chapter manifest a complicity with that national ideology in promoting an imagined separation of spheres to preclude social diversity and strife. Aestheticism was product-oriented, much as the British nationalist ideology justified the means and costs of colonialism by idealizing its ends. Viewed as narratives of a particular kind, the writings of Arnold and Pater provided the 1890s with articulations of a desired cultural self-image. In the face of these ideological impediments, revisionary aesthetic theorists were compelled to acknowledge the particulars of material existence while always answering to the ruling class's fantasy of itself and its desired status. The ramifications of this double objective were enormous in terms of the impact progressive texts were to have on literary judgment. As I will illustrate in the following chapter, their attempts to placate possible mainstream objections resulted in the further marginalization of politically motivated feminist and "mass"-appeal texts. My observations concerning class elitism informing the dominant aesthetic ideologies are equally applicable to women's marginal position in relation to aesthetics. But the status of women in this conflict is more intricate than that of the working classes, since women could not be excluded quite so completely from aesthetic discussions. Women could not be eliminated from the High Culture paradigm, nor could they be remanded to Low Culture as easily, since they had traditionally served an important function in it. However, even though women had been producing "quality" fiction throughout the Victorian era, the aesthetic tradition outlined here did not account for women as artists, nor did it account for them as subjects of High Art, except in the most rudimentary ways. Subsequently, we find an odd and at times strained identification of women with mass culture.

In the aesthetic ideology of the 1890s we also find a repression of women similar to that of the "masses" and an idealistic emphasis on individualism that served to stratify social reality and to undermine feminism's problematization of female cultural subjectivity. The exclusion of women from aesthetic formulations was noted and theorized in political terms by Olive Schreiner, a late Victorian feminist author and activist:

> The males of the dominant class have almost always contrived to absorb to themselves the new intellectual occupations, which the absence of necessity for the old forms of physical toil made possible in their societies. The females of the dominant class or race, not succeeding in grasping or attaining to these new forms of labour, have sunk into a state in which they have existed through the passive performance of sexual functions alone. (1911, 28)

This early observation concerning the monopolization of intellectual matters by the late Victorian dominant culture (bourgeois patriarchy) highlights its ensuing marginalization of women, its according to women the sole status of compromised subject matter. Even at its most progressive, the Victorian aesthetic tradition failed to acknowledge women as subjects of serious aesthetic inquiry, and women's presence in theoretical discussions is nonexistent. Quite conveniently, middle-class women were excluded from those discussions because of their marginal place in them. As the most culturally visible class of women, middle class women had for so long been the property of bourgeois morality and the bourgeois domain, they were seen to represent qualities and values of which they were actually symptomatic: prudery, narrow-mindedness, and social complacency. If middle-class women embodied dominant Victorian values publicly displayed, they were likewise excluded from areas concerning interior quests for truth and beauty. Consequently, the late Victorian period features a positioning of women as vacuums or receptacles for problematic cultural values. Judith Williamson observes that in terms of the larger cultural economy, although women serve as a variable that can be used to balance the insufficiencies and discordances of capitalist patriarchy, "Women, the guardians of 'personal life,' become a kind of dumping ground for all the values society wants off its back but must be perceived to cherish: a function rather like a zoo, or nature reserve, whereby a culture can proudly proclaim its inclusion of precisely what it has excluded" (106). It becomes apparent that literary economies function in much the same way. The implications of Pater's and late Victorian aesthetics for gender are carried over into some of the less conventional texts of the period. Revisionists of Victorian aesthetic ideology such as the Pre-Raphaelites (with the notable exception of Christina Rossetti) consistently saw women as an impediment to progress and to the true artistic endeavor—that is, the artist's highly spiritualized quests for truth. Representing a cross point between Ruskin and the later aesthetes in what Andrew Lang describes as their "representational fidelity" and their commitment to "the genius of beauty," the Pre-Raphaelites also challenged notions of decorum and traditionalism in art and society, but used women as the vehicles through which they would rebel against conformity (1975, xii). Whereas their artistic ideology professed a primary allegiance to the visible world, their poems, prose, and paintings mythologized women by focusing on their spiritual and psychological makeup. With Ruskin's support, Dante Rossetti and Leigh Hunt added to "representational fidelity" a symbolism that imparted romance, fantasy, and a sense of wonder to otherwise mundane subjects. Harking back to earlier, Romantic models of women in art, both the poetry and paintings of the Pre-Raphaelites abound with allusions to an ideal woman who is desirable only insofar as she remains distant, unknowable, unreal. This is generally true of Dante Rossetti's writings, including "The Orchard Pit" (1886), "The Blessed Damozel" (1850), and "My Sister's Sleep" (1850), in all of which the female is caught in a symbolic bind somewhere between good and evil, always posing as a threat to mankind. In his poem "Jenny," for example, Rossetti's attempt to rescue a prostitute from her fallen state in the eyes of society results in little more than a different kind of exploitation. Jenny is portrayed as perpetually elusive, perhaps even as the ultimate unknown, and the scholar-narrator leaves her much as he had found her, except now deciphered; he tosses a coin into her hair at the end, having made use of her for his particular purposes by appropriating her intellectually.[8]

Even Carlyle and Ruskin, whose aesthetics were not as insular as those of the later aesthetes, could not accommodate the "exteriority" (social presence) of women. In their limited function as symbolic objects in art, women were traditionally treated as blank slates upon which male artists could write. Lacking meaning in themselves, women could be perpetually constructed and revised in various ways. Talking about Thackeray's depictions of women in *Henry Esmond* in her chapter on "The Historicity of the Female," Sedgwick remarks on the appropriation of the female and her negotiation as a symbolic figure in masculinist, High Victorian art in terms that both resemble those of Gayle Rubin and support my own observations about late Victorian women's relation to art:

> ... both woman-as-virgin and woman-as-whore take on sexual significance within the context of circulation, exchange, and the gift;

and what women make of women, as moral or social figures but most signally as sexual creatures, occurs primarily . . . under the pressure of a signifying relation in which both the sender and the intended recipient of the message are male. (151)

"Woman" had long served her purpose in masculinist art, where she functioned as a variable whose significance could be altered to accommodate the need of different historical and cultural moments in the perpetuation of elitist aesthetic tradition. When she was no longer needed to typify domestic virtue, as she did in the bulk of mainstream novels of High Victorianism, she had to be adjusted to assist a new vision, as she did for the Realists: that of a society in transition. In light of all this, the feminist-authored and Realist heroines appear to subvert appreciably a long tradition of women's objectification, particularly as they went about naming "woman" for themselves and constructing an alternative literary aesthetic. First, feminists had to invent a means of gaining the general public's attention and also a way of asserting their political consciousness in the midst of an aesthetic and literary market that invariably relegated women to the role of artistic commodity.

Attempts to appreciate the social implications of late Victorian aesthetic ideology are assisted by the oppositional literature of the age and by texts that respond to or challenge oppositions to the status quo. As I illustrate below, the latter are by and large nonprogressive and arguably even reactionary texts that function by appropriating social and aesthetic resistances and then reinstating them into the mainstream of normative late Victorian discourse. Both oppositional and reactionary texts can be understood best in their relation to the three main ingredients of the cultural setting described in the previous chapter: England's colonizing interests, changing definitions of class, and the women's movement as a challenge to patriarchy. Feminists, in particular, appreciated the dynamics and implications of late Victorian aesthetic ideology in all their complexity, and dissected and challenged them through the popular literary mediums available to them, new journalism and the novel.

~3~
THE POLITICS OF PUBLICATION: WOMEN IN THE LITERARY MARKETPLACE

XXIV
Misread by man, [the] sign of his misdeed
Was held as symptom of her nubile need
And on through history's length her tender age
Has still been victim to his adult rage;
He, by his text, with irony serene,
Banned her resultant "manner" as "unclean";
The censure base upon himself recoils,
Yet leaves the woman wan and cumbered in his toils.

"Ellis Ethelmer," *Women Free* (1893), 12

♦ ♦ ♦

In the previous two chapters I have worked to characterize the 1890s as a troubled time that marginalized women politically and culturally and as a decade that featured both political resistance and cultural conservatism. In this chapter I look more specifically at the status of feminists in the literary world, primarily as authors, and consider their efforts to resist and challenge mainstream appropriation through their writings.

The restrictions imposed on writers in general by the circulating library system were especially oppressive to women authors writing in the context of debates concerning woman's place in society and the feminist movement's agitation for women's rights. This was particularly the case with the popular women novelists we may now call "feminists," that is, women who were either actively involved in the women's rights movement, such as Mona Caird, Sara Grand, and Olive Schreiner, or those who challenged patriarchy solely through their writings. The social agents who exerted an influence over feminist writing in the 1890s included those who, like Mudie, Salisbury, and the aesthetic theorists, set the tone and boundaries of social discourse and imposed new terms on the debate by promoting conservative and socially incongruous definitions of women. At a time when vast numbers of women were working to challenge and transcend gender stereotypes, the conservatives and aesthetes intervened in that process by promoting either traditional or counterrevolutionary models of womanhood. Mudie's own position on women and on gender relations was clear in his patronizing stance toward the "young girls" he wanted to protect from moral corruption. This broad category actually extended to women of all ages, since the common perception viewed all females as childlike and vulnerable to moral corruption. Progressive women writers, new to writing as a "profession" in the literary marketplace and utilizing their skills in order to gain financial autonomy, were even more suspect and harshly scrutinized by Mudie. As Gueneviere Griest shows, "new authors were hurt the most by circulating libraries, because publishers did not want to chance low circulation" (1970, 184). Since the vast number of new authors were women, it was they who suffered the most from Mudie's censorship, which was not interested in promoting unestablished or unconventional writers. Like more mainstream authors, feminists and other women writers "demanded the right to choose their subjects *and* their readers" (137). In the midst of a tradition invested in subordinating female subjectivity to patriarchal law, a tradition that did not allow for resisting or politically based opposing definitions of female nature (either as subject or as creator of art), women who reacted against this marginalization resorted to public protest in voicing their objections. One of the most powerful tools available for gaining a public voice was the "new journalism," Mudie's successors in controlling the literary market, because it afforded individual feminists the opportunity to reach a vast number of readers at one time. The popular publications that comprised the new journalism became a public forum in themselves, and progressives did not fail to appreciate their potential usefulness. Writing for the popular press enabled the feminists not only to make their case known but also to comment on their society. Whenever possible, women's rights advocates turned to reputable mainstream journals such as *Nineteenth-Century* and *The Westminister Review*, as well as to newspapers and to mass-appeal periodicals, to voice their opinions on especially controversial subjects such as marriage, divorce, the vote, and education for women.

Feminists made such extensive use of these popular publications that at least one member of the public, Eliza Linton, expressed her hostile reaction to these developments in an essay, entitled "The Partisans of the Wild Women," attacking not only feminists but their sympathizers as well. Linton objects especially to how opinionated, vocal, and public women had become, always calling "attention to their feats" (1892, 463). Linton makes an intriguing analogy between feminists' visibility and the objectionable (to her) manner in which the press has enabled this phenomenon. According to this formulation, the feminist movement appears as a corollary to the "decadence" of the press. In her apparent ignorance, Linton sees this relationship in reverse: "If we contrast the Radical penny paper with the older journals," she says, "we see the decadence, not only of style but of thought and principle, which this new ideal of womanhood, this standard of decency, has brought about." In acknowledging the *radical* feminization of the press, Linton unwittingly implicates the journals' commodification of women when she ponders, "[h]ow far is it a consideration of pence and profit, and what will best sell the edition whereof the buyers and patrons are the unsatisfied and idle?" (463)

Very often, extended debates were carried on through several consecutive issues of a single journal. *The Contemporary Review*, for example, published a feminist essay entitled "How We Marry" (Cameron, 1896) and then compromised its potential impact by following it with a number of other essays on the same subject, the majority of which were conservative if not antifeminist. In this one of many examples, the voice of tradition was an extremely hostile one, that of W. J. Knox Little in an essay entitled "The Doctrine of the Church of England" (1895). The exchange between women's advocates and antifeminists carried on in journals served to inform, to influence, and to divide readers. It was so extensive, and the subject of women was exploited to such an extent, that the abundance of opinions and views published there created considerable confusion as well, particularly for those who did not want to participate actively in the debate. Yet claiming neutrality was not a real option, ultimately, as "The Cult of Cant," published in *Temple Bar* in 1891, illustrates. Its anonymous author asks for some reasonable mediation between the many factions publishing on various causes in the journals and wishes to see some order restored to public discourse and to popular feeling. Interestingly, the author of this essay characterizes "cant" as woman-dominated chaos, as a predominantly *female* disarray that only patriarchal order can restore to sanity and order. The author also feels that the "New Morality" (belonging, presumably, to progressive voices) has "turned . . . common-sense, true morality and the established law . . . out into the street as refuse," and awaits the day when "a more manly spirit rules the English world" and represses this "enervating cult of cant" (193). Invariably, those who opposed women's public visibility and radicalness did so because they felt feminists' agendas threatened the hierarchical status quo, not only as it pertained to gender, but to national identity as well. As was the case with the labor movement's consensus at the Second International, women's rights advocates were also not likely to identify with British national and colonial ideologies. Rather, like Olive Schreiner, they would construe gender and national/cultural interests as corollaries.

Mainstream publications were not neutral nor disinterested enough to refrain from interfering with the objectives of its contributors. As Feltes has argued, in practical and political terms, the popular press was a necessary evil. Progressive writers recognized it as a potentially empowering medium, but the ways in which they were presented to their desired readers often undermined their efforts because their texts were sensationalized. It was not only specific editors, but the whole structure of new journalism that undermined progressive writers' projects. Feltes's observations make clear these writers' awareness of the subtle and often not-so-subtle censorship their texts met with in the hands of new journalism's proprietors:

> Hardy's phrase, "this unceremonious concession to conventionality," too nervously compresses a production process determined by the forces and relations of magazine production, by the ideologies of "class" journalism and, by the late 80's, of the "new journalism." These constituted a fully capitalist mode of literary production, of which the "anticipatory censorship of editors and publishers" was but the most explicit manifestation. (1896, 74)

Women writers and late Victorian women's issues were exploited as cultural commodities to help boost circulation rates, and it was clear to feminists, at least, that this was not a reliable medium. Editorial intervention was extensive to the extent that often, the novel in serial form differed greatly from the final version of the novel in volume form; "occasionally a novelist would rewrite a serialized novel before it appeared in book form . . . other novelists, however, found revision beyond their power" (Doughan 1989, 9). Despite the fact that this practice distanced authors from their texts by allotting many of the editorial decisions to the publishers, several women's novels were serialized in journals, and feminists used the forum to publish political essays. Even beyond the serial's revisions, novels would undergo further scrutiny and censorship. Mary Cholmondeley's *Diana Tempest* was serialized in *Temple Bar* over the course of ten issues in 1892 and published as a volume in 1893, while Mudie was still the formidable first reader of novels. *Red Pottage* (1899), published in a single volume after Cholmondeley's many attempts to find a publisher for it, was authored by a woman familiar and experienced with the literary establishment and who thus wrote in opposition to its dictates. It sarcastically confronts several of the problems by which women authors were confined, not the least of which was censorship of their writing and also of their ideas.

Under these same conditions, Sarah Grand published a series of stories under the guise of "realistic portraits" in *Temple Bar*, stories that bear little ideological resemblance to her novels published either in the three-volume format (*Heavenly Twins*) or in a single volume (*Ideala*). "Janey, A Humble Administrator—A Study From Life," published in 1891, is a sentimental portrayal of a working-class woman's life and her ignorance, emphasized by the middle-class narrator's perceptions and descriptions of that world, which attempt to engage the sympathy of middle-class readers. In what might be construed as a condescending tone resembling Matthew Arnold's, Grand describes Janey as "delicately emotional, I knew, for I had heard her Tennyson and Longfellow, and seen her transparent skin suffused with pale pink flushes of pure pleasure when I came to the passages that specifically appealed to her" (74). Apparently, Janey is remarkable and perhaps even redeemable because she illustrates qualities generally considered to belong to the middle class, such as the deep appreciation of the finer, redemptive literature. Nowhere do we see in "Janey" or in the other characterizations for mass consumption in the series the critical insights evidenced in Grand's novels. Nowhere is the New Woman evident in these works, either in the heroines or in the narration. Furthermore, "Janey" betrays and negates Grand's politically sophisticated view of literary aesthetics as expressed in the novel *The Beth Book* (discussed in the next chapter), by utilizing conventional and classist conceptions of literature's function. Perhaps an explanation for this inconsistency is to be found in the fact that progressive women writers who wanted to court the journal market had to abide by its proscriptions, since the value of exposure overrode the limitations journals imposed. They also worked piecemeal and under constant supervision, a situation in which "[the publishers'] control of the product . . . did not need to be negotiated; it was a given" (Feltes 63). Monetary gain and even economic survival were at stake for women writers, and this dependency threatened both the contents and purpose of their writings published in the more lucrative journals. The case of Margaret Oliphant supports the importance of monetary motivation in women's publication history, as I illustrate below.

A substantial segment of 1890s women writers were part of the phenomenon known both today, as then, as "the New Woman," the women's rights advocate who threatened to unsettle the middle-class Victorian ideological and material domestication of women and the rigid separation of social spheres already being shaken by the assertive "masses." In courting public sentiment and seeking to instigate changes in perceptions of gender, feminists such as Schreiner, Caird, and Wostenholme Elmy had only indirect and mediated access to the public, the new readers among the "masses" who were already being preyed upon by news of national prowess and ideologies of economic affluence. Besides, their story did not constitute "news" as much as it did critical evaluations of the past and present—that is, cultural criticism. And insofar as feminist fiction constituted an important component of popular discourse on gender relations, mainstream masculinist thought and discourse did not consider that the feminists were addressing "fact" or that their stories and criticisms could constitute insightful, "truthful" revelations. Actually, feminist fiction, otherwise known as "sex-conscious" fiction, was harshly criticized for distorting "reality," as it was in "The Fiction of Sexuality" (1895), an essay by James Ashcroft Noble that was published in the widely read *Contemporary Review*. In this essay, the author's objection is to feminists' "present[ing] men and women as merely conduits of sexual emotion," a practice he perceives as being "as ludicrously inartistic as it is to paint a face as a flat, featureless plain." Noble adds, with some confidence, "'George Egerton' would not accuse me of overstatement" (493-494). Another critic, Gerald Stanley Lee, sums up in "The Sex-Conscious School in Fiction" the general consensus against gender-interested literature:

> It is one of the fundamental criticisms upon the sex-conscious school that prevails at present that it . . . lacks the moral imagination, the spiritual and intellectual range, to sweep its objectors aside, to carry its treatment through, on the theme it chooses to take, into the power and reverence and beauty and awe of life that always belong to the truth on any subject, and that cannot belong but to art, from the beginning of the world. (Lee 1900, 78)

Speaking as an authority on civilization, art, and truth, Lee's criticism of feminist fiction is that "it has but one topic, a topic the only conceivable sin of which, either in life or art, is its being focused on itself" (79). In addition to lacking "spiritual range," according to Lee, feminist fiction does not revere beauty or "truth" but utilizes both in demystifying their subjects by way of creating a more humble art; that is, an art that serves a political cause.

Feminist fiction is seen as weak and ineffectual, according to this perception, because it does not represent reality as an "awesome" and mysterious entity. Criticisms such as these caused feminist novelists to be branded as "intellectual degenerates," self-absorbed creatures whose art amounted to little more than "self mutilation" in the form of "protest." Feminist writers were unacceptable, in Lee's estimation, primarily because they were viewed as regressives who hindered the progress of the coming age, the "Century of Facts"—and of men (81). The very definition of progressive change was challenged, and the existing dichotomy of "sense" and "fact" recast and attributed to feminists.

Even the aesthetes, whose cultural agenda clearly did not include the privileging of facts as it did elusive "internal" truths, excluded women's works from their publications. The aesthetes were nearly exclusively a male movement, although some women writers and poets, Egerton and Schreiner among them, were included when their literary styles were seen to override their gender-interested agendas. As in the case of Egerton, specifically, these women writers published under male pseudonyms. Their identities remained unknown until after they had established a readership, as a quick glance at a list of literary women's history with pseudonyms reveals. According to Kahler-Marshall's findings, *all* late Victorian women writers published under names other than their own at one point or another; this can be taken to indicate that, "protected by their masculine pseudonyms, they could presume to have opinions on matters more intellectually challenging than those believed suitable for women" (1985, xi).[1] Women writers masked the gender specifics of their texts to enhance their marketability but undermined their authority in the process. To counter this inequity, but also to profit from engaging the market of unrepresented authors, publishers such as Fisher Unwin and John Lane made it their mission to promote new authors, and women in particular. Lane, the first editor of *The Yellow Book* and subsequently the publisher and supporter of several women writers, stands out as an anomaly among fin de siècle publishers, who for the most part urged women to confine their writing to domestic or sensational themes. The exceptions to this rule were far too few, although John Lane is a notable one, as is Heinemann, who was "quick to recognize new literary movement[s]" and was invested in discovering new authors (Mumby 1956, 278). Encouraged by the favorable reception of George Egerton's *Keynotes*, Lane initiated "The Keynote Series" of publications, which was to include titles such as Ella D'Arcy's *Monochromes*, Grant Allen's *The Woman Who Did*, and Egerton's own sequel to *Keynotes*, *Discords*, all of which were clearly presented as pro-woman literature.

Feminists gradually became aware that they could not benefit from aligning themselves with male-dominated political and social organizations, and turned their attention to formulating analyses highlighting gender differences, both in their fiction and in nonfictional tracts. In opposing economically, politically, and socially maintained definitions of women and power relations, feminist discourse such as the texts by Elmy, Schreiner, and others I discuss here responded to practical constraints that served as instruments of this marginalization; feminists addressed, specifically, those imposed through publication practices, exclusivism in education, and professional/employment standards. Feminists were openly and harshly critical not only of male dominance, but of oppression in general, and they often took up the banner for other causes in their writings. More important, as a critical philosophy, feminism was astute in pointing out the relationships between the oppression of women and other forms of oppression. This may well explain why they were considered so subversive and radical: They failed to sympathize with or support nationalist sentiments, just as they were in support of the labor movement. As Mona Caird argues in "The Evolution of Compassion" in 1896, "the annals of conquered lands, of subordinate classes . . . bear testimony to the same startling fact" that "the spirit of tyranny still rages among us; . . . it is still defended in government, in religion, in opinion, and in the most intimate relations of life" (638).

The market for literature advocating women's rights was limited and their audience was by extension small, and so several feminists saw the benefit in establishing or at least controlling their own modes of literary production. By the mid-1890s a handful of journals not only catered to women, as several commercial "ladies'" journals such as *The Ladies' Treasury, Leisure Hour,* and *The Ladies' Gazette* had been doing for decades, but also sought to provide the "new" woman with a safe and fair forum. In addition to these progressive journals, the most prominent of which was *The Woman's Journal,* there were also printing presses owned and operated by women's rights activists, as well as a female-operated publishing establishment called Victoria, which issued many feminists' nonfiction works. Promoting the employment of women and led by the activist Emily Faithful, the Victoria Press published many feminist texts, including the progressive *Englishwoman's Journal* (1858-1864) and *Victoria Magazine* (1863-1870). But once again, these were special-interest journals, and as such were only marginally influential. The primary objective of the Victoria Press was not the promotion of feminist ideas as much as it was the professional education of women in the printing trade. Even so, by the 1890s, the Victoria Press had been overshadowed by more affluent and powerful journal establishments.

As David Doughan has observed in his study of women's periodicals, "undiluted women's rights literature was comparatively rare, and much of the activity of the nineteenth-century feminists occur[ed] in areas that . . . would be defined as philanthropic, syndicalist, moralistic, or religious" (1989, 68).[2]

Some progressive women writers did seek to make "undiluted women's rights literature" possible by revealing the intricacies and complexities of reading and text evaluation, by stressing the reciprocity of readers and texts, so that texts could not be said to simply "corrupt" their readers. In the process, they also worked to create the kind of audience they desired. "Vernon Lee" (Viola Piaget) sought to educate readers of fiction on this subject, following her own damaged reputation as a novelist caused by readers' hostile reactions to *Miss Brown* (1884), though the same readers continued to praise her nonfiction. Two essays published in *The New Review*, "Of Writers and Readers" (1891) and "The Craft of Words" (1894), work to create a critical reader who would not dismiss controversial subject matter as immoral. In the first essay, Piaget illustrates that reading is an active process and that both reader and writer contribute to the effects and meaning of a book:

> written words are not in themselves anything, but merely the suggestion of something. We do not remember a book, nor even a chapter, nor even . . . a page: we remember its contents, and sometimes its manner of conveying this. We do not assimilate books as we do music. . . . We digest books; now, digesting means dissolving. . . . Readers do not know, as a rule, how much of a book they are themselves creating. . . . The writer, if he be candid, must know . . . how entirely he depends upon the contents and movements of the reader's mind. ("Lee" 1891, 532, 534)

In the second essay Piaget is much more radical and explicit in exposing the "art" of writing as a deliberately interactive process, and demystifies the ways in which texts works in relation to readers' reception. In this second discussion, the author effectively describes authorial, textual, and cultural or readers' ideologies as they inform both the production and consumption of texts:

> Whatever we are doing, so long as we are writing, we are manipulating the consciousness of the Reader. . . . Why all this manipulation and manoeuvering? Why not photograph, so to speak, the contents of the mind of the Writer on to the mind of the Reader? Simply because the mind of the reader is not a blank, inert plate, but a living crowd of thoughts and feelings. . . . All writing, therefore,

is a struggle between the thinking and feeling of the Writer and Reader. ("Lee" 1894, 580)

Unlike Moore's description of the "sympathy" that ought to be allowed to exist between writers and their readers in "Literature at Nurse," Piaget's analysis of readers' reactions to texts highlights the "struggle" over differences in orientation and the text interpretations they yield. Hence, while it appears that Moore "firmly believed solutions to be outside the novelist's province," as has been argued, both inter- and extratextually, Piaget is making the more radical argument (Fernando 1977, 87). Apparently, she feels the need to *create* a receptive reader rather than appeal to one, and she is mindful of the power of readers to prejudge and exclude those whose ideas differ from their own. Piaget's model of reader and writer, but also of texts, demystifies them all and reveals them as negotiations in meaning and privileged realities. This critical project of enlightening readers out of their complacency did not go far enough in creating a friendlier readership for women and feminist writers, and while they were being used to sell periodicals, the feminist authors' political mission was still compromised.

As a result of the compromises exacted by new journalism publications and the relative ineffectiveness of the smaller women's journals, the need for a reliable literary forum was so great that the radical feminist organization, the Women's Emancipation Union, added the production of fiction and nonfiction to its otherwise entirely activist agenda. Mrs. Wolstenholme Elmy ("Ignota"), its president, wrote a volume titled *Woman Free* published under the pseudonym "Ellis Ethelmer" independently in 1893 by the Women's Emancipation Union. Illustrating the advantages of claiming independence from the formal and moral constraints imposed by the standard literary market practices, *Woman Free* serves as an excellent example of the autonomy women writers gained as a result of controlling the production of at least some of their texts. The sonnets serve as a chronicle of man's injustices to women, and do not fail to address the male appropriation of language itself and, apparently, women's oppositional literary utterances. A disparity that at the present renders women alien to one another ("How shall he write what she alone may tell?") is projected resolved at some distant point in the future:

> And "winged words on which the soul would pierce
> Into the height of love's rare Universe"
> Shall native flow from them as mother tongue
> In softest strain unto listening infant sung;
> Till, the sad memories of unmeant wrong

> Solving in music of conciliant song,
> Man's destiny with Woman's blended be
> In one sublime progression—full, and strong, and free.
>
> ("Ethelmer" 1893, 31)

But while it appears to be a sonnet sequence, *Woman Free* is actually a critical analysis of late Victorian patriarchal oppression of women, with ample documentation of its exploits. The major part of the text consists of the "Notes & C" section, which appears as an appendix to the poems and which promotes a basic knowledge of the history of the women's movement. It is primarily a metacritical treatise that documents man's injustices to women, women's own oppositional writings and actions, and the ongoing debates concerning the rights of women, ranging from classical perceptions to modern psychology, although it innocently professes to be a mere "gathering together of which scattered rays—thoughts and experiences from many an observant mind—into one focus, to offer light and warmth to suffering manhood and humanity" (222). In addition to documenting hundreds of sources on religion, science, literature and art, Mrs. Wolstenholme Elmy uses this appendix as a place of authority from which she can exclaim: "Are not . . . English injunctions to womanly and wifely slavery as trenchant and merciless as any ascribed to so-called 'heathenism?' And is not the fuller truth that the spirit of the male teaching against woman is the same all the world over, and no mere matter of creed—which is nevertheless made the convenient vehicle for such teaching . . ." (161). *Woman Free* is further empowering to the women's cause because it provides other 1890s feminists with a platform. In the "Notes" are quoted Elmy's contemporaries Mona Caird, Lady Florence Dixie, among others, as well as her own earlier political writings. There is no doubt that such an extensive and thorough (about 230 pages) indictment against patriarchy, which could easily be considered excellent feminist scholarship today, could not have found endorsement among late Victorian publishers. These textual strategies are significant because the overlap and blurring of the lines between fact and fiction effect a textual strategy also apparent as a common feature in feminist novels as well.

When independent publications of feminist texts was not possible, feminist writers resorted to a wide range of subversive means to publish their views and to establish their public visibility. For example, once again under the pseudonym "Ethelmer," Mrs. Elmy published an essay entitled "A Woman Emancipator: A Biographical Sketch" in *The Westminster Review* in 1896, of which she herself is the subject. Elmy prefaces her essay with a quotation from a text published under her own name and highlights her own accomplishments as a feminist, including a promotional reference to the newly formed Women's Emancipation Union:

> This Union claims for women, "equality of right and duty with men in all matters; . . . equality of opportunity for self-development; . . . equality in industry; . . . equality in marriage. . . ." Such are the words of its honorary secretary, Mrs. Wolstenholme Elmy, by whom the co-operation and membership of those in sympathy with the announced views will be cordially welcomed. (428)

There is something startling and intriguing about this kind of text and its mode of publication because it unsettles notions of subjectivity and authorial voice, and challenges presumptions such as Homans's assertion that women's texts tend to literalize the figurative and symbolic structures of patriarchy. For, insofar as "women might and do embrace this connection" of literal language with nature and with woman, as Homans argues, which would render them "selfless mediator[s]" through whom "language is being transmitted without the messenger's interference," texts such as this ask us to see women writers as something other than the conduits of patriarchal discourse (Homans 1986, 257). They become, instead, active agents whose political agendas and texts are self-directed and self-serving insofar as they are subversive of established discursive hierarchies. Wolstenholme Elmy's handling of her material in *Woman Free* is highly figurative and symbolic in its implicit assertions concerning the status of "scholarship" in relation to gender. The "Notes" to the sonnets, although meant to literalize the feminist premises of the sonnets and the sexist discourse against which the poems rebel, constitute a symbolic structure because they cryptically imply their own coherence without the assistance of narration or commentary from the author.[3]

In light of the fact that feminists were being commodified by the "new journalism" market and thus being made "figures" of sorts for the sake of a superficially constructed reader-author identification that rarely elicited what Moore called "sympathy," feminist writers had two practical options from which to choose: either to be published by an independent agent such as the small feminist presses and thus achieve only limited publicity, or to court that greater establishment of mainstream publishers through whom they could reach vast numbers of readers. The second option appealed to many, and since the novel was the most popular—yet still malleable—literary form, they had to find ways of satisfying those readers' expectations as well as transforming them through it. Feminists made use of the novel as a tangible medium with which they could experiment, as well as a political and ideological tool turned against itself.

NEW WOMEN AND LITERATURE

Any effort to recover the tradition and significance of late Victorian women writers needs to take into account the fact that women novelists occupied an important place in the literary market of fin de siècle England: Their books were best-sellers. Women produced more novels in the last twenty years of the nineteenth century than in all of the history of English literature until then. As authors, they were highly visible, yet very few of their works survive today. Writers such as Margaret Oliphant, Marie Corelli, and Mrs. Humphrey Ward have fallen into obscurity. When their writings are alluded to in critical studies, it is often unfavorably, usually as distractions from so-called serious—generally Realist—literature of the period. Even feminist critics such as Elaine Showalter have been reluctant to praise feminists writers' accomplishments and their status as authors. For example, in *A Literature of Their Own*, a pioneering study that brought to light neglected women novelists, Showalter examines the literary and political significance of late Victorian "feminist" authors. In delineating the tradition of women writers in Britain, Showalter places the late Victorian "feminist" writers between the earlier "feminine" writers of the eighteenth and early nineteenth centuries and "female" writers such as Doris Lessing and other contemporary women writers. In this configuration, the feminist phase precedes that of "self-discovery," suggesting that women novelists who were also advocates of the feminist causes and who wrote as feminists did not achieve self-discovery. Showalter's evaluation of late Victorian feminist writers hardly makes them sound appealing. This may be due to those writers' disregard for what literary criticism has long associated with aesthetic "quality." More likely, Showalter's critique of these women as feminists and as writers stems from her inattention to the many kinds of discursive practices they employed in their novels. Showalter's complicity with an aesthetic tradition that privileges nonpartisan and presumably apolitical literature, even when that cause is feminism, introduces a number of interesting problems for feminist analysis because it can only view feminist visions and actions as self-contained and self-determined:

> In retrospect, it looks as if all the feminists had but one story to tell, and exhausted themselves in its narration. They represent a turning-point in the female tradition, and they turn inward. Beginning with a sense of unity and a sense of mission, a real concern for the future of womanhood, an interest in the "precious speciality" of the female novelist, they ended, like Sarah Grand, with the dream that by withdrawing from the world they would find a higher

female truth. Given the freedom to experience, they rejected it, or at least they tried to deny it. (Showalter 1977, 215)

Showalter's harshness is understandable and even, to an extent, justified. Feminist authors were caught in the middle of an ongoing debate that often necessitated their responding to affronts to their status as women and as professional authors. In fact, as I argue in the next chapter, much of the feminists' project centered on initiating a rhetorical exchange with ideologues who sought to maintain traditional gender roles in society and literature. Such defensive stances do not often lend themselves to the consuming activity of self-discovery and are a hinderance to the creation of a self-denied subjectivity. But all this posturing on the part of feminist novelists was precisely an attempt to construct a female identity in the face of opposition, and is thus oppositional itself.

This problem in self-representation is perhaps illustrated best by Schreiner's short fiction in the collection entitled *Dream Life and Real Life* (1893). Two stories, "The Woman's Rose" and "'The Policy in Favor of Protection . . .' — Was it Right? Was it Wrong?" describe the potential power of women in contrast to the misogynistic myths surrounding woman's nature and her relationships with other women. The first story examines relationships between women as traditionally antagonistic and revises that model to promote the kind of alliance feminists advocated: The story's theme conveys that all women are situated similarly under patriarchal oppression and would benefit from joining forces. An older woman gains insights on her status as a woman in society by reflecting on her past and seeing past socially endorsed impulses of jealousy among women. The heroine's ruminations result in a feminist awakening that aligns her with other women in sympathy and in action. The story's resolution is the author's own affirmation of the great possibilities for women's betterment, particularly as it diverges from male interests:

> Men were curious creatures, who liked me, I could never tell why. Only one thing took from my pleasure; I could not bear that they had deserted her from me. I liked her great dreamy blue eyes, I liked her slow walk and drawl; when I saw her sitting among men, she seemed to me much too good to be among them; I would have given all their compliments if she would once have smiled at me as she smiled at them. . . . (Schreiner [1893] 1981, 56)

This final statement is clad in pure conjecture since the narrator "knew" that women's relationships with other women "could never be," primary because women identify more closely with men than they do with one another. The heroine reveals her affection for the younger woman by giving her a rose, thus dispelling the narrator's misgivings about women's solidarity and identification with one another. Schreiner suggests here that the main obstacle to women's solidarity is the same patriarchal cynicism and misogyny internalized, and that feminist visions must include the hope that all women will reach their true potential at a distant point in time, perhaps in a different world altogether: "When my faith in woman grows dim, and it seems that for want of love and magnanimity she can play no part in any future heaven; then the scent of that small withered thing comes back: —spring cannot fail us" (62). Despite their hypotheses and assertions concerning woman's "nature," then, it appears that feminists were acutely aware of the level at which ideology serves to corrupt and divide. In fact, as their novels reveal, they were all too sensitive to it. Therefore, when Schreiner asks, "as we row hard against life, is it only a delusion of the eyes which makes us grasp our oars the more tightly and bend our backs lower?" she is differentiating between ideology and social reality (1911, 115). Reflected in such statements is the awareness that female and feminist subjectivities, as well as the literary female identity in the feminist novels of the 1890s, are to be understood as ideological constructions that have patriarchal social reality and oppositions toward it as their base. While late Victorian aesthetic and literary debates centered on the relevance and literary adaptation of notions of "fact," which was understood to represent a highly problematic social reality, as I have suggested, progressive women novelists were caught in a web of ideological obscurity and in semblances of "truth" that they would often come to metaphorically define as "dreams." Amid what Ann Ardis has termed the "violent rhetoric" surrounding women's rights activism, feminist writers ran as much risk of appearing sentimental as of being too radical (1990, 11).

These examples indicate that in trying to arrive at an understanding of the character of feminist and the specific subjectivity of women in the 1890s, we must not look to the feminist novelists as if they possessed a fixed or essential identity that motivated the issues and questions they raised. Instead, we must look to the social, ideological, and political structures that shaped their changing character; structures that, as Felski argues, "are only constituted through the practices of social agents who produce these structures anew in the process of reproducing them" (1989, 56).[4] It remains to be seen what forms female subjectivity took in specific feminist novels, but there was a cyclical relationship between two kinds of subjectivities attached to women during the late nineteenth century—the social and the literary—and these subjectivities constituted responsive relations and influences. The two most recent studies on late Victorian feminist literature, Ardis's *New Women, New Novels* (1990) and Showalter's *Sexual Anarchy* (1990), agree in emphasizing the significance of the relationship between the New Woman's social and literary identities. As Ardis illustrates, the main respect in which the New Woman differed from the earlier feminist, the "independent woman" who demonstrated a limited awareness of her own ideological marginalization, was the latter's "challeng[ing] the naturalness of sex, gender, and class distinctions" (17). Hence, insofar as it acknowledged and challenged ideological appropriations, the New Woman novel's character was contingent on its concern with social acceptability, the extent of which has not been conclusively decided by Showalter and Ardis. Both agree that the New Woman's literary subjectivity served as a tool for social change specifically by taking issue with its social contexts. As an example of the dual subjectivity Showalter and Ardis highlight, the New Woman was not one phenomenon but many. Her social and political identity had yet to be ascertained, although, loosely defined as the women's rights advocate, she emerged as a singular creature in mainstream literature. Even so, there was general agreement among women's rights activists that the New Woman was not in the least new: One could point to a centuries-long women's history comprised of exactly the kind of self-determined rebellious woman late Victorian feminists championed. Such histories were being compiled by feminists such as Olive Schreiner (*Women and Labour*), Mrs. Wolstenholme Elmy (*Woman Free*), and Mona Caird (*The Morality of Marriage* [1897]). It would not do, then, to ignore the feminists' own critical views of the New Woman's identity. Similarly, it would be erroneous to assume that the production of any "new" identity or changed status for women in society was divorced from the production of previously established relationships between gender and power, idea and practice, social role and self-definition.

Detailing the literary subjectivities of the New Woman, A. R. Cunningham bases her observations on Stutfield's analysis and remarks in an early essay that two types of New Woman fiction, the "Purity School" and the "Bachelor Girl," exhibit the characteristics of the different social stereotypes of the women's activist (1973). These novels "paved the way for more realistic characterizations of women in fiction to match their social emancipation and to lift the 'bar' on literature," according to Cunningham, and so had a long-ranging effect on enabling the production and function of literature promoting a politically invested realism (182). Gail Cunningham concurs that the "Hill-Top" or "Purity School" variety featured a bold, independent heroine who turns her attention to the "woman question" and to moral problems associated with the institution of marriage, "to show that purity could be based only on knowledge of life's darker facts" (1978, 58). The heroine's intelligence and struggle for independence were used to dispel hypocritical Victorian notions of what constitutes women's happiness. This kind of novel aimed for frankness in discussing subjects that were considered taboo, such as sexual relations, and was not well received by the general reading public; Cunningham cites Sarah Grand as an example of this category. The second kind of New Woman novel, the "Bachelor Girl" or "neurotic" type, featured a more introverted and sensitive heroine, usually confused about what the ideals for the emancipated woman should be. These New Women were far less sensational than the first type; they suffered in their attempts to confront the implications of a more far-reaching emancipation, and their revolutionary acts were self-destructive. George Egerton and Mona Caird most closely fit this type.

More productive than categorizing New Woman novels in this way and more telling of the New Woman novel's production, are the many ways in which these novels did not seem to share a common style or a specific *aesthetic* mission. Furthermore, Cunningham's categories often overlap in a number of ways; for example, the Purity School worked to problematize notions of purity at the same time that it reinforced that value, since philosophically for members "purity could be based only on the knowledge of life's darker facts," and they "encouraged plain speaking between the sexes" (58). The two types of feminist novels Cunningham describes reflect both their specific authorial ideologies and the novels' final forms as literary products. In fact, the differences between various feminist novels ultimately serve more as an indication of their authors' negotiations with the cultural economy including textual and general ideologies than as expressions of distinct feminist philosophies or specific authorial ideologies. Given that there were at least these two types of New Woman novels, including numerous variations, there is little indication in the feminist literature of the 1890s that feminists were caught in the bind of gender-identity/subjectivity Showalter described, since they were clearly not confined to a singular feminist vision and hence not a singular characterization of the New Woman. Feminists' fictional representations of New Women reveal that feminist enlightenment posed problems only within the context of a forbidding society that problematized women's attempts at self-definition. In both types of novels, the central motivation shaping feminist characterizations of New Women was the desire to create a space in which some of the deliberations feminists were engaged in might at least be articulated, regardless of whether a neat resolution to the dilemmas exposed could be provided. This distinction is evidenced in the fact that although the protagonists in feminist novels are often put into some very limiting situations for dramatic purposes, the authors themselves—in the guise of wise narrators—are without doubt past such dilemmas.

In working to define what I have thus far distinguished as the social mission of feminist novelists and texts, we must also take into account the fact that in the 1890s "it became easier than ever before to earn a living as a professional creator, because of the striking growth of the daily periodical press," and many women turned to writing as piecework, as if it were no different from factory work.[5] But as late as 1887, "'woman writer' and 'professional' were construed as contradictory terms," as Tuchman points out, evidenced in part by the fact that the prominent Society of Authors accepted women into its membership only reluctantly, and then accepted only those women authors who were already widely known (Tuchman and Fortin 1989, 192). Alluding to her low status in the mainstream literary market, Margaret Oliphant notes in her *Autobiography* ([1899], 1988) that she considered her novel-writing to be labor rather than an artistic process, and one in which High Victorian judgments concerning artistic integrity did not play a major role. This text offers an especially revealing account of women writers that is helpful precisely because it lacks the analytical and political insights present in feminists' discussions of their status in the publishing world:

> I went home to my little ones, running to the door to meet me. . . and that night, as soon as I had got them all to bed, I sat down and wrote a story which I think was something about a lawyer. . . . [It] almost made me one of the popularities of literature. . . . The story was successful, and my fortune, comparatively speaking, was made. It has never been very much, never anything like what many of my contemporaries attained, and yet I have done very well for a woman . . . I never could fight for a higher price or do anything but trust to the honor of those I had to deal with. I can't tell . . .whether it was really inferiority on my part. Anthony Trollope must have made at least three times as much as I ever did. . . . (70)

At least in this evaluation of her career as a writer, Oliphant is careful to make clear that she took up writing as a trade and that the rewards she desired for her literary efforts could have been nothing more or less than monetary. As this passage indicates, when Oliphant evaluates herself as a writer, it is primarily in terms of the money she gains by it, and she compares her own status as a writer to that of Trollope, another writer who suffered critical scrutiny because he wrote for money. Oliphant is aware that marketability and status are not indicative of real artistic or aesthetic merit and does consider the possibility that gender determined her value as a writer among publishers in the marketplace. Although there is a long tradition of writing strictly as a money-making enterprise in Victorian literature, with Scott, Dickens, and Trollope as prime examples, it is late in the century, with the literary market's dramatic expansion to include vast numbers of new authors and especially women, that the relationship of the nonestablished women writer to this market becomes especially important. Ernest Baker, a historian of the novel, describes Mrs. Oliphant as someone who "was no friend to the women's movement of her day" and who wrote "the novel of commerce"; Baker also criticizes Oliphant for "calmly and perhaps unwittingly shunn[ing] the more serious realities. Her characterization is not much more than skin deep" (1936, 209). Such criticisms of her work support Oliphant's own assertions that her work was not treated with the same seriousness as that of others; it is difficult to find the literary bases for such criticisms today, since her novels compare well technically with those of other novelists of the period. Oliphant's *Autobiography* attests to the fact that even when women writers did sell well, they were undervalued by the literary establishment on purportedly "aesthetic" grounds. Gaye Tuchman and Nina Fortin's discussion, "The Critical Double Standard," which looks at the contractual relationships between publishers and women authors, substantiates Oliphant's suspicions and concludes that "women novelists . . . were generally in a more precarious financial situation than men were" (1989, 194).

Oliphant grudgingly acquiesced to publishers' demands, although her novels do not fail to engage critically some important social issues of her day, and wrote the "problem" novels characteristic of women writers, such as *Hester* (1884), which examines the lives and conflicts of two generations of women. As she indicates in her *Autobiography*, she lacked the autonomy she would have wanted as an author since she depended on her writing for her living. Even within her compromised status as a "popular" writer and her view of herself as a producer of commodified texts, Oliphant values her experiences as a woman, mother, and wife, as they informed her writing. Ultimately, as the quoted passage suggests, she sees the combination of these apparently disparate elements that shaped her writing as constituting her own literary aesthetic. Hence, even a self-proclaimed nonfeminist such as Oliphant, who authored the reactionary "The Anti-Marriage League" (1896), saw that the literary aesthetics of women's texts are comprised of a different reality from those of men.[6] The case of Margaret Oliphant and a large number of other women writers in the last two decades of the nineteenth century suggests that women's novel writing fell under the domain of what Hobsbawm calls the "service" industry. Women's writing filled an occupational vacancy created by the unprecedented number of new journals and serials, with many authors producing as many as a dozen novels a year to earn a living. Women's writing also met a perceived need for moral instruction, similar in nature and function to that provided by and expected of vast numbers of women educators. Like education, writing that did not qualify as "fine" literature came to be undervalued as women's domain.

Several kinds of mainstream women's novels had different agendas concerning women's issues in relation to late-nineteenth century proscriptions of women, and not all of these advocated women's emancipation. For example, novelists such as Mrs. Humphrey Ward reacted against the feminist agitation for women's emancipation. Mrs. Ward can be viewed as "conciliatory," in Lovell's terms, or as reactionary in her response to feminism; she served a late Victorian need for reassurance that feminism had not done away with the traditional, domesticated, self-negating woman.[7] Like her social and political activities, including her role as leader of the Anti-Suffrage League, Mrs. Ward's novels work to bridge the gap between feminism and dominant cultural perceptions, incorporating society's fears and misgivings into her own fictional representations. Thus, her heroine, Marcella, is punished for presuming to violate gender boundaries and is reformed through humiliation. In this novel, the heroine is tamed by her love for both social status and an aristocrat. Early in the novel Marcella is adamantly opposed to the subservience expected of women, even as she accepts Alduous's marriage proposal: "I shall *never* be a meek, dependent wife," she declares, and "a woman, in my mind, is bound to cherish her own individuality sacredly, married or not married" ([1894] 1984, 121). By the end of the novel, Marcella has lost not only her rebelliousness but also her voice and her politics; having become that dependent woman she rebelled against earlier, she sits at her husband's feet, repentant of her ways. The narrator rejoices that Marcella ". . . had given away all rights—even the right to hate herself. Piteously, childishly, with seeking eyes, she held out her hand to him, as if mutely asking him for the answer to her outpouring—the last word of it all. He caught her whisper" (560). Marcella is transformed from a rebellious young Pre-Raphaelite beauty into a self-sacrificing wife who looks back on the New Woman she used to be with shame and amusement. With the heroine reformed and repentant, the husband stands as the only authority from this point on, and does, literally, have the last word in the novel.

Clearly, as novelists such as Mrs. Ward illustrate, it will not do to treat the literature produced by women in the 1890s as separate from the social reality of the period. This is particularly important, since the New Woman novels were a powerful component of feminist activism in the 1890s, and typical separations of literature from "real life" mislead us into underestimating the political function of the feminists' literary project. In 1897 Hugh Stutfield remarked in his essay "The Psychology of Feminism" that "everybody who writes nowadays must have a mission," suggesting that by the 1890s the function of the novel itself was polarized and socialized to the point that it was expected to express its author's position on a variety of controversial issues (107). Stutfield's observation suggests that in the midst of much social and aesthetic controversy, novelists were forced to situate themselves socially as well as politically within the literary marketplace. This was a highly problematic mission for feminist authors, because at the same time that they worked to assert their newly politicized identity, they were also being commodified by the literary establishment at large. The 1890s' woman became a source of artistic inspiration for writers in general, and she faced the danger of appropriation as "the emergence of the New Woman as a social phenomenon was matched by an increasing interest [in her] among novelists" in general (Cunningham 1978, 18-19). (See Chapter 5 for further elaboration on this point.)

A powerful example of the conflict between authorial ideology and the commodification of texts is in the work of Marie Corelli, whose novels were widely popular because they embraced and reinforced patriarchal idealizations of women, while her nonfiction prose advocated women's liberation. Her very popular first novel, *A Romance of Two Worlds* ([1886] 1976), valorizes spiritual independence from mundane problems and celebrates the Victorian aesthetic of "beauty equals truth," with beauty representing a curious combination of female attractiveness and spiritual purity.[8] The heroine in this novel embarks on a supernatural journey into alternate states of being and learns how to turn away from the here and now in anticipation of a universal afterlife. At a time when gender relations were a highly controversial issue and marriage in particular was critically investigated by Divorce Reform activism, Corelli's novel negates these issues' importance as pressing social problems and offers an overly simple, sentimentalized solution: Should women not gain marital bliss on earth, they can still have it in heaven; a marriage of souls is celebrated as a desirable alternative to problematic gender relations on earth. By contrast, Corelli's essays, published mainly in journals, challenged patriarchal ideology through bold feminist proclamations. "The Advance of Woman," in *Free Opinions* (1905), calls for a vision of liberation that would include the elimination of women's identification with patriarchy and advocates an emphasis on difference between the sexes: "In claiming and securing intellectual equality with Man, [woman] should ever bear in mind that such a position is only to be held by always maintaining and preserving as great an unlikeness to him as possible in life and surroundings. Let her imitate him in nothing but independence and individuality" (182). The problem that Corelli's work represents may simply reflect the complexity of her personal politics concerning women, since she remarks, in the same essay, that she would "detest" women's involvement in Parliament, because women would be "degraded" in "'scenes' of . . . undignified disputation" (181). Even so, this can hardly be a satisfactory explanation for the disparity between her novels and other prose, because her fiction offers no indication that she recognized the need for woman's liberation from patriarchal structures. Rather, her fiction embodies conservative late Victorian notions advocating a separation of spheres promoted in response to feminist intrusions on the public domain. If this novel does express Corelli's feminist philosophy, she appears to value the interiority of women exclusively. Since she proclaims herself a women's advocate in her journal articles (once again, a market that was significantly different from the novel market) and states her own brand of feminism, one that emphasizes woman's difference from and superiority to men, it is likely that Corelli conformed to mainstream expectations of fiction in order to gain success as a novelist. So successful was she that staunch Queen Victoria proclaimed Corelli her favorite among late Victorian authors (Masters 1978, 103).

Much of the feminist fiction of the 1890s was subject to the cultural appropriation of self-determined subjectivity that I have described in the first chapter. Despite their material bases and practical implications, the marginalization of feminist text was represented in social rhetoric as being based strictly on ideological—moral, religious, "cultural"—grounds and hence as lacking in popular acceptance. In feminist discourse, practical restrictions were represented as segments of the rhetorical controversy concerning feminist activism. In this way, the specifics of women's literary marginalization in the late nineteenth century were often obscured in discussions concerning cultural hegemony, literary value, and aesthetics. Since the "aesthetics" debate did not favor women's literary status, as I have already suggested, the feminist message in women's writings often took second place to other, more widely cultural considerations. Tuchman and Fortin offer an example of how this displacement of feminist literary objectives was implemented: "During the . . . 1880s and 1890s, critics emphasized what today are called 'literary values.' Women were still compared to women, but critics used new terms to claim that women failed if they dealt with topics deemed suitable for men: Some were said to have sacrificed 'art'" (186). Citing this phenomenon as an example of how the last two decades of the nineteenth century, "the period of redefinition," differed markedly from the earlier (1840-1880) "period of male invasion" during which men appropriated what had formerly been a female-dominated genre, the novel, Tuchman and Fortin point to the ways in which women novelists were subsumed in the late Victorian literary marketplace while male novelists reigned as high-literary figures. Women's political agendas were so closely scrutinized and censored along aesthetic lines, in fact, that an 1894 review of George Eliot as a woman and as a writer proclaimed her inferior to Mrs. Humphrey Ward, citing the latter's *Marcella* as exhibiting a kind of "philosophical enthusiasm" Eliot lacked (Tuchman and Fortin, 184). Implicit in this reviewer's argument is that Mrs. Ward's "enthusiasm" is worthy of praise because it constituted polemical expressions of reactionary traditionalism and a forthright criticism of the political and social unrest wrought by the feminist of her age. Mrs. Ward's "philosophical enthusiasm" called for that very same separation of the spheres that literary ideology sought to preserve, while Eliot's works, specifically *Middlemarch* and *Mill On the Floss*, problematized those systems. As I have already argued, *Marcella* can be described as a reactionary novel, since its "philosophical enthusiasm" lies in its negating feminist philosophy, its mission to reinstate more traditional definitions of womanhood. Proving Tuchman's point, this critic of Eliot seeks to discredit the earlier period in the history of the novel, that dominated by women like Eliot.

Complementing the rather covert criticisms of feminism found in fictional works, expressions of censure included the clamor of blatant antifeminists such as Eliza Lynn Linton and others, writers whose essays encouraged outrage toward the New Woman and served to shape public opinion against feminism.[9] In light of the biases it had to contend with, of which antifeminist fiction is only one example, much of the feminist literature of the 1890s works not so much to express the author's own political philosophy or even to reflect the feminist community's sentiments, but to augment some of the misrepresentations and slander issued by antifeminists. Therefore, they are novels with a double purpose; in addition to external interference, a number of problems within the feminist movement itself complicated feminists' attempts at self-definition and unified purpose. For instance, the class-identity conflict between middle-class women activists and the vast numbers of working-class women they claimed to represent may explain why it is so seldom that we find working-class protagonists in feminist novels, a common enough occurrence in other novels written by nonfeminist men and women in the 1880s and 1890s. Characters in feminist novels often turn to the slums of London as sources of experience, wisdom, and growth toward independence, but those settings are rarely central to the narratives themselves. Even with their reservations, feminist novelists adopted several strategies that enabled them to transcend the limitations imposed by the novel form, so that they could create what they viewed as more accurate representations of New Women. The novel was used by feminists as a medium through which to engage their readers' sympathies and to sway popular opinion concerning gender relations. Feminist fiction was thus both an extension of and a substitute for feminist social activism. Courting popular sentiment gave the feminist novels their propagandistic character, so that artistic and "aesthetic" quality was ultimately not as much a concern among these writers as were influence and their texts' ultimate impact. The novel enabled various expressions of feminist ideas, but it also modified and was modified by them. Every feminist assertion concerning the "true" character of women appeared in the context of then-current controversies concerning not only women, but human nature, morality, and social propriety. When feminist writers put forth their theses on women, they intervened in such public discussions and pitted themselves against more prominent and socially sanctioned assertions. Thus, what I am naming the "feminist novel" works deliberately to acknowledge, question, and oppose specific voices and gender assumptions in status quo, mainstream Victorian discourse. Mainly, feminists set out to insert themselves into the monolithic patriarchal aesthetic ideology that would confine them to the domain of "interested" or extraliterary literature, as, by the 1890s, "men used their control of major literary institutions to transform the high-culture novel into a male preserve" (Tuchman and Fortin, 204).

In conclusion, because it appears in the context of a number of appropriations and negotiations, the feminist novel and the nonfiction writings of the 1890s I have examined here can best be viewed as "systems," as Pierre Macherey has put it, including the silences it seeks to articulate as well as those they incorporate into their projected totality (1989, 100). The silences of which the feminist novel is partly comprised—namely, that genre's battle with both ideological and material modes of production—render it an open-ended text, requiring that we read it alongside other "texts," including social debate and the premises and consequences of social agitation. The "silences" to account for in reading these texts, then, include feminists' textual exchange with reactionary elements and testify to the conditions of their production—including their readership.

LATE VICTORIAN FEMINIST DISCURSIVE AESTHETICS

"Purpose!" he ejaculated: "It is hardly likely I shall write a novel with a purpose. I leave that to the ladies."

Sarah Grand, *The Beth Book* ([1897] 1980), 455.

♦ ♦ ♦

Given the publication constraints specific to the 1890s that I have outlined in Chapter 3 and women writers' efforts to gain and enlighten their audiences in late Victorian culture, the feminists' project in writing novels can best be understood as a series of ventures toward discursive mediation and the disruption of normative Victorian conceptions of gender. The feminist novel's desired impact, that of disrupting mainstream cultural systems, stems from the fact that novel writing for feminists of the nineties served a primarily social and political function. Defined along the lines of Homi Bhabha's analysis of oppositional writing, the feminists' goal was to "re-situate [themselves] as critical subject[s] while maintaining a position of effective agency and rejecting the temptations of [patriarchal] essentialism or [institutionalized] pragmatism" (1990, 7). Indeed, one of the prominent features of 1890s' feminist novels, at the outset, is that they set out to directly confront repressive social ideologies, including the dominant Victorian aesthetic ideology, as an intellectual discipline that minimized the significance of both women and of women's rights activism. The feminists' mission, in the novels they produced, was to assail and dismantle the privileged authorial and cultural perspective and the ensuing categorizations concerning literary value. This was a necessary but difficult task since the old adage about appropriate pronouncements stemming from women earlier in the century still applied in the 1890s: "It would be presumptuous in a woman to speak authoritatively in a woman's voice of ['facts']. Where she could legitimately speak was of course from sympathetic feeling," as Lovell has argued (1987, 87). Hence, feminists turned to the novel as a familiar medium and experimented with it in the process of making some fairly bold gestures toward women's emancipation. I would add, however, that part of the appeal to sympathy was a political ploy as well: Feminists wanted to earn the "sympathy" of their readers, which Moore also acknowledged as being of the utmost importance to late Victorian authors, in the context of an already claimed reading public. Also, given their history of failures in instigating legislative change, their mission had to foreground cultural change and social support as well. The project for feminist novels was, as Gail Cunningham has observed, to "integrate the demands of art [with those of] propaganda" (1978, 69).

In this chapter, I consider the feminist novelists' explicit arguments with late Victorian aesthetic ideology, the complex character of the feminist heroine, and then examine the ways in which feminist authors sought to stylistically subvert literary and cultural proscriptions they found limiting. As I argue in Chapter 2, Victorian aesthetic theory ranging from Ruskin and Carlyle to the Pre-Raphaelites and Pater had traditionally conceded to women primarily the role of object in art and culture. In such normative, sexist treatises, women figure as variable signifiers upon which different and often conflicting meanings could be imposed. Hence, the challenge to feminist novelists was to create a more meaningful and direct correspondence among the constructed subjectivities of their female characters, their own authorial and political agendas, and the social context in which their narratives appeared—that of feminist agitation and the reactionary controversy it engendered. As a result, in the majority of late Victorian feminist novels, heroines are literary creations who bear some significant relation to social reality while they challenge the gender and widely cultural prejudices prevalent in late Victorian England. In literature, as in society, the feminists' goal was to free woman from her passivity, to make her an active agent in her own existence; thereby, the feminist novel's heroine was a disruptive agent in herself, insofar as she embodied the goals and struggles of the feminist movement as a whole.

My point here is that "feminist" novels are distinguished from the many other woman-authored novels of the period by their emancipatory mission and their explicit protest against various examples of patriarchal ideology and oppression. Patricia Stubbs also distinguishes them from earlier woman-centered and authored works by emphasizing their partisan political character and their argument with patriarchal ideology. In *Women and Fiction*, she notes that "it was only towards the end of the Nineteenth Century that novelists began to go beyond structuring their work around the dislocation between ideology and reality and started to attack the ideology itself" (1979, xiv). Following decades of women's activism, the feminist novel at the close of the century was informed by the movement's many successes and failures, and was thus in a critical position to work to transcend specific and isolated moments and temporal concerns. Stubbs's observation concerning the distinct character of the "feminist" novel is further supported by an essay entitled "The Psychology of Feminism" (1897), in which Hugh Stutfield distinguishes "feminist" from other woman-authored writings and highlights the radicalism of the former. In his view, nonfeminist novels of his day appear to "follow in man's footsteps, philosophizing and preaching after the manner of the leading male thinkers of the day," while the feminist novel's dominant note is "restlessness and discontent with the existing order of things" (104). Indeed, writers such as Mrs. Humphrey Ward and Eliza Lynn Linton, though they address the "woman question," could hardly be said to be doing anything more than reinforcing the patriarchal status quo; for these writers, the concept of ideology as an agent of repression is obfuscated by their esteem for tradition, and in their novels patriarchal values serve a central function in their explorations of the woman problem. Both definitions of the feminist novel agree in emphasizing feminist fiction's nonidentification with, and rebellion toward, patriarchal thought. Therefore, while nonfeminist literature of the period is characterized by an incorporation of patriarchal ideology, the feminist novel managed to initiate an argument with patriarchal ideology to complement feminists' arguments with society via political protest.

Keeping these distinctions in mind, I want to elaborate on the feminists' engagement of literary and social repression by outlining some of the means by which the feminists, as authors, sought to communicate their oppositional message to general audiences, defying the prohibitions of the literary marketplace. Feminist novelists sought to revise traditional notions concerning women by criticizing and revising that cultural history and tradition, given that by the 1890s the novel came to be "the literature of the people" (Griest 1970, 102). For feminists, novel writing constituted an effective means of intruding on the cultural imagination so that the "story" of women's lives could be rewritten from a radically politicized perspective, with a different awareness or "subtext" informing their narratives, that of female advocacy and the exposure of women's victimization by patriarchal tradition. Therefore, most of these novels "were treatises first, novels second," as Stubbs has argued, although the novel as a genre would undergo some significant modifications as a result of having thus been used as a political medium for feminism (117). As I will illustrate, insofar as cultural ideology was the impetus of feminist novels' main opposition to the status quo, narrations of the "externals" of women's social lives were complemented by explanations of how oppression works; this second item on the feminist literary agenda forged new strains in narratives, while the question of conscious and unconscious subversion lent the novel "interiority." By the 1880s feminism had made such an impact that even nonfeminist novelists were writing, quite complacently, "[she] rebelled as a girl does against every such injurious picture of women" (Oliphant [1884] 1984, 304).

The issues that surface as themes in feminist novels of the period reflect the feminist political agenda, but also serve to highlight their authors' preferred issues. Nonetheless, they all make it a point to at least comment upon—in passing, sometimes—the basic items of man's immorality, societal hypocrisy, and the need for women's education. Given the basic similarities in political aims and premises among individual feminists, and given their common collective goals, woman's "nature" is constantly being defined and redefined in feminist novels. In fact, the issue of what a woman is *really* all about was open to question and was perpetually posed as a question, as Oliphant did not fail to notice, even from her position outside the feminist movement. As she notes in *Hester* ([1884] 1984), "a sense of helplessness began to take the place of indignation.... Was that what they called the lot of woman?" (405). The essence of womanhood was only to be guessed at. While feminists' "specifically political arguments centered upon the issues of equality and representation," as Philippa Levine illustrates, their many differences and "ethical arguments extended from a simple declaration of injustice to a belief in woman's moral superiority and fitness" (1987, 60). Feminist philosophy of the nineties illustrates different conceptions of woman: Some feminists saw themselves as morally superior to men; others saw women as pure in every way; while yet others stressed power as inherent in untapped, unappropriated female sexuality. Reflecting the philosophical divisions within the women's rights movement, which mainly had to do with their different perspectives on the woman question and their different resolutions toward it, feminist fiction of the 1890s features a number of distinct approaches to the woman question. In a sense, while feminist authors described the same general social reality as individual authors, they had different stories to tell about woman's status in society and about "the eternal feminine," or woman's authentic, uncompromised character. Hence, feminist authors offered slightly different explanations for woman's predicament, and also different solutions to it. The politically based differences in approach evidenced in feminist texts are compounded by the many literary and aesthetic mediations in their story's telling. These external as opposed to authorial interventions render the feminist novel of the nineties an openended, uncertain text. Ultimately, given the divisions within the feminist movement and the complexity of late Victorian feminist philosophy, especially as it was closely bound with an equally complex social reality, the feminist novel also gives expression to a radical point of view that does not compromise dissonance as it radically revises normative ideological proscriptions of gender. Quite unilaterally, feminist novels of the 1890s confront gender assumptions by revealing their cultural and political manifestations. In this respect, one is perhaps most enlightened by the sophistication of the feminist novel's scrutiny of the insidious politics of oppression through analyses that compare well to contemporary feminist critique.

Feminist novelists of the 1890s sought to account for, and responded to, material and ideological intrusions on their political agendas as well as on their texts, and to dismantle them so that they could begin to infuse literature and society with a feminist consciousness. Feminists could hardly afford to forgo the use of the novel as a forum, even with the challenges it presented; fiction was a great deal more popular than nonfiction in the nineties, and between 65 and 90 percent of all books circulated were fiction (Altick 1957, 231). Serving as an extension of social activism, the novel enabled feminists to intrude upon speculations concerning literary value and to define their own literary agendas and philosophies so that their novels would get the kind of reading their authors desired. Most important, fiction enabled feminists to subvert a dominant aesthetic ideology that would otherwise have undermined their project and their validity as authors, and to theorize and expose the exclusivism of commonplace aesthetic practices. This same act of literary self-assertion enabled them to enact an alternative, feminist literary aesthetic. Extended narratives afforded feminists the opportunity to retell, and in the process politically translate and revise, the story of women's lives. Their novels include social perceptions of women, harsh criticisms of patriarchy and the subordination of women, recognizable social and literary types, and various means of problematizing those types while blurring distinctions between "fact" and "fiction." Of necessity, given the restrictiveness of late Victorian literary aesthetics, feminist narrative strategies were also subversive of the standard novelistic form itself, the control of which was seen to lie, hierarchically, in the domain of patriarchal repressiveness.

REDEFINING LITERARY "AESTHETICS"

Much like the dominant cultural and political ideologies of the 1890s, literary aesthetics posed a threat to oppositional writers such as the feminists, especially since aesthetic ideology of the nineties concerned itself with defining "good" "art" and distinguishing it from mere preoccupation with "facts." Since, as Tuchman observes, "unlike men, women never possessed the power to define the nature of good literature," it follows that feminists would seek to gain some control over the labels attached to their texts (Tuchman and Fortin 204). For feminists, also, the subtler implications of value judgments concerning what Walter Pater termed "the finer feelings" and acceptable reconstructions of the real in literature were manifested in the controversy on the suitability of narrativizing women's troubled lives. But it isn't true that "when women served as critics, they displayed their internalization of male standards," for feminists did explicitly take issue with such discussions, and appear to have been aware of their importance (Tuchman and Fortin 204). As I illustrate later, feminists scrutinized mainstream fictional representations of women and quite clearly attempted to intrude on this male-dominated domain. Feminists often expressed and published their critical readings of male-authored texts. The challenge that women posed to aesthetic ideology was external—that is, effected outside literary texts themselves—and internal, implemented from within the novel. Some even went as far as to attempt to *create* the kind of enlightened, critical reader their novels required, as the case of "Vernon Lee" illustrates in Chapter 3. Writing in opposition to the cultural aesthetic and literary standards of their day, feminists attempted to instill in their readers a critical consciousness that would effectively end their complicity with mainstream literary valuations. Commendably, writing within the confines of a single narrative, feminist novelists did engage in contradicting and revising their male colleagues' critical formulations concerning "good art." Tuchman's oversight relies on the traditional generic definition of the novel that disallows the possibility of intertextuality and that feminists managed to alter; that is, feminists did serve as literary critics, but they did so primarily through their fiction. The novels I discuss in this chapter also serve to illustrate that feminist writers had not, in fact, "internalized" male critical standards quite as thoroughly as Tuchman suggests, and that they were in the precarious position of having to produce "good" fiction (as judged by the established literary standards) that was also politically invested, novels whose desired effects were not literary, primarily, but functional and sociopolitical. Apparently, feminists were aware of oppression along social lines across the board, and so in highlighting the political ramifications of aesthetic ideology, they often allude to other power inequities perpetuated by the dominant aesthetic ideology, such as class, and draw parallels between the two as being intrinsically similar. Middle-class insularity and complacency are depicted by Caird, Cholmondeley, and Grand as being both socially and emotionally crippling for women since they perpetuate dependency and a primary allegiance to social class in the women they serve to oppress. For example, feminist heroines tend to reject social institutions such as marriage and the family, and often leave their gilded cages to seek independence by exploring their potential in other contexts: They become uprooted single women living and working in cities, merging with the big, unnamed and uncharted class of the "masses." Such women forfeit notions of what is "good" and "proper" in order to begin to make sense of their own lives and to consider more authentic and worthwhile values. Feminist heroines such as Caird's Hadria, Cholmondeley's Rachel, and Grand's Beth, are shown to reach true independence and self-actualization precisely because and when they occupy a place on the fringes of social and class divisions. Hence, for these feminists, aesthetic ideology is very much bound up with extraliterary and artistic considerations.

The kinds of negotiations entailed by the feminists' positioning in relation to aesthetic ideology, readership, and literary expectations are illustrated clearly in the introduction by "Sarah Grand" (Frances McFall) to *Heavenly Twins* (1893), entitled "Proem." This essay merges and confuses form, so that the narrative that follows, which initially appears to be fiction, must now be interpreted as bearing a problematic relation to nonfiction prose. In its uncomfortably close association with fiction, Grand's preface works to establish fiction as the narration of "true" stories. One of the most important feminists of her age, Grand had long stood in opposition to public opinion and the expectations established by Victorian literary and aesthetic ideologies. Grand was president of a branch of the National Union of Women's Suffrage Societies and was a also active in campaigning against the Contagious Diseases Act, both in her public life and in her novels. As a sexual reforms activist who published extensively, she was also familiar with the dangers of being co-opted by the mandates of "popular taste" as interpreted by the publishing industry. Indeed, it was not until she began to write the "sentimental" novels deemed more appropriate to women writers that she gained a substantial readership.

Heavenly Twins centers on how patriarchal society degrades women both sexually and morally, and constitutes a literary protest against the immorality of the Acts. At a time when sexually overt literature was being decried as "ludicrously inartistic" and a nuisance, this novel's highly controversial subject matter necessitated justification and experimentation with form (Noble 1895, 494). In "Proem," Grand criticizes aestheticism's claims to truthfulness by pointing to the material determinations of both art and aesthetic judgment. Uncovering the underlying self-interest of the literary establishment, she writes, "there is no faith in the fetish he has helped to make, or in a particular kind of leather that sells quickest because it wears out so fast" (1893, xi). A critical account of aesthetic ideology and its implications, the "Proem" is Grand's indictment of the aesthetic standards of both "philistines" (such as Mudie and the growing number of booksellers) and antisocial figures (such as the aesthetes) whose proclamations were generally frivolous and of no immediate political consequence, but whose power to influence notions of literary value and importance cannot, in retrospect, be underestimated. *Heavenly Twins* was reviewed at length only after it went into second printing, having sold out its first. Consistent with her attempts to subvert the critical constraints on her own writing, Grand demystifies works of art by defining them as subjective utterances of the artist amid problematic contexts. Likening art to the innocent chime of a bell that comes to be complicated by its listeners, a comparison also made by "Vernon Lee" in her "Craft of Words," Grand offers a model of aesthetics based on the bell's constancy as contrasted to the flippancy of its dubious listeners. In this analysis, it is the listeners/readers who are the cause of the problem of art's reception, since the privilege of judging the beauty and value of the "chime" invariably falls to those who

> knew the music well [and] who spoke their "truth" [about it] but [also to] others [who] maintained that it could not be true just for that reason; while others again, although they confessed that they knew nothing of the distance sound may travel under special circumstances, ventured, nevertheless, to assert that the chime the people heard on those occasions was ringing in their own hearts. (i)

Rather than support a notion popularized by the aesthetes—namely, that art offers a sifted, subjective perception of reality and hence a higher and purer truth than does social reality—Grand argues that this position is only one of several informing the evaluation of texts. Grand's attention to audiences' predispositions and her systematic categorization of the process of art's reception attests to her awareness that her own text would receive only the kind of reading her audience was prepared to give it. The categories of readers she describes in the preceding passage suggest that she believes her readership would not be a sympathetic one. Grand also makes clear that her novel's reception would not be one that she could value for its own sake or as indicative of her work's intrinsic value, because it would primarily reflect the wider network of ideological and cultural biases informing those readings. Grand's analysis mirrors the kind of censorship Jameson has termed "the bourgeois censoring ego" (1981, 8).[1] In Jameson's terms, Grand is reading both her audience *and* aesthetic ideology as "symbolic texts" that signify the power structure that informs and underlies them. Having asserted this critical awareness, and having worked to unsettle the reader's complacency by pointing to the relevance of his or her positioning in relation to her text, Grand proceeds to write her own version of womanhood, finally producing a story that makes some startling assertions about the hypocrisy of late Victorian culture and morality. *Heavenly Twins*, which came to be viewed by many as an "unspeakably revolting . . . ridiculously overpraised book," promotes a redefinition of gender oppression that includes the sexual, societal, and psychological or "spiritual" debasement of women (Noble 493). Grand portrays a society infested with dishonesty and a superficial concern with keeping up appearances, but also a diseased and degenerate world that compromises and sacrifices woman's virtue.

In an argument similar to Grand's, Caird's *Daughters of Danaus* ([1894] 1989) once again presents a critique of aesthetic ideology as a precursor to social critique. The novel opens with a debate that aims to address the question of aesthetic value by revealing the High/Low cultural judgments permeating late Victorian aesthetic ideology. Caird's analysis invests aesthetic ideology with class-based associations by exposing the realities of unequal opportunity as being constitutive of artistic expression and judgment. She thus promotes a broader understanding of art as a product and of the artist as a social being. In the novel's opening scene, a group of children, "The Preposterous Society," argues the question of self-determination versus determination by social circumstance. Hadria, the heroine of the novel, argues for social equality and a kind of socialism that would engender sympathy for, and identification with, the oppressed. Her argument, remarkable for its emotional intensity and intellectual rigor, reveals that the art and reality to which one has access is privileged, as is an idealistic view of art in general:

> Given (say) great artistic power, given also a conscience and a strong will, is there any combination of circumstances which might prevent the artistic power (assuming it to be of the highest order and strength) from developing and displaying itself, so as to meet with general recognition? . . . There seems to be a thousand chances against it. . . . Artistic power, to begin with, is a sort of

> weakness in relation to the everyday world, and so, in some ways, is a nice conscience. I think Emerson is shockingly unjust. His beaming optimism is a worship of success disguised under lofty terms . . . perhaps the very greatest of all are those whom the world has never known, because the present conditions are inharmonious with the very noblest and the very highest qualities. (11-12)

Intimating that the "worship of success" can only be complicitous with the hierarchies promoted by the aesthetic and cultural status quo, Hadria turns her attention to the multitudes to whom injustices have been done, the same multitudes, "all those unknowns," whom, as she points out later, society has "silenced." Both the obstacle *and* project of this novel, Caird realizes, is as much to deconstruct prejudice and elitist assumptions as to begin to construct an alternative, empowered existence for her silenced heroine: "'what a frightful piece of circumstance *that* is to encounter . . . to have to buy the mere right to one's liberty by cutting through prejudices . . . *that* particular obstacle has held many a woman helpless and suffering. . . .'" (15). Speaking as a representative of women, whom the novel reveals as having been similarly silenced, Caird equates her own status as a woman to that of the lower classes and the "masses," and insists that they are quite capable of producing great art but have been systematically ("conditionally") prevented from doing so. Her own definition of "success," along these lines, is breaking that silence by producing art that, she acknowledges, would not meet with acceptance and "general recognition" in her culture.

Having thus outlined the philosophical argument she means to pursue, Caird constructs a plot that bears out her position's validity. The heroine's frustration as a woman and artist in male-dominated society works to illustrate her own earlier philosophical argument. During the course of the novel we discover that the greatest tragedy of all, and the circumstance that leads to Hadria's tragic undoing, is her parents' and husband's (hence, authority's) discrediting and undermining her musical ambitions. Caird poses this invalidation as one of the main obstacles to Hadria's growth as a woman, for, even though the heroine's repression leads her to look for freedom in all the wrong places, such as an illicit love affair with a man who is her moral inferior, the most urgent reason for her ultimately leaving her husband is the desire to develop her musical talent. Through her narrator, Caird comments on the dangers women encounter in their desperate need for acceptance and support, and bemoans "the hero-worship that is latent in us all," false and compromising alliances with men that stem from the redundancy and meaninglessness of women's constructed lives and render women "ready to believe in the professions of the devil himself" for a mere "touch of poetry" (189). Given how they are situated socially, women must consider the freedom to create art a privilege and a rare opportunity amid repressive middle-class societal expectations as executed by Hadria's marriage and her parents, and amid duties that are enforced by hypocritical notions of moral rectitude. In this novel, then, Caird is fictionalizing the single issue that directed her social activism and that she explored more fully in *The Morality of Marriage*, her study of marriage as a morally corruptive institution (1897). This novel serves as an extension of the argument she was to continue to make in different ways and through different forms during her life. As such, it is an important articulation of Caird's specific political position as a feminist activist.

Another instance of feminism's literary challenges to dominant aesthetic ideology is *Red Pottage* ([1899] 1985) by Mary Cholmondeley, a relative recluse who was greatly influenced by the writings of Sarah Grand. The last and boldest of five novels, *Red Pottage* was avidly read and widely discussed for months following its publication because it scandalized Victorian society by satirizing it. Accurately described as "angry" by many critics at the time of its publication and since, *Red Pottage* seeks to discredit the aestheticism of the 1890s by mocking its stereotyped features that made their way into the popular imagination.[2] Making sure to place herself within one of the most popular trends in the popular literature of the 1890s, the sentimental narrative of manners, Cholmondeley adopts certain features of aestheticism's distinctive style in order to criticize it. In her depiction of Lady Newhaven as the socially corrupt woman, Cholmondeley's narrative style complements her caricature of the "society" lady, who has been created according to the "mode" as a reactionary caricature of womanhood and who was commonly depicted by the aesthetes in their art and self-representations: "*Tableau* — A beautiful, sad-faced young married woman in white, reclining among pale-green cushions near a bowl of pink carnations, endeavoring to rouse the higher feelings of an inexperienced though not youthful spinster in a short bicycling skirt. Decidedly, the picture was not flattering to Rachel" (106). Juxtaposing the socially and sentimentally affected Lady Newhaven to Rachel, the New Woman "in a short bicycling skirt," Cholmondeley diagnoses aestheticism's ramifications for women as decadent and corruptive. Cholmondeley encourages a critical stance toward Lady Newhaven by positing the truly liberated Rachel as an observer of the former's affectation. She contrasts the two women, granting Rachel the powerful position of critical observer, and then incorporates feminist criticisms of aestheticism into the narrative's workings. Through Rachel's subtle yet potent dislike of Lady Newhaven, the latter appears as a caricature of her potential womanhood.

Whereas Lady Newhaven's "attitude had the touch of artificiality which was natural to her," Rachel represents the kind of woman who is more authentic because she disregards the dictates of fashion and style as elitist dissociations from "Low" Culture and because she can claim partial membership to the lower classes (11). Rachel's "naturalness" includes her identification with the masses, having once been very poor herself; she can thus see through the seductive superficiality of "high society." Her critical stance toward the melodrama of Lady Newhaven and her society comes from her familiarity with an entirely different reality. Upon first meeting her, Rachel's lover observes:

> Something in her clear eyes told him, as they told many others, that small lies and petty details might be laid aside with impunity in dealing with her . . . he felt her eyes were old friends, tried to the uttermost and found faithful in some forgotten past. Rachel's eyes had a certain calm fixity in them that comes not of natural temperament but of past conflict, long waged. . . . (21)

In the case of both Rachel and Lady Newhaven, characteristics that may be construed as "natural" are shown to be determined by experience that is class-specific. Because she has crossed class lines, Rachel possesses a knowledge and substance absent in the elite, and she serves as the measure by which the reader can evaluate the lives and self-images of the privileged. On the contrary, as a sheltered member of the aristocracy, Lady Newhaven's self-image is narrowly defined by aesthetic representations of women, so that she fashions her own life in such a way as to imitate art. A self-stylized lady of leisure and indulgence, Lady Newhaven is selfish and destructive, living out a melodramatic romance that results in tragedy. In fact, in this plot Lady Newhaven's self-centered whims are the cause of two deaths: that of her husband, whose fallacious attempts at chivalry lead him to commit a mock-heroic suicide; and that of her lover, who, having been debased through his affair with her, cannot reconcile himself to being loved by someone as virtuous as Rachel. The kind of self-importance and sensationalism exhibited by Lady Newhaven and her circle is similar to the kind of "snobbery" Hobsbawm associates with the neo-conservatism and insularity of the upper classes anxious to protect their class status from merging with that of the mobile middle classes at the close of the century (1987, 174). It is significant that the means by which they maintained their cultural and social superiority were primarily social and ideological. In scrutinizing the self-indulgent Lady Newhaven, who has made an aesthete's "art" of her life, Cholmondeley at once accuses the dominant *fin-de-siècle* aesthetic ideology for its misogynistic tendencies and unrealistic pretensions, and links the biases it promotes to the perversion of class and gender identities.

In addition to illustrating the negative social ramifications of aestheticism's claims through her representation of the decadent aristocracy, the major portion of Cholmondeley's critique of late Victorian aesthetic ideology is expressed more directly through the character of Hester, the figure of the author in *Red Pottage*, through whom Cholmondeley initiates a discussion of literature's social function and women's status as authors. This proves an important and strategic undertaking for Cholmondeley, since the issues she raises pertain directly to her own novel's legitimacy and its ultimate harsh appraisal in the literary market. The many heated debates between Hester and her middle-class minister brother, Mr. Gresley, who "had not a high opinion of the feminine intellect," typify and expose the late Victorian controversies concerning the purpose of literature. Is it to educate readers in conventional morality, or to refine emotion and sensibility, a critical process with unpredictable results? (263) Gresley reveals his ignorance as a reader, but also his self-righteousness. After reading the novel, he concludes that it isn't appropriate reading material because he does not recognize the situations it depicts: "he had never felt like that, and his own experience was his measure of the utmost that is possible in human nature" (259). Interestingly, part of Gresley's argument is that his judgment is superior and must override that of the general public; in fact, he derides Hester for having "pander[ed] to the depraved public" (263). While Hester's own position is substantiated quite forcefully by the plot as she risks her life in order to produce and protect a novel she views as her "child," Gresley's formidable censoring influence must finally be judged as blatantly immoral, especially as he burns Hester's novel because it represents him as the tyrant he is. Thus, the descriptive accuracy of Hester's novel, its fidelity to social reality rather than to moralistic idealization, come under attack, while its lack of governing conventional morality and its refutation of the Christian ideal of martyrdom bans it from existence. Hester's challenge to traditional middle-class pretensions, in short, causes her novel to become permanently censored out of existence.

Cholmondeley's "anger" toward this type of mistreatment as a violent abuse of privilege and power is complemented by attempts to protect and shield her own text. In her own novel, *Red Pottage*, the text that frames Hester's contested text, Cholmondeley resists an allegiance to High Victorian literary aesthetics in two ways. First, she prefaces each of the chapters with quotes from such nonconventional figures as Dante Rossetti and Omar Khayaam, including some of the more oppositional statements from George Eliot's fiction, thus distancing herself from mainstream values ("The only sin which we never forgive in each other is difference of opinion—Emerson," begins this critical chapter, and "It is as useless to fight against the interpretations of ignorance as to whip the frog—Eliot," another). Second, the postscript to the novel undermines any novel's presumed conclusiveness and insularity by asserting that it does not convey any absolute truths about life and morality—there are other novels, other readings, and this has been a single page out of life. Hence, although *Red Pottage* culminates in tragedy, Cholmondeley remains optimistic. Holding to her purpose for writing this novel, she states that each of life's occurrences is a single step toward what she calls "the Perfect Day," a moment that she envisions as bringing an end to the injustices she has described:

> WE turn the pages of the Book of Life with impatient hands. And if we shut up the book at a sad page we say hastily "Life is sad." But it is not so. There are other pages waiting to be turned. I, who have copied out one little chapter of the lives of Rachel and Hester, cannot see plainly, but I catch glimpses of those other pages. . . . Hope and Love and Enthusiasm never die. . . . How, then, can life be sad, when they walk beside us always in the growing light towards the Perfect Day. (375)

In addition to undermining her novel's possible misreadings, then, Cholmondeley's postscript challenges the authority granted certain texts and uses the narrative as a means of obfuscating the generic proscriptions of the novel. Furthermore, she initiates a discourse of endless change and possibilities, so that it finally becomes possible for her readers to ponder what may have happened had Hester's brother not interfered with her work, had the indulgent aristocracy not been so self-serving, had love and friendship not been subjected to the influences of a life-denying, morally decadent society. It becomes possible to question and challenge the very structures that determined this tragedy from the outset. Through this same strategy the tragedy of Hester's life is diffused and divested of any, even a textual, permanence.

One of the most explicit fictional expositions on the relationship between art and society, and the most volatile refutation of late Victorian aesthetic ideology, is found in the militantly feminist semiautobiographical novel *The Beth Book* ([1897] 1980) by "Sarah Grand" (Frances McFall). Grand published the novel under a pseudonym, thus gaining some dissociation from her social identity as a women's rights activist. In this narrative, Grand makes clear the antagonistic relationship between aesthetic ideology and progressive politics through a rebellious heroine who comes to define herself as a women's rights advocate. In a series of overt references to the commodification of literature, Grand presents Beth as an author who becomes educated in the dangers of appropriation faced by women writers of the period. When she writes with the purpose of interpreting and narrating her own experiences as a woman, and thus reaffirming the central importance of the realities of women's lives as opposed to writing in order to satisfy literary standards, Beth also uses those experiences to construct an analysis of women's oppression. Her own experiences as a woman come to serve as a paradigm for the emancipation of women in the novel, suggesting that for feminists there is a close relationship between life/fact and literature. Beth's narratives invariably work to illustrate that woman's potential and identity are not acknowledged by society but are actually minimized so that women may become suitably subjected by and subservient to men who, feminists argue, are their inferiors. For example, Beth finds she is demeaned by her dealings with her husband and "was angry with herself, and grieved because she had fought Dan with his own weapons . . . [but] fight him she must with something, somehow, or sink for ever down to the degraded level required of their wives by husbands of his way of thinking" (408). Power is located in action, according to Grand, and through her writing, Beth discovers that it is all too easy to compromise her integrity to her subject matter—women—because she must answer to external literary standards and her readers' expectations. According to Beth's analysis of late Victorian literary mandates, aesthetic ideology sets and enforces literary categories that negate the author's lived experiences and views as a woman; she discovers that the aesthetic standards of her day render politically invested oppositional discourse virtually impossible:

> The works of art for art's sake, and style for style's sake, end on the shelf much respected, while their authors end in the asylum, the prison, and the premature grave. I had a lesson on that subject long ago, which enlarged my mind. I got among the people who talk of style incessantly, as if style were everything, till at last I verily believed it was. I began to lose all I had to express for worry of the way to express it. (460)

Beth puts an end to her frustrations toward the aesthetics and politics of "art for art's sake" by affirming her commitment to writing that is inspired by concerns other than writing itself, writing that makes reference to realities other than the textual. Undermining the main claims of aestheticism that facts demean art and that the truth is to be found mainly in the artistic expression, she concludes, "If you have the matter, the manner will come, as handwriting comes to each of us; and it will be as good, too, as you are conscientious, and as beautiful as you are good" (461). To emphasize the point, Grand has her "new man," Arthur Brock, exclaim in support: "the positive right and wrong . . . are facts, not ideas. I believe that there is good and evil, that the one is at war with the other" (501-502). Thus, Grand revises the aesthetic formula of truth equals beauty and vice versa by underscoring the author's responsibility to her readers and to social reality over intangible notions of "truth."

Having tried the route of becoming a popular mainstream author, Beth eventually chooses feminist activism and politically invested writing because these do not compromise her own personal integrity nor that of her writings. The heroine's ultimate resolve to make content rather than style her top priority in writing reflects Grand's own resolution of her problematic status as a writer, which *The Beth Book* exemplifies. The narrative voice at the end of the novel, geared toward a defined reader—"you"—and resembling advice, is a political act in itself, insofar as it its meant to inform and encourage other women who aspire to become writers. Also, it is significant that Beth's writing finally takes the form of speeches, texts over which she has total command, echoing George Moore, and that enable a more direct relationship with her audiences, unlike the novels whose marketability and integrity she had tried to negotiate without much success. Beth chooses not to write for publication but to lecture in public, to explicitly educate other women in all the ways that she was not educated. As a feminist, Beth joins the ranks of other women engaged in the same struggle for self-determination as she, and shares her experience and wisdom with them in an effort to lead them toward "the woman's summer," or a more empowering future. Accordingly, Beth's definition of "success" centers on her public accessibility and visibility, and not necessarily on her acceptance by the general public:

> The postman came beladen, and there were brought to her pamphlets, papers, cards, letters, telegrams, a fine variety of praise, abuse, sympathy, derision, insults and admiration. Quietly Beth read and knew what it meant, all of it—success! and the success she had most desired: that her words should come with comfort to thousands of those that suffer, who, when they heard, would raise their heads once more in hope. . . . Beth was one of the first swallows of the woman's summer. She was strange to the race when she arrived, and uncharitably commented upon; but now the type is known, and has ceased to surprise. (495)

Implicit in Grand's narrative is the final message that the woman writer with a feminist agenda may use the novel as her forum at her own peril, since it stands in opposition to her social mission. Furthermore, when women writers do attempt to communicate certain truths through novels, they are likely to be frustrated and daunted in their endeavors. Beth serves to set a literary precedent for Grand's own female readers and paves the way to authorial "success" and effectiveness: "now the type is known."

Recurring allusions to the occupation of writing in feminist novels illustrate feminist authors' concern about the edicts of the late Victorian literary market and their position within it. For many of these novelists, literary success was synonymous with political agency and effectiveness. Or, when that is not possible, success signifies public visibility and appeal to women readers. For instance, literary integrity is aligned with political commitment in Miss Du Prel, the reactionary character in Caird's *The Daughters of Danaus*. Indicative of the intimate, direct relationship feminists saw themselves as having with their texts, Miss Du Prel's writings, romance novels, are as accurate a reflection of her identity as a woman as her actions and self-proclamations. She illustrates the relationship politics and writing were seen to possess, for the feminists, in that her shortcomings are most clearly exposed by her fictional writings: She writes conventional romance novels in which the heroine's struggles are rewarded by a socially lucrative marriage. Miss Du Prel perpetuates patriarchal oppression through narratives in which woman is mindful of her "Nature" and gains societal acceptance for it. Thus, Caird, at least, assumes a direct correspondence between women's politics and the texts they produce. Furthermore, she makes clear that authors' politics cannot help but be revealed by the kinds of narratives they construct. Feminist authors such as Caird, Cholmondeley, and Grand generally exhibit considerable concern and sensitivity over the corrupting influence of traditional texts that promote fantasies of female dependence and subordination. Given the uniformity of these feminists' assumptions concerning the power of texts, the feminist novel can best be viewed as metafiction in its purpose and function. They are novels about novels as much as they are about women.

THE "NEW" FEMALE SUBJECTIVITY

In addition to addressing the question of aesthetic judgment and promoting a feminist understanding of the function of literature, feminist novelists of the 1890s worked to construct an empowered female identity. It needs to be said at the outset that this was not an easy task, since on many levels late Victorian culture appears to have disapproved of women's self-examination and investigations into female subjectivity. Cultural and artistic representations of the activity of women's self-examination amounted to "admonitions to woman not to peek into the mirror of self without the tempering influence of a man to guide her. Only a truly perverse woman... would dare to do so" (Dijkstra 138). And, in fact, a casual perusal of late Victorian representations of women intently glaring into their own images in mirrors or into one another's eyes suggest that mainstream culture found this concept threatening or unappealing, at the very least.[3] Fulfilling their texts' primary objective of revising their readers' perceptions concerning women and constructing a New female literary and social subjectivity, proved to be an "aesthetic" project as well: It challenged the dominant aesthetic ideology's stance claiming the inherent incompatibility between social reality and "the soul of things." In working to accomplish their primary goal of arguing the case of women who were socially, morally, and spiritually harmed by gender inequalities, the feminist novelists changed and "modernized" the novel through the psychologization of their female characters.

Studies of late Victorian women's novels have long credited feminist writers with having lent interiority to the novel, or with having "psychologized" it. However, this "psychologization" has generally been taken to suggest that the main effect of the feminist narrations of heroines' hidden struggles with patriarchal morality was almost exclusively literary and only coincidentally political, if at all. Hence, Holbrook Jackson has characteristically aligned the New Woman novel with the Realist tradition because it falls into the category of the "problem novel." The late Victorian feminist novel was viewed as being "still more modern" than most because of its emphasis on "temperament and psychological analysis represented by such writers as George Egerton and Sarah Grand." Credited with having made an "important contribution to the fiction of the period," critics have listed the feminists' having "express[ed] that modern revolt of women" as secondary (Jackson 1913, 219). In a similar gesture, Ernest Baker's description of these novels obscures the relationship between feminists' political agendas and their literary styles: "The authors took themselves and their duties as seriously as if they were George Eliots... they narrowed their vision as to see life as made up of problems, which is as much as to say that they reduced it to a series of abstractions. Fiction almost ceased in their hands to be an art concerned with the concrete material of the human world" (1936, 213). Patronizing observations such as Baker's tend to discount the fact that the feminist novelists' emphasis on introspection and "psychoanalysis" served to point to the specific negative effects social institutions such as marriage and the family had on women as social beings. In this sense, the introspection or internal monologue that many feminists engaged as a narrative device served to articulate a system of "silences" as described by Pierre Macherey, silences that are indicative of the societal injustices against women and that, despite feminist articulations of women's concerns, were still a reality in women's everyday lives (1989, 100). "Psychologization" enabled the feminist novelist to reflect and at the same time eradicate such silences. In addition to being trivialized as subliterary and peculiar, such feminist narrative strategies as these were also often construed as "aestheticist," which, as I note later in the chapter, have further ramifications for readings of feminist literature.

In constructing politically informed narratives of women's lives, feminist novelists had to negotiate their political agendas with the novel's adherence to certain conventions, particularly expectations concerning fictional representations of women. Invariably, the most reliable source of positive identification among these novelists, their heroines, and their readers was to revert to the literary convention of the woman as victim. Yet to court such a potentially compromising stereotype in their novels, when they blatantly rebelled against it in their social activism and nonfictional writings, confronted feminist novelists with a dilemma that was all too real: How might they liberate their women characters (and, by extension, attain the power of self-definition themselves, as women and as authors) from such a disempowered position without alienating their readers? And how might they do so and still construct viable liberated female characters? The novels I examine here reveal that the woman-as-martyr model had to be utilized yet revised so that it could be useful without being too incriminating. In the case of *Ideala* by Grand (1888), even a stereotype characteristic of feminist heroines is used and discarded to be replaced by a more revolutionary one. Most univocal cultural depictions of women had proven either too limiting or, otherwise, self-contradictory. The woman as shrew, as morally fallen, or as all-virtuous and pure, all ideological manifestations of patriarchy's means of objectifying women, are sorted through and restructured to create one new whole. Hence, quite literally, a "new" female subjectivity was called for, especially since the feminist political mission included showing women a way out of oppression. In the novels I examine, this kind of liberatory female subjectivity was achieved by combining more than one possible characterization of women, often utilizing the traditional model of Victorian womanhood and complementing it with more analytical depictions of the New Woman's contemporary predicaments. Therefore, the ideal heroine in feminist novels is often not a single woman but a composite of a traditional type and an enlightened, rebellious nonconformist, a feminist. In their combined wholeness, these heroines testify to their authors' and feminism's projected definition of the *truly* liberated woman. The New Woman is thus the woman who has severed some (although not necessarily all) attachments to Victorian patriarchal valuations of women. The true feminist heroine has experienced gender-based oppression personally and has not failed to notice its workings—she is enlightened as to its political underpinnings and eventually is able to see her relation to systematic sexism. She thus gains a new subjectivity, one that makes her own oppression apparent to her.

In *Red Pottage*, Mary Cholmondeley finds that she cannot equate self-sacrifice with virtue, and offers an antidote to male-defined women by combining the traditional model of Victorian womanhood embodied in Hester, the martyr and "angel in the house," with the New Woman as typified in Hester's alter-ego, Rachel. Hester, a model of the suffering and victimized Victorian woman writer representative of the invalidism that symptomatized the social marginalization of Victorian middle-class women, is joined with Rachel, a socially and economically liberated woman. In Cholmondeley's narrative, patriarchal stereotypes of women and the hold that marriage has traditionally had on women are merged to produce the feminist heroine whose evolution the narrative witnesses. This heroine is free of both marriage and other forms of patriarchal control. Following her lover's death, Rachel's romantic involvement is supplanted by a renewed loyalty to Hester. Her abandonment of Hester would have been equivalent to self-betrayal for Rachel, since, throughout the narrative and their entire lives, the two women complement one another perfectly: Hester's vulnerability is supplanted by Rachel's boldness, her poverty by Rachel's wealth, her fear and weakness by Rachel's courage and strength.

Cholmondeley seeks to address the realities of victimization yet resists the perpetuation of the tradition of the martyred heroine. Cholmondeley refuses to make the martyr her heroine, although insofar as the woman writer's struggle for self-expression is a practical concern, it is one of the central themes of the novel. When Hester is on the verge of dying after her novel is declared immoral and burned by her brother, Rachel saves her friend's life by making her commitment to their friendship primary among her relationships. Seeking a way out of victimization so extensive that not even living in a city could remedy it, the two women leave England together to explore new countries, different cultures, to discover new possibilities for themselves as women. In the novel's "Conclusion," the two women make a circumspect appearance when the tyrannical Gresleys indulge in some gossip about Hester and Rachel. Contrasting the Victorian model of womanhood Hester used to represent to the emancipated New Woman she is becoming with Rachel's help, the gossips observe that whereas Hester used to nurse sick friends and relatives and give of herself unconditionally, now "she and Miss West are . . . in India. And they mean to go to Australia and New Zealand, and come home next spring." The relationship between Hester and Rachel is completely mutual and interdependent. Rachel's devotion is reciprocated by Hester, who, "[d]irectly poor Mr. Scarlet died, . . . left her room, and devoted herself to Miss West, and Dr. Brown said it was the saving of her" (373). Indicating that Hester's own long-standing illness and invalidism "was not a valid illness," as these characters observe, but an expression of her struggle against the tyranny of her brother and his family, Cholmondeley echoes Grand in her astute analysis of patriarchal control of women as a social disease that is also shared by those perpetrate it and who are not immediately injured by it. Both authors characterize patriarchal oppression as debilitating for women, not only socially, but spiritually and physically as well. Both authors also suggest that the antidote to the disease of oppression can only be emotional and physical distance from those very real constraints.

In Caird's heroine in *The Daughters of Danaus* we discern the traditional victim and martyr, the woman who would negate her own ambitions and desires in order to satisfy social convention. In this instance, Hadria's victimization is effected through what is perhaps the most insidious form of oppression, Cobbe's "customary" emotional manipulation mentioned earlier. As evidenced very early in the novel through the philosophical debates of the "Preposterous Society," Hadria realizes that her society's values are hypocritical and self-serving, and that she should not feel compelled to comply with its dictates. Even though she recognizes that women are manipulated into acquiescence, Hadria does not have courage or support enough to live as she sees fit. Her political awareness and emotional fortitude are incongruous, and this renders her inactive and impotent in her own life. Hadria's potential dual complement and "better half" is her sister Algitha, who leaves the parental homestead to do what she calls "humane," or philanthropic, work in London. Although she is clearly tired and worn when she reappears after having been away for some time, Algitha has managed to do what Hadria cannot, as long as she remains under the overpowering emotional control of her parents and husband. Algitha is free to live life as she chooses and finally to marry a man with whom she is far more compatible, emotionally, philosophically, and politically, than is Hadria with her "proper" social match, the very conventional Temperley, whose sole object in marrying was to secure a woman who would serve as social director in his life. Algitha's philanthropy, or her active love for her fellow human beings, enables in her a love and consideration for herself that Hadria has yet to discover because she is self-sacrificing. Caird draws out the distinct differences between Algitha's social responsibility and activism and Hadria's sense of obligation to serve her husband and parents. Algitha's independence serves to shed an unfavorable light on Hadria's binding duties, her society responsibilities, and to emphasize her subservience and dependence. Significantly, Algitha gains a social, public significance through her philanthropic work, while Hadria remains bound by the directives of her husband and parents and the bourgeois values they impose on her. Algitha has escaped her family's and society's unrelenting expectations of her as a woman, and serves to inform Hadria through her critical perspective; as she puts it, "[h]ere, once my day's work is over, it is over, and I have good solid hours of leisure ... I hear all sorts of opinions, and see all sorts of people" (48). That the city and a commitment to serving the general public have served to liberate Algitha is apparent, since it is there that she is able to assume an identity different from the one imposed on her in her community and home, as it is imposed on Hadria as well. Margaret Oliphant also offers a telling description of the challenge posed by the New Woman to conceptions of womanhood in late Victorian culture. While she does not write as a feminist, Oliphant represents the New Woman as superseding and displacing the traditional conceptions of women, and represents them as doing so in a gentle and subtle transition. In her novel *Hester* ([1884] 1984), the enlightened New Woman depicted through Hester consists of an amalgamation of valuable characteristics of the older, traditional Victorian woman embodied in Hester's aunt, Catherine. Although Catherine herself is considerably unconventional in comparison to Victorian gender definitions, having reigned in her family as the sole controller of family finances and the family bank, she is a bitter, antagonistic, and generally unattractive matriarch. Catherine's relationship to her own power is problematic to herself and has made of her a cold, impersonal, fearsome opponent in even the most intimate interpersonal exchanges. As a representative of the older liberated woman who lacks a critical understanding of patriarchy, Catherine instinctively dislikes Hester for her pride and willfulness, for not knowing her place as a poor relation. When Hester is made not one but two attractive marriage offers, Catherine advises her to marry in order to avoid a fate like her own. According to Catherine's experiences and wisdom, a financially independent woman who chooses not to marry can only end up an old maid whose power is mistrusted and resented. The two women represent two different phases in the women's movement, with Hester representing the more enlightened and self-determining New Woman.

This novel's development cultivates the sense that New Women like Hester have more options than their predecessors and that they need not forfeit power for love and happiness. Hester is baffled by the number of choices and opportunities for change she is offered throughout the novel, none of which preclude her happiness. Rather, Hester opts for "choice" rather than the "chance . . . to make a suitable marriage," for which Emma, an eager and eligible young woman, keeps obsessively preparing herself (248). Having asserted herself repeatedly and having refused to be intimidated by Catherine's antics as she resists submitting to social pressures to marry, Hester becomes Catherine's confidante and friend. The old comes to appreciate the new, in the novel's resolution, as Catherine learns that Hester's powers, more self-determined than hers, are valuable. She concedes to the young woman, and "ma[kes] Hester her representative in conversation," trusting that with her unabashed certainty and bold courage, Hester is better suited to see to both their interests than Catherine may be herself (494). Significantly, unlike the feminist heroines I have discussed thus far, Oliphant's heroine in *Hester* is one whose liberation is effected from without, that is, socially and by circumstance, while the rest do not and clearly cannot rely on societal sanction and assistance in changing their lives. On the contrary, feminist heroines instigate change from within; unlike Hester, they begin with an oppositional imagination—they do not inherit it.

Self-definition combined with sociopolitical awareness and commitment to women in general are the primary ingredients in the creation of the truly "new" female literary character. Political commitment is exemplified as a feminine virtue by Grand's heroine in *The Beth Book*, whose growth culminates in her becoming a feminist activist. Aptly described as a "portrait of the artist as a young woman" by Showalter in her Introduction to the novel, *The Beth Book* offers an account of how a young girl comes to be empowered by political activism. This is a highly polemical novel because it advocates several revisions to the status quo of Victorian womanhood and because it proposes woman-centered vision as a viable alternative and antidote to patriarchal control. Beth's sole source of moral direction as a child is her maiden aunt Victoria, who is marginal enough to provide the child with a sense of propriety and moral self-command without imposing restrictions on her. The formal education that is financially provided by this aunt is forfeited so that her brothers can establish themselves in careers while Beth "runs riot" (233). Although Beth is exceptionally rebellious and fiery in temperament and cannot make logical sense of her family's values, it is expected that she will abide by the rules set out for all young Victorian women, and Beth does in fact attempt this much. For example, she attends Miss Blackwood's, a school that was actually "a forcing house for the marriage market" (318). Also, she marries a man who is unworthy of her and remains loyal to him despite his corrupt politics and his personal failures; both his enforcement of the Contagious Diseases Acts exams and his participation in vivisectionism, both very prominent controversial subjects of the day, are objectionable to Beth. Grand's characterization of the oppressive husband is typical in feminist novels protesting women's social oppression as immoral, and includes sexual infidelity and emotional and moral degeneracy. Once she is convinced that her husband is as immoral as the society that endorses her marriage is hypocritical, Beth is able to challenge her husband and to act as her own best advocate; in this instance, she addresses him as the liberated, feminist woman she will become by the end of the novel: "'Be careful!' Beth flashed forth. 'If you make such assertions you must prove them. The day is past when a man might insult his wife with impunity. I have already told you I won't stand it. It would neither be good for you nor me if I did'" (393). Like other feminist heroines, Beth ultimately goes to London, the center of feminist activism in the 1890s. She lives on her own, working as a nurse to the poor, and it is there that she discovers her purpose in life. She finds that she is committed to social work, much as many late Victorian women did, but Grand develops her heroine even further by having her realize the inadequacy of philanthropy as a facilitator of self-emancipation. At the end of the novel, Beth is free to choose her destiny from the many possibilities open to her, none of which is mutually exclusive: writing novels, marrying an idealistic American "new man" who serves as a contrast to her first husband, and joining feminists in their social and political campaigning. At the novel's conclusion, Beth has both love and political commitment to the women's cause and to her own empowerment.

In contrast to the emancipated and justly rewarded Beth, Grand's other famous character, Ideala, is both an idealist, as her name indicates, and, in some respects, the "ideal" woman. *Ideala: A Study from Life,* Grand's first novel, defines the New Woman by exploring and analyzing her marginalization and by offering a critique of the "neurotic" type of female heroine. Grand's characterization of Ideala is such that it undermines preconceived notions of womanhood by making her simultaneously naive, impulsive, and courageous. As a representative of the "neurotic" type, Ideala perpetually wavers in indecisions: "Her nervous system was highly strung; she was too sensitive, too emotional, too intense . . . even her love of the beautiful was carried to excess" (23). Reflecting on her failed marriage, Ideala condemns the morally inferior men who reign over women; "Oh, if I could save other women from that!" she says, and is praised by the narrator when she does not set herself apart from other women since "what she says of other women is true of herself" (187). Yet, for the most part, Ideala falls short of Grand's conception of the "ideal"

New Woman because she is far too naive and idealistic; that is, she lacks the kind of political consciousness that would enable her to address both her own predicaments and those of other women, with valuable insight such as that possessed by the narrator; "she cared little for people in general," we are told, "and had few likings" (10). This shortcoming on Ideala's part is accounted for by the fact that she lacks an active community of progressive women and is merely philosophical about issues pertaining to women's repression, never taking any action to remedy the problems she acknowledges. Ideala's political naiveté is illustrated by her stating that she "despises" conventional women because "they could do better if they would":

> They know the higher walk, and deliberately pursue the lower. Their whole feeling is for themselves, and such things as have power to move them through the flesh only. I would almost rather side on the impulse of a generous but misguided nature, and have the power to appreciate and the will to be better, than live a perfect, loveless woman, caring only for myself, like these. I should do more good. (8)

Grand's own demonstrated sympathy toward the women Ideala despises, and toward Ideala herself, presents the latter in a critical light. Resisting any possible oversimplifications of Ideala as a formulaic characterization of the budding New Woman, Grand points out in her preface to the novel that Ideala is not a conclusive or definitive portrait of the New Woman, but of a woman whose "life was set to a tune that admitted to endless variations" (9). This is in partial fulfillment of the feminist vision of the truly liberated woman, since the New Woman is not definable according to any existing model of liberated womanhood because women are simply not liberated yet. In fact, *Ideala* states unequivocally that at the center of the problem of the lives of women like the heroine is the fact that "women have never yet united to use their influence steadily all together against that of which they disapprove" (188). The best these novelists can hope for is a "feminist," that is, a woman in pursuit of liberation from patriarchy, not only her own, but all women's. Interestingly, Ideala is reclaimed and redeemed by Grand in *The Beth Book*, where she appears not as a victim but as a victor and an agent of radical change, as she convinces Beth that she is right to leave her husband; thus, the fictional heroine experiences an evolution from a state of subservience to that of revolutionary possibility not only within individual novels, but across textual boundaries as well.

Feminist novelists of the 1890s were in many ways less naive than has been supposed, in that they did not fail to note the ways in which women's indoctrination into patriarchal ideology would be the main obstacle they would encounter. Women themselves often fell short of this ideal of the woman emancipator, and feminist novelists are revolutionary to the degree that they understand and portray these failures. Their novels negate and contradict stereotyped perceptions of women as they work to reconstruct a feminist character true to their social and political objectives. Just as Cholmondeley does away with the literary type of both the shrew and the virtuous martyr by mocking Lady Newhaven out of existence and "marrying" Hester to Rachel at her novel's conclusion, the sharpest criticism of conventional women is found in Caird's character, Miss Du Prel, in *Daughters of Danaus*. A potentially empowering role model because she is unmarried and self-supporting through her writing, Miss Du Prel cannot offer Hadria much inspiration or support because she is not ideologically and politically liberated, but only financially. Her philosophy concerning women is conservative if not altogether reactionary in comparison to that of Hadria, as she aligns herself with the principles of the then-popular Social Darwinism. Her advice to Hadria reveals her as something other than the cynical and disappointed woman she appears to be in earlier parts of the novel:

> A woman cannot afford to despise the dictates of Nature. She may escape certain troubles that way; but Nature is not to be cheated, she makes her victim pay her debt in another fashion. There is no escape. The centuries are behind one, with all their weight of heredity and habit; the order of society adds its pressure—one's own emotional needs. Ah, no! it does not answer to pit oneself against one's race, to bid defiance to the fundamental laws of life. (71)

Here Miss Du Prel addresses the "woman question" and the "eternal feminine" inadequately because she essentializes women as "natural" in a formulaic definition that proscribes nature as dangerous, deceptive, and evil. Miss Du Prel's views on women are an articulation of the various translations of Darwinism that popularized horrific images of women as usurping vampires, as elemental and decadent, and as frighteningly sensuous and impulsive. This is a closely accurate description of one manifestation of late Victorian challenges to feminism, since, as Dijkstra argues in *Idols of Perversity*, it reflects the profusion of negative depictions of women in male-created art during the 1890s. Arguments based on Social Darwinism, Dijkstra asserts, "became steadily more virulent and apparently unassailable because they appeared to have the full support of 'nature'" (165). In addition to being a theory of human nature and a justification of gender inequalities, it is an oppressive translation of women's history, and one that feminists sought to revise. Yet, like other mainstream notions concerning women, this one was readily and widely accepted, by women as well as men, and informed various arguments against feminism, insofar as it imposed on women a fatalistic destiny.

Caird presents Social Darwinism as harmful to women, and Miss Du Prel serves as the author's argument against it insofar as she herself is clearly victimized by it. She is utterly unhappy because she has not married yet, and her literary success and financial independence are inadequate compensation for her failure to fulfill her nature. More important, Miss Du Prel's conventional view of woman's nature and possibilities endangers Hadria's spiritual and emotional well-being, as her advice entraps Hadria even further than she is already—that is, ideologically. In this way, Miss Du Prel, whom Hadria had at first seen as a New Woman and a source of inspiration because she is seemingly autonomous, acts as a neutralizing or "reconciling" agent in Hadria's life, insofar as she is always trying to subdue her rebellious spirit. When Hadria does assert herself, Miss Du Prel stops being a friend and distances herself from Hadria's life and struggles; she becomes a disapproving spectator and tries to intervene in favor of preserving Hadria's marriage and status as entertaining hostess. If she cannot be married herself, Miss Du Prel wants to be part of the proper society circles of marriage and family life, even marginally, and she acts as an agent of conformity.

The type of woman Miss Du Prel represents is elsewhere depicted in her most advanced degeneration as posing mortal danger to womankind. The most dramatic example of how women can victimize one another is in the novel *The Real Charlotte* ([1894] 1986) by Edith Somerville and "Martin Ross" (Violet Martin), which is devoted to analyzing woman's psyche in her fallen, misogynistic state. The biting sarcasm and irony that dominate in this novel suggest that the authors are not merely conducting an analysis of women's lives, but are angrily protesting against them. Charlotte, the old hag in the narrative, is duplicitous and opportunistic, and sacrifices her young cousin, Francie, in order to obtain false power through her romantic and professional associations with men. Francie is victimized by Charlotte in league with her lover, so that she dies tragically, ignorant of her cousin's motives and actions. In its entirety, this novel powerfully illustrates the message of the dire, corrupting consequences of women's identifying with the interests of men and the patriarchal systems as opposed to identifying with other women. Also an example of the old confronting the New Woman in woman-authored fiction of the period, Charlotte bears many similarities to Catherine in *The Beth Book;* Charlotte's relationship to money and power is far too tenuous, and so she is mean-spirited and selfish with it. For feminist novelists, marriage and the rituals that accompany it appear to be the foremost oppressive patriarchal institution from which women must liberate themselves; it also is the one that has co-opted women's sympathies and support the most extensively.

The point here is that since all too often women themselves served to perpetuate their own subordination and to oppress other women (Hadria's mother is also presented as an example of this problem), feminist novelists employ male characters to emphasize the point that biological sex is not the determining or even the main ingredient for a feminist consciousness. In several instances enlightened men serve as parallel selves to the feminist novel's heroines. In *Ideala,* Grand does away with Ideala's best friend in the novel, the morally upright, tradition-bound woman, because she is by all indications harmful to women. Rather, Ideala's story is narrated by a man who can sympathize with the heroine's predicament. Responding to Ideala's confusion over whether she should leave her husband, whose repeated infidelities have caused her physical, psychological, and spiritual harm, her woman friend advises her to stay in the marriage in order to keep her place in society and to save her reputation and that of her friends. Emotionally bound by what she comes to view as her social obligations, Ideala despairs and becomes fatally ill, having given up her only opportunity to know real love and happiness. In contrast, the narrator had encouraged Ideala to pursue her own happiness at any cost. At the very end, the sympathetic narrator concludes that Ideala might have lived and been happy if not for her friends's well-meant but ill-advised attempts to help her and had Ideala been more self-interested and less concerned about others' wishes. Likewise, in Caird's novel, the perfect model of gender liberation is not a woman but a man. When Hadria is separated from her perfect parallel in the novel, her sister Algitha, Professor Fortescue serves as a source of inspiration and wisdom for Hadria. Unlike Algitha, who has accepted her sister's unhappy fate and even sees it as based on choice rather than compromise, Professor Fortescue serves to validate Hadria's discontentment. Unlike the woman friend in *Ideala,* the professor feels that when a woman finds herself in an unhappy marriage, "the thing to do is to get out" (272). Insofar as Professor Fortescue is committed to encouraging Hadria to find happiness and freedom away from her oppressive marriage and social obligations, he is more truly a feminist than the socially progressive but not woman-focused Algitha. At the same time, portrayed as a complex and emblematic character, Professor Fortescue represents the dilemma feminist authors had to confront in relation to what they considered their constituency, women at large: A committed feminist, the professor has vowed never to place himself above women or to impose his views on them or "advise" them; he "could not assert what [Hadria] calls his 'rights' without insulting her and himself." Therefore, his dramatic influence on Hadria's life is limited, because "one dare not advise," he says; "it is too perilous" (272). Much like the feminists who saw that they had to challenge gender ideology at all levels, Professor Fortescue's function in Hadria's life is that of a mentor, a source of knowledge, experience, and critical insight, all of which come to inform her reevaluation of herself and her views of women, insofar as his views are subversive of the status quo:

> "It is the fashion, I know," he said, "to regard woman as an enigma. Now, without professing any unusual acuteness, I believe that this is a mistake. Woman is an enigma certainly, because she is human, but that about ends it. Her conditions have tended to cultivate in her the power of dissimulation, and the histrionic quality. . . . Let a man's subsistence and career be subject to the same powers and chances as the success of a woman's life now hangs on, and see whether he does not become a histrionic enigma." (226)

In addition to his function in completing the characterization of Hadria, Professor Fortescue is also Caird's mouthpiece and serves as extratextual function as well: He expresses her particular brand of feminism, one that is blatantly antithetical to George Egerton's vision for liberating women from oppressive societal definitions that will be discussed later. Professor Fortescue's treatises on womanhood work to present definitions of women as materially and culturally produced. The professor's social consciousness is so great that he serves to translate Hadria's general frustration into a politically sophisticated account. Caird's plot, with its emphasis on the social and practical means through which women are entrapped in traditional martyr roles, is analyzed in Fortescue's philosophical statements, articulations that function as the space in which the events of the novel are explained to readers in feminist and gender-political terms. Caird makes this point even more deliberately in a paratextual reference to Olive Schreiner's philosophy, Caird's mention that "the sharpness of the insult lies in its not being intended" calls to question the characters' political identifications (171).

Apart from being a reflection of the fact that there were a number of women's rights advocates among men in late Victorian England, the male feminist protagonist in novels such as Caird's disputes the essentializing notion that all women are inherently supportive of the women's cause. Male narrators sympathetic to the plight of women suggest that the consciousness from which one speaks on women's behalf is primarily a matter of gender politics and not "natural" or biological sex. In this sense, feminists such as Sarah Grand and Mona Caird subscribe to the notion of "false consciousness" or of "male-identified women," and such conceptions inform both their characterizations of women in fiction as well as their analyses of women's oppression. Furthermore, the duality feminist novelists create and highlight by combining progressive and reactionary or traditional women characters serves to illustrate a political problem: namely, that the liberation of women is often achieved at a price, and that this may account for the conservatism of many women. In Caird's account, Hadria is coerced into taking her sister's place and compensating for Algitha's freedom by catering to her parents' desire for an obedient daughter. Caird suggests that women's independence is often obtained at the cost of personal sacrifice — what is sacrificed for the sake of family unity and peace are woman's desires and her complexity. Exchanging one woman's happiness for that of another is the means through which the patriarchal economy is maintained, as Gayle Rubin has argued in "The Traffic in Women." Insofar as women are deprived of self-definition and are defined in relation to patriarchal cultural practices according to Rubin's analysis women can at best attain the status of gift object exchanged among men, primarily through marriage (1990).[4] Feminist novels show that women are often complicitous in this compromising exchange, although the most favorable characterizations are afforded to women who have somehow managed to transcend the limits and dictates of the patriarchal economy by joining other women in a joint search for liberation. In addition to serving to characterize the women late Victorian feminists sought to liberate, the novels I point to here also provide feminists and nonfeminists alike with a formula for criticizing and transcending conventional models of female subjectivity. Furthermore, they work to suggest that the ways in which women are marginalized in patriarchy are all too often subtle and coercive in nature. Women are to be held as accountable as men in contributing to patriarchal oppression of women, particularly within their own primary domains, marriage and the family, which perpetuate "custom"-ary marginalization. Woman is asked to fit the mold of her society's dictates; she is compelled to appear and be, for all practical purposes, one-dimensional, not a subject, but an object. The only way out of this predicament, for women, is the substitution of this model with one that is more self-serving: Women must change their own and each others' minds.

THE FEMINIST LITERARY AESTHETIC

Feminist authors' redefinitions of the female literary subject and their contradictions of patriarchal aesthetic ideology are constitutive of late Victorian feminist literary aesthetics, but nowhere are they made more explicit than in self-conscious, "independent" stylists such as "George Egerton" (Mary Chavelita Dunne). Writing for literary and otherwise independent as opposed to "new journalistic" journals and hence, significantly, outside the novelistic form, feminists such as George Egerton were able to write without consideration for normative narrative features and were more outspoken, harshly critical of convention, and stylistically innovative. Egerton's position on the woman question is problematic and sets her apart from the general consensus among the feminists of her day. She is reluctant to idealize women, and in a letter, she bitterly denounces them: "Don't tell me I don't know women—I do—and put them ten grades lower than men in every way. We have less sentiment, less religion and a long way less straightness" (DeVere White 1958, 10-11). Egerton further distanced herself from the more common feminist positions by proclaiming women "hermaphrodite[s] by force of circumstance," a formulation most feminist philosophies of the time could not accommodate as long as they were embracing conceptions of "the eternal feminine" and of woman's innate difference and superiority from men. So out of the ordinary was Egerton, even when compared to other feminists, that one reader speculated that "it were better to believe her a hermaphrodite than a typical woman of our time."[5] Writing beyond the constraints of the novel market and catering primarily to the more permissive readership of literary journals enables George Egerton to offer a much more direct analysis of feminist literary aesthetics as they relate to the status of women in the late nineteenth century. Egerton is most insightful when she addresses the issue of the feminist writer/artist confronting questions of gender identity and woman's repressed subjectivity, and the product of this quest "leave[s] an unpleasant taste in our mouth." She reveals that these are the determining forces beyond her own literary style, which was often misconstrued as purely aestheticist by critics of the period. Aligning Egerton to the literary ideology of the aesthetes, her stylistic and formal innovativeness was seen to bear little relation to social politics, and *Keynotes* has thus long been perceived as "a study in impressionism" (Jackson 143).

In *Keynotes* ([1893] 1983), a collection of stories that was to become very popular and that has been classified as "the first work of the neurotic school," Egerton includes a number of pieces that challenge the status quo of both gender and aesthetics by problematizing the essence of women as well as her function as a feminist author (Mix 1969, 64). The context created by John Lane, the publisher of *Keynotes* and other woman-centered works in the Keynote Series, was such that it at least professed to grant women authors considerable authority and autonomy over their subject matter and its treatment. It made gestures toward a "womanist" aesthetic; this was, however, an aesthetic that feminist authors themselves would have challenged as long as it did not exhibit a feminist consciousness and as long as it did not hold assumptions about the positive features of an essential femininity. In fact, Egerton herself subverts such views through this work. When it was first published, *Keynotes* was promoted as featuring "knotty questions in sex problems" and was characterized as woman-centered and revolutionary:

> The chief characters of these stories are women, and women drawn as only a woman can draw a word-picture of her own sex. The subtlety of analysis is wonderful, direct in its effectiveness, unerring in its truth, and stirring in its revealing power. Truly, no one but a woman could thus throw the light of revelation on her own sex. Man does not understand woman as does the author of "Keynotes."[6]

One story in particular, "A Cross Line," clearly contradicts the aesthetic ideology that good art can at best reflect Egerton's vision of the "interiority" of masculinist culture. It juxtaposes the complex interiority of women against the oppressive exteriority of men. The story points to this female force as directing and shaping the author's writing style, her authorial voice, into a disruptive voice that Julia Kristeva (1980) terms "jouissance" or language lacking symbolic order, and Egerton simply calls "laughter."[7] Insofar as "A Cross Line" resists participation in patriarchal or symbolic structures, Egerton's deliberate ambiguity here both contains and problematizes mainstream formulations of female subjectivity, and by extension, all "knowledge" and possible styles:

> Her thoughts go to other women she has known, women good and bad, school friends, casual acquaintances, women workers—joyless machines for grinding corn, unwilling maids grown old in the endeavor to get settled, patient wives who bear little ones to indifferent husbands until they wear out—a long array. She busies herself with questioning. Have they, too, this thirst for excitement, for change, this restless craving for sun and love and motion? Stray words, half confidences, glimpses through soul-chinks of

suppressed fires, actual outbreaks, domestic catastrophes, how the ghosts dance in the cells of her memory! And she laughs, laughs softly to herself because the denseness of man, his chivalrous conservative devotion to the female idea he has created blinds him, perhaps happily, to the problems of her complex nature. Ay, she mutters musingly, the wisest of them can only say we are enigmas. (21)

In this story Egerton decides that, aesthetically at least, she will not symbolize women as the aesthetes would, nor will she represent them as figurative mysteries. Much like the self-proclaimed feminist Professor Fortescue, Egerton rejects the mystification of women as "enigmas," and this resistance leaves the author without a concrete characterization of women. Unlike Arthur Symons's aesthetic formulation, in which the "external" is a "superficial" and minimalistic reflection of a much more truthful, valuable yet elusive interiority that "good" literature will reveal, Egerton points to the confusion that is created by this ideological polarization. She contradicts the argument that art is true and "good" only insofar as it remains dissociated from social reality and only as long as it expresses what Symons calls "the soul of things" by making her writing inclusive of both "internals" and "externals." Writing as a feminist but also as a member of the "aesthetic movement" by virtue of having her works published primarily in *The Yellow Book* amid aestheticism's most volatile advocates, Egerton violates the aesthetic code of the aesthetes by writing for and from the public realm, the "mass culture" that Andreas Huyssen describes as being culturally circumscribed as "feminine." By extension, she renegotiates the disparity between the "internals" and "externals" of aesthetic formulations as they differ in men and women when the context that lends them meaning is the repressiveness of patriarchy. It may be, as Lovell has asserted, that feminists emphasized women's *inner* strengths in order to avoid comparison with the working classes. However, it seems more likely that feminists were doing just the opposite and that they were not deliberately dissociating themselves from the "masses," even in the case of Egerton.

Egerton's project here, as in the "psychological stories" in the book that followed, *Discords* (1894), is mainly to address the question of "what it feels like to be a woman," as Patricia Stubbs has observed (110). More significantly, Egerton places herself in a polemical position, aesthetically, because she "... seems to historicize George Moore's model of the artist's exploration of 'nature,'" and creates, in the process, the kind of narrative we can term "anti-naturalistic" (Ardis 1990, 99). Insofar as Egerton attempts to construct a new definition of "Woman" that is neither presumptuous of her "natural" character nor sets limits on that definition, she is rejecting notions of the "natural female" in preference of what was more optimistically termed the "eternal feminine." What these stories and "Cross Line" in particular reveal is that whereas patriarchy can at best create a monolithic definition of women, among women themselves there are not one but many separate and alienated identities, as one woman is hindered from identifying with another. The "laughter" to which the narrator's musings succumb erupts because she does not know any more about women than men do, but also because she must in good conscience allow for that multiplicity in her representations of them. Her laughter reveals the anxiety that results from this not knowing, but also from the frustration produced by the writer's unwillingness to partake of the myths that dismiss the realities of women's lives and foster the dichotomy of "internal" versus "external" being. Having situated herself thus at the outset, Egerton's politicized aesthetics compel her to speak only of and for herself. She is forced to limit her explorations to her own nature and subjectivity and to add to this awareness her observations of the "externals" of other women's lives. In the process, she discovers that her own identity is fundamentally comprised of other women's anonymity, silences, and misrepresentations. Hence, Egerton's "laughter" disrupts the theological sense that this narrative of other women's lives might make. It also acts as a disruptive force for the reader, since her many questions concerning woman's identity and "nature" remain unanswered.

Stories such as "A Cross Line" makes manifest feminists' objectives in representing women as being distinct and exempt from the traditional Victorian assumptions concerning woman's nature and her relation to culture. Just as feminist activists such as Millicent Garrett Fawcett pointed to the infusion of "custom" into notions of naturalness and cultural definitions as mentioned in Chapter 1, feminist fiction produced women who defied cultural stereotyping and hence resisted the threat of commodification. As Ardis suggests in her analysis of Egerton's work, "the precedent Egerton sets for other New Women . . . [is the] acknowledgment that 'nature' is something defined by culture as the place where culture's most cherished ideas and ideals can be kept safe from history" (100). The space I have alluded to earlier in my discussion is inclusive of the self-serving contradictions of late Victorian culture, since it accounts, and provides for, refigurations of an "eternal feminine" that is riddled with discrepancies concerning woman's nature that are imposed from without; that is, feminist narratives are inclusive of the confusions and distortions produced by history and cultural ideology. Simultaneously, their characterizations of women resist the national fantasy of the concrete English subject. Hence, even if we were to accept that 1890s' feminist novelists "had one story to tell and exhausted themselves in its narration," as Showalter suggested early on, neither their project nor ours can be a simple one because that story, the patriarchal oppression of women, is complicated (215). Given that feminists were attempting to invest an old word, "Woman," with new meanings, and that they did so through a controlled if contested medium, the novel, it is a story in which both authors and their literary characters must answer to a number of plots and subplots, thematic and incidental truths and untruths. Returning to the definition of oppositional writing with which I began this chapter, it helps to see the feminist texts I have discussed here and specifically the feminists' arguments with the aesthetic and cultural ideologies of their age as a disruption that facilitates articulations that do not comply with, but actually oppose, repressive social and discursive structures. Bhabha's hypothesis makes it possible to understand how oppositional writing can in fact find its place in a culture of "nonsense" such as late Victorian culture, one that disowns its own oppressive practices and is permeated by "lies" and negations. For oppositional writing to be effective in such contexts, then, there must be "a certain slippage between human artifice and culture's discursive agency. To be true to a self one must learn to be a little untrue, out of joint with the signification of cultural generalizability" (Bhabha 1990, 216). Conceivably, then, there is a need to appropriate certain means of repression, especially in discursive practices. There is a need to tamper with the recognizability of cultural stereotypes such as those evidenced in the feminist texts I have discussed here. Hence, it would not have been very productive for feminist novelists to thrust their emancipated heroines upon readers without the accompanying traditional, self-denying and martyred woman of Victorian literature and imagination. By the same token, they could not have made their argument effectively without incorporating into their discussions the influence of class and aesthetic elitism. The feminists' struggle for social and literary self-determination produced texts that open themselves to socially and historically based readings, precisely because of their inculcated, apparent awareness of late Victorian "culture's discursive agency." Feminists both used and manipulated cultural and literary conventions to create texts that are, paradoxically, both open-ended and self-referential.

⁕5⁕

DEFINING THE POLITICAL: THE "REALISTIC" APPROPRIATION

> . . . as soon as a book is written all right passes from the author to the book itself.
>
> . . . the creator passes into nothingness and the thing created lives on?
>
> About that there can surely be no doubt.
>
> George Moore, *Esther Waters* ([1894] 1964), xvi

◆ ◆ ◆

In the midst of women's activism and much feminist writing, male writers, and in particular those espousing the doctrines of Realism, created some unconventional female characters. They are even more remarkable than the feminist novelists for doing so, first because they were not especially committed to feminist philosophies and politics, and second because they implicitly professed to write as nonpartisan observers. Therefore, it is useful to consider how male-authored novels featuring the New Woman and addressing the woman question differ from feminist novels. There are several significant differences between feminist and Realist novels as cultural products, which I will concentrate on here. The most apparent difference is the enthusiasm with which the latter were greeted in public, in contrast to the censorship and harsh scrutiny experienced by the feminists. Here I want to examine the Realists' literary project, as well as to suggest some similarities between it and that of the feminists, and to consider its political implications. First among the questions to ask about these writers is: Were they really feminist in the way that the authors discussed in Chapter 4 were feminists? That is, how important was women's liberation to them, and what were their views regarding this problem? By extension, are their works to be read as intrinsically "feminist" according to the definition that is suggested by the works of the feminist authors?

As I argue in the last chapter, the feminist literary project paralleled, and was meant to supplement, social and political efforts to combat women's subordination. Hence, the social and political realities affecting women's lives constituted what Homi Bhabha would term a "significant sub-text" that informed feminist fiction (1990, 214).[1] In reading the Realists it is necessary to complicate the notion of a text's "subtexts" further. For instance, according to Bhabha's analysis, there are repressed subtexts in both dominant and marginalized discourse; these subtexts stand outside of the "non-sense" discourse in the latter and consist of "normalizing strategies" or an "anomalous containment of cultural ambivalence" (1990, 205) which comes of the "coercion of the native subject in which no truth can exist" (212). In contrast to feminist texts, Realist literature and especially their novels featuring New Women often touched on women's struggle for emancipation as an already conspicuous feature of the age. We rarely find Realists writing feminist tracts motivated by any consideration other than their literary agendas. Their version of the New Woman (the literary creation, as defined in the previous chapters) was of only secondary or minor importance in their literary aesthetics and social views. Hence, grouping "the decline of religious faith, feminism, the barriers of social caste and the battle against moral censorship" in that order as their "common concerns," the Realists accepted the New Woman as a type of social problem they would work into their narratives (Stonyk 1983, 214). The Realists' treatment of the New Woman and the "woman problem" is significant because the Realists were the canon at the close of the century, regardless of the fact that they were writing against the grain and were therefore subject to challenge. Still secure in its privileged aesthetic place within literary tradition, Realism was challenged primarily for its choice of subject matter, which was mainly centered on the New Woman and the working-class "masses." The New Woman was co-opted by the Realists as if she were conclusively defined, and this appropriation of the New literary heroine, whom feminist activists were in the process of constructing, is problematic. Nonetheless, in retrospect, the Realists' use of female types can be viewed as something other than merely a literary strategy, for insofar as literature exhibits a reciprocal relationship to social life, this appropriation had political ramifications for women. Macherey's observation on the use of "types" in novels is apt here:

If the novel involves a use of "types," this is because those types have between them relations other than real (the real relations between types are determined by the real existence of the social groups of which they give a fictional image), *relations determined by their very nature as types*, ideal relations: in which case the function of the type will be to confuse rather than to clarify. (1989, 288; emphasis added)

Given that they were once removed from the "reality" of the women's emancipation struggle, the Realists' use of the New Woman as a literary and even a social "type" interferes with the feminists' political project, which focused first and foremost on exposing and describing woman's "real" position within patriarchy and on revising her social function and her relation to other women. Paradoxically, then, the Realists' agenda, which aimed to address "reality" directly, worked to undermine the reality both of women's lives and of the realistic imperatives in feminist literature.

Much has been written about the predominance of the New Woman theme in feminist-related novels written by the Realists in the 1880s and '90s, but not enough about the treatment this theme was given, especially in light of the fact that feminist authors were first in constructing this social and subsequently literary figure. Having illustrated the feminists' efforts to construct a politically inspired heroine in Chapter 4, it remains to be seen how the Realists, as relatively progressive individuals, wrote about this phenomenon of the woman who challenged societal and gender stereotypes. These writers particularly need to be considered beside feminist authors' efforts to transmit through literature messages countering misrepresentation and marginalization. The Realists present an interesting problem, especially since their aesthetic philosophy values the literal. To begin with, it appears that Realists made use of the New Woman not only as a strictly literary "type," but also as a figure representing other social issues and concerns on their literary agendas. This is by far the most important and most problematic aspect of their use of the New Woman, because it presents Realism as politically elusive at the same time that it characterizes the differences between feminists and Realists as politically motivated authors. Their novels reveal that the Realists co-opted feminist formulations in order to explore issues relevant to their literary aesthetics and used the relative embodiment of feminism, the New Woman, as a metaphor. While the feminist authors I have discussed in Chapter 4 utilized the New Woman type to inform their attempts to construct a truly liberated, "feminist" heroine, the Realists use her as a preexisting vehicle through which they can comment on society at large. It is arguable that they had little interest in her particular political significance, just as they were not very invested in her progress socially. Given this central difference, we need to locate the shifting valuations of the literal and the figurative in the works of the Realists, particularly those dealing directly with women's issues, in order to examine the artistic and political relationship of women as subjects and men as artists in their novels. Furthermore, "myths" of gender current in the late nineteenth century and "myths" concerning the aesthetics and politics of literary production need to be considered as instrumental in the production of the Realist New Woman novel.

First, knowing the problems confronted by feminist authors in gaining recognition, we need to ask: What was the status of Realism in the aesthetic and literary context of the late nineteenth century? Lovell and Tuchman have surmised that Realistic fiction has always been the privileged literary form in English literary tradition. Lovell, in particular, speculates that the reason underlying this privilege is that Realistic fiction adheres to notions of the scientific and objectivity in relation to social reality; that is, it reinforces the ideology of the author as truthful and detached teller of true stories. Furthermore, she elaborates, "realist story-telling is governed by what currently passes for probable and plausible cause and effect in the social world. Non-realist story-telling recognizes different constraints" (1987, 156). Novelists such as George Gissing, George Moore, and George Meredith, as well as Henry James, who concerned themselves with acknowledging woman's changing subjectivity, did so in ways that are interesting in terms of what they themselves were arguing against as well as in relation to typical characterizations of women. During the 1880s and 1890s the argument for Realism was being made all over again. In the midst of ideological and cultural questioning and ongoing redefinitions of class and gender, literature professing to be neutral in the debate on either side was unequivocally considered suspect. Hence, the subject matter and approach of 1890s realistic fiction in general was objectionable to many readers, precisely because it addressed issues already rendered controversial by the women's movement and the working-class "masses." Many readers and critics found Realist fiction to be morally objectionable and highly unlikely as an aesthetic doctrine, and sources document its growing defensiveness toward its aesthetic doctrine. One account complains that "the army of successful novelists" object to being labeled "realist" and may go so far as "to protest against my describing his books even as 'fiction.'"[2] Yet Realists had a distinct traditional advantage over women in the last two decades of the nineteenth century. Tuchman and Fortin's observation concerning male writers' instrumental role in literary evaluation and categorization highlights the extent to which male literary figures were able to influence literary judgment, while women were subordinated to it:

> Unlike men, women never possessed the power to define the nature of good literature; when women served as critics, they displayed their internalization of male standards as universal standards. Men were in a position to invade the field of novel writing where women had once been prevalent. From 1840 to 1917 men made the high-culture novel their own. (1989, 204)

In addition to being well served by patriarchal literary tradition and hence attaining literary authority whereas feminists who likewise experimented with literary forms did not, Realism's self-definition also did much to imbue it with literary authority. Insofar as it foregrounds art's problematic relation to its social and political contexts during the nineties, Realistic fiction is legitimated by its claim to being art imbued with fact and with the authority of truthfulness. As noted by Ann Ardis, Realists defined their writing as entailing "no authorial commentary, no attempt on an omniscient narrator's part to mediate" (1990, 64). It is in the latter half of this explanation and in its apparent basis in some kind of omniscience (despite Realism's rhetoric) that we can locate Realism's primary task as being advocacy of its own legitimacy.

Realism's theoretical/aesthetic underpinnings are similar to those of Pater. In formulation as well as in execution, both Realism and aestheticism claimed a privileged proximity to "truth" and a freedom from external influence or partnership. Insofar as it proclaimed a privileged literal proximity to "the truth" about social life, Realistic fiction had at its core an unwavering faith in its own artistic merit. However, as an aesthetic philosophy, Realism exhibits certain internal "contradictions":

> The originality of the concept of Realism lies in its claim to cognitive as well as aesthetic status. A new value, . . . the ideal of realism presupposes a form of aesthetic experience which yet lays claim to a binding relationship to the real itself, that is to say, to those realms of knowledge and praxis which had traditionally been differentiated from the realm of the aesthetic, with its disinherited judgments and its constitution as sheer appearance. (Jameson 1980, 198)

The "reality" Realists relied upon for their legitimacy was not so objectively construed by the feminists, whose objective was to unsettle its oppressive underpinnings. Furthermore, Realism's assumptions concerning a singular definition of reality bears a close resemblance to patriarchy's oppressive rhetorical stance, historically. By definition, the power to name and diagnose social realities was never the domain of women or of the lower classes, but of bourgeois males. To add to Tuchman's point about literary authority lying in the male domain, the claim to a privileged access to the "real" is a predominately patriarchal one, particularly in the context of Victorian culture, where scientificity called for noninterested attention to an objective, singularly defined reality. However, since power inequities in class and gender informed the contents of literature at the end of the century, the "realistic" text's professedly unmediated relationship to reality is clearly an empowering quality, as it grants the text an authority not subject to scrutiny. It exempts the text from accountability for its relation to those power inequities. This favorable positioning of the Realistic novel was further reinforced by a literary and aesthetic tradition that differentiated literature along class lines and aligned "literary" fiction with mainstream bourgeois values and with agreed-upon representations. Yet this alignment is questionable now in the same way that canon formation practices are suspect, insofar as Realism sought to claim a space in the literary marketplace at the same time as the feminist authors.

The ways in which the Realists made use of extant social material in their works are important, as they enable us to read them both within the context of their literary philosophy and in view of their sociopolitical significance. At the outset, the following observations are instrumental in understanding the Realists' function in relation to their politically implicating subjects. First, rather than perpetuate or respond to literary practices already in effect, the Realists sought to change the literary standard altogether by attributing a different kind of truthfulness to their works. In promoting their particular literary philosophy of aesthetic integrity, they were exempting themselves from any preconceived standards of literary judgment. Yet they did not confront the same problems concerning popularity and the subversion of their authority as progressive women novelists did. Second, the Realists' political and social affiliation with the women's movement was gratuitous since they were not bound by any of the internal dilemmas concerning feminists' diverse beliefs. Their work was neither politically nor philosophically embedded in the controversies and arguments surrounding women's status in late Victorian society, except insofar as these implicated their literary representations of them. Thus, these writers had a literary, not a political, interest in the New Woman; she appeared to them already socially contested and politically problematized by the feminists through their social activism and their novels. Whereas for the feminists the New Woman was a social and political mystery, for the Realists she appeared as a literary given. Finally, it remains to be seen whether the Realists' works are truly feminist; that is, do they work to deliberately further the cause of women's emancipation and to oppose patriarchy, as do the novels discussed in Chapter 4? The only certainty at the outset is that they took issue with various manifestations of the New Woman and made her part of their literary agenda. The heroines depicted by these novelists are New Women in that they all defy some feature of the traditional feminine roles. Realists wrote of sexual behavior with frankness and employed as mouthpieces women who were unusually independent, insightful, and free from convention's dictates. Yet the Realists' use of the New Woman as a literary subject is intricately bound with the literary issues they had to work out for themselves. In many ways, the New Woman enabled the Realists to examine issues pertinent to their literary and aesthetic projects. Realists sought and found ways of situating themselves in relation to social reality that were new to the Victorian tradition of the novel, while they distinguished themselves by challenging the status quo of woman's proscribed nature and her place in the Victorian imagination.

The Realists appear to uphold the identification of women and the "masses" that did so much to impede the women's and labor causes. Utilizing their characteristic sympathy toward the working-class "masses" as an underrepresented and thematically challenging group to write about, the Realists combined two contentious subjects in their novels: Women and the working-classes became the working-class heroine. But unlike the feminists, who were willing to accuse their female characters of false consciousness (even while they account for class as contributing to this problem), the Realists valorize their heroines for being elemental in their sentiments and actions. The heroines in realistic novels are for the most part working-class women; when they are middle class they are generally women who have not made woman's place in society an issue for themselves, although it may be a real personal concern. Yet, interestingly enough, the one most obviously elemental aspect of their being—their sexuality—appears to be either compromised or reasoned away by the Realists. Finally, these women, like Meredith's Diana, are not representative of other women in their ideas, feelings, or actions; they are presented as exceptional women and do not represent the societal New Woman at all. Most of all, they do not view themselves as members of a gender class, nor do they define their concerns and troubles along class lines. Their troubles are individualized in their consciousness and the narratives they appear in. For example, Moore's Esther Waters is, in her simplicity and in her lack of awareness, essentially a nonpolitical being. Not bound by middle-class conventions, she appears to be the embodiment of feminist ideals in practice, but these are never articulated or preached. She is the New Woman minus the philosophical, political, and ideological underpinnings for which she was notorious. This aspect of the characterization of the New Woman is important since she was unpopular during the 1890s primarily because she was much too obtrusive. In fact, a large body of antifeminist literature of the decade criticizes the New Woman for speaking too much "cant"; in other words, for having and articulating a philosophy and cause of her own, and for being too vocal.[3] Feminist activists, who invited the harshest criticism of all, were particularly disliked for being "restless and ambitious persons who are less than women, greedy of notoriety, . . . with strong passions rather than warm affections" (Linton 1979, 21). Since self-assertion was generally considered the chief characteristic of the New Woman, and this is the characteristic Esther lacks, heroines like her can be viewed as New Women who are silenced politically. This silence may be due to Esther's subordinate status as a working-class woman, informed by the common gender and class biases and the general discriminatory view that the working-class masses lacked "interiority." Realists agree that for the working classes to act is human, to be aware or conscious of one's subjectivity unimaginable, and to possess a critical consciousness is to transcend societal limitations of class as well as of gender (Huyssen 1986, 45).[4]

It is easy enough for Moore to advocate the cause of a woman who has no political agenda of her own. As a model of womanhood as it "really" exists, Esther Waters is not a political model, but a model of apolitical and—in the novel—depoliticized existence. The events that take place in Esther's life happen in a haphazard way, ranging from seduction and discrimination to moral support, so that even they are not made sense of by Moore. Life's occurrences are not politicized; in the final analysis, their political and social significance is not an issue in Esther's life. For example, Moore describes the forces that shape Esther's life and being, and ultimately her moral character, as accidental. Quite naturalistically, Esther is a passive recipient of life's happenings:

> Never had she felt more certain that misfortune was inherent in her life, and remembering all the trouble she had, she wondered she had come out of it alive; and now, just as things seemed like settling, everything was going to be upset again. Fred was away for a fortnight's holiday—she was safe for eleven or twelve days. After that she did not know what might happen. . . . Ah! if she hadn't happened to go out that particular time she might never have met William. (201)

Cultural bias against the working classes allowed Realists like Moore to posit his heroine and the problems she confronts in the context of a reality that is, by the Realists' definition, deterministic. This reality serves as a depoliticized setting in many ways, if by political we mean—specifically in the 1890s—symbolic actions and reactions, negotiations of (and struggles for) power, and challenges to established class and gender hierarchies. In the 1890s' context of social and cultural revisions of women and socioeconomic classes, one's political identity included all of the above public pronouncements concerning oppression and its opposition; the absence of these features in Realist novels could not go unnoticed by the feminists. In fact, the Realists' essentializing and conventional characterizations did not escape the notice of their more enlightened female readers, and it may help us to know that there is a body of literature from the 1890s, mostly published in journals, in which women read men's texts and evaluated their representations of women. These readers acted as a controlling influence on the Realists, as did protests against Realistic "frankness." Most important, these readers held Realists accountable for their attestations to be representing reality accurately. An essay on Hardy, for example, argues that Hardy did not convey or even have a sufficient understanding of woman's nature, and as a result mischaracterized women in novel such as *Tess of the Durbevilles*.[5] Writing as one who has "a long career of novel reading," Edith Slater wrote in 1898 that the women who appear in men's fiction are "saints, or Jezebels, or monuments of obstinacy or colourlessness, or a hundred other things; but they are hardly ever women" (575). She observes that men always seem to accept their women "ready-made" without troubling to reexamine or analyze preconceived notions of womanhood and femininity. Finally, Slater suggests, the women characters one encounters in male-authored novels are little more than "preconceived ideas" applied to a number of imagined plots, reflecting little of the reality of women's characters and lives. There are "stock virtues" and "stock vices" attributed to women over centuries, and these simply become transported onto current contexts. Slater surmises that male authors create conventional female characters and are so noncritical toward their own notions of womanhood because "nothing is easier than to make things fit in with a pre-conceived idea" (571). In short, she accuses such writers of being complacent and consequently conservative in their views and depictions of women. The degree to which these accusations are justified may be determined by examining some of the novels themselves.

GEORGE MOORE

Initiating a late Victorian literary trend of external artistic influences, George Moore went to Paris to be instructed in alternative views of art and its functions. He returned to England as an oppositional force in his own right, producing texts such as *Esther Waters* (1894), which discount traditionally hierarchical views of class. If the central operative ideology in Moore's representations of women remained bourgeois, the characters and themes of his novels were nonetheless aberrations in that they challenged existing definitions. Research, observation, and minute description would override the imaginative (and political) component of art and literature for Moore, and the chasm between art and life would be bridged as never before. When Moore asked that writers be allowed to produce literature appropriate to its age without interference from those controlling the market, and when he criticized market practices for their moral censorship, he was raising the same objections already voiced by Mrs. Humphrey Ward, when she pointed out that Mudie was not stocking enough copies of her novels and was thus subverting her efforts to gain a wide readership (Griest 1970, 209).[6]

Moore's formulations concerning the purpose of art problematized notions of authorial integrity and is reminiscent of the argument between Ruskin and Whistler two decades earlier. In attempting to break away from the contrived forms that he believed constituted British fiction until that time, Moore emphasized what appeared to be the incidentals of life or the "casualness" with which life-altering decisions are made (xi). Moore himself realized that his was not an altogether neutral project, nor one that could allow for the objectivity and detached observation he advocated. When all was said and done, the author's relation to his subjects was a complicated one in which power, validation, insights, accuracy, and authority were critical components. These intricacies in the relationship between author and subject, artist and matter (life), required a judgment call on the part of one or the other, but never both, it would appear. Generally, the literary subject was subordinate to the author, as Thomas Hardy did not fail to notice in his critique of Realism's claims:

> The most devoted apostle of Realism, the sheerest naturalist, cannot escape, any more than the withered old gossip over her fire, the exercise of Art in his labour or pleasure of telling a tale. Not until he becomes an automatic reproducer of all impressions whatsoever can he be called purely scientific, or even a manufacturer on scientific principles. If in the exercise of his reason he select or omit, with an eye to being more truthful than truth (the just aim of Art), he transforms himself into a technicist at a move. (1891, 316)

Moore's attempt at a resolution of this conflict between literary purpose and authorial function was to seek a favorable, positive relationship between the two. The active ingredient in Moore's portrayal of Esther's life and of life among the working classes in general is an ideological and sentimental argument based on the assumption that the lower classes are good-natured; the circumstances of their lives are figured around this given. Whatever they might be construed to mean in the context of 1890s' class and social relations, in *Esther Waters*, courage and wholeheartedness can salvage all situations, appease threats, resolve calamities. This can be the case since Esther's social agency is not an issue and since her life and destiny are commanded by chance and coincidence. Esther is so good-natured, in fact, that she may easily pass for a simpleton. She is as susceptible to forceful seduction as she is to love, as her relationships with the two men in her life illustrate. While she is settled in her life with a supportive and understanding employer (an unkind caricature of the New Woman), Esther allows herself to be swept off her feet by her child's father when he reappears after a many years-long absence, and she sacrifices her own security in order to be with him because he seems to need her.

Moore emphasizes his concern over his relationship to his characters but also over the question of "accuracy" in realistic literature in his preface to *Esther Waters*. The introduction to the novel frames the narrative in such a way that the writer is granted authority by the heroine, who asks him to write her story. Esther surfaces out of Moore's subconscious to say "I have come here to defend my life," and finds, instead, that she must first transform her medium (the narrator) if he is to be of use to her, to understand her at all (xvii). Esther's ghost infuses Moore with unprecedented awareness, he claims in the preface, and prepares him to undertake the task of writing her life. Moore thereby suggests that this novel is authored definitively by Esther herself and that he is merely a qualified conduit through which she must pass to reach the public. Thus, at least on a philosophical and moral level, Moore removes himself from a potentially uncomfortable position as interpreter of life and as potential appropriator of women's experiences. At the outset of the narrative Moore does away with the role of the artist as mediator between art and life, and it was perhaps his deliberate avoidance of moral and ideological censorship, his reluctance to make Esther's life more palatable that caused the novel to be banned from libraries and to incite his outrage toward literary censorship. *Esther Waters* is not an apology, after all, but an explanation, a justification for a kind of social existence that Victorian morality still condemned as depraved and animalistic. Interestingly, Moore's advocacy is not so much of the working-class woman but of his characterization of her, which, as I have indicated, compromises her potential. This novel serves as an example of how, even though characterizations of women were informed by the existence of the New Woman type, mainstream, Realist novels that concentrate on female heroines nonetheless did not serve to enhance the feminist model, but co-opted it and imbued it with familiar, conventional understandings of class and gender. In this respect, Realist novels are quite conservative.

GEORGE GISSING

Alongside Moore, George Gissing stands out as a critic of bourgeois nineteenth-century morality and as a revisionist of the novel. His connection to Realism is evidenced by his use of the novel to address predominant problems at the end of the century, such as the marginalization of women, class bias, and literary exploitation. His fiction deals with labor, gender, and authorship in a critical manner. Yet Gissing's female characters are also problematic because they occupy an ambivalent position somewhere between emancipation and servility to tradition. Some of his women are "odd," some "emancipated," some misogynistic caricatures of the mythical evil usurper of male power. *The Emancipated* ([1890] 1985) bears a title that would have provoked instantaneous association with New Women and the women's movement, but actually concentrates on both sexes equally, does little to further or support the women's cause, and does not promote more equal or better relations between the sexes. The main female character, Miriam, is a widow and a Puritan by faith. She is in Italy in order to recover from a period of mourning following her husband's death. The epitome of traditional Victorian virtuousness in women, Miriam is repressed and reserved, and resists enjoying the natural beauty, art, and architecture of the country. Art can "emancipate" Miriam and presumably all women, according to this narrative, as it is aesthetic appreciation that enables her to break free of conventional morality and ultimately to fall in love. In a plot that includes elopement and a failed marriage and divorce, and that champions passion's reign over reason, Miriam stands out as a paradigm of Victorian repressiveness, and so the reader is relieved to see her come out of it and into a more independent existence. Miriam undergoes a spiritual rebirth and eventually gains a heightened awareness of herself, a process initiated and aided by art, in the most literal sense. In a scene following her transformation, the heroine looks at two portraits of herself, drawn by her lover: One is of the old, reserved Miriam, and the other of the "emancipated," New heroine:

Yes, she recognized them. They were both portraits of herself, but subtly distinguished from each other. The one represented a face fixed in excessive austerity, with a touch of pride that was by no means amiable, with resentful eyes, and lips on the point of being cruel. In the other, though undeniably the features were the same, all these harsh characteristics had yielded to a change of spirit; austerity had given place to grave thoughtfulness, the eyes had a noble light, on the lips was sweet womanly strength. (437)

Apart from the obvious point to be made concerning Gissing's praise of the "sweetness" of women, the narrative works to subvert gender to the transformative powers of art. The kind of artistic appreciation promoted here is dissociated from any moral significance or content. Art itself remains privileged and inviolable, although individual subjects, say women, are transformed by its powers. In fact, according to this narrative, art is valuable when it is appreciated for its own sake and on its own merits alone, echoing aestheticism's claims.

Paralleling late Victorian imaginings of women, Gissing's novel about novel writing, *New Grubb Street* ([1891] 1985), includes an attack on aesthetic adulteration and portrays women as morally and emotionally corrupt beings who cause man's demise. Published in three volumes under the constraints of the circulating library market, this novel is a chronicle of two very different kinds of writers, one strictly commercial and profit-interested, the other writing in earnest and resisting commercial pressures. *New Grubb Street* sets up a number of binary oppositions that reveal the author's estimation of literary integrity and gender relations, and suggest a relationship between the two: author/hack, virtuous being/social parasite, woman as martyr/woman as vampire, literature as art/fiction as commodity are aligned to correspond to one another in negative terms throughout the narrative. Women and men are likewise situated in antagonistic relationships, but whereas virtue for men corresponds to the pursuit of a higher ideal in art, virtue in women represents self-sacrifice and subordination to men even when they qualify as serious and respectable scholars, as does Marian. *New Grubb Street* also offers some unfavorable representations of middle-class women, especially the antiheroine of the novel and the cause of Edward Reardon's demise, Amy Reardon. Amy manipulates her husband into overworking in order to maintain her bourgeois lifestyle; she wants money and fame, is socially ambitious, and her vulgar materialism thwarts Edward's idealistic desire to produce a literary masterpiece. Despite his self-sacrificial attempts to please her, Amy leaves her husband in poverty and hardship and joins her mother, who is much like her. She ends up selfishly happy, even though her husband and child die, and marries Jasper Milvain, the hack writer, who is now the embodiment of social and literary vice as a successfully exploitative agent in the book-selling and promotion market.

The model of ideal womanhood in this novel, and the contrast to Amy Reardon, is a martyr, Marian. In an age that Gissing represents as far too product-oriented while undervaluing artistic integrity and aesthetic quality, Marian is destined to lose to those whose priorities are personal profit and self-interest. Interestingly, Marian is a writer as well, but is not featured as such in the novel. The fact that she does the bulk of her father's research, writing, and reviewing is explained as being an extension of her female virtue. She is a good daughter doing her duty to her father, a caring and giving woman of whom no man in the novel is ultimately truly worthy. Given Marian's status in the novel and her juxtaposition to Amy Reardon, Patricia Stubbs's criticism of Gissing is most appropriate and applicable to this novel as well. Granting that *The Odd Women* is in fact an insightful account of the serious problems encountered by women who are considered socially "superfluous," Stubbs still notes elements of conservatism and gender bigotry in Gissing's view of women in relation to patriarchal institutions:

> The domestic dream and the idealized wife play a characteristically contradictory role in Gissing's work. They are partly used as vehicles for his criticism of what he saw as the selfish, empty-headed, incompetent woman. . . . They are also used as an indictment of the would-be emancipated woman who attempts to throw off the oppression of existing social or sexual relations. (1979, 153)

Marian is a puzzling characterization of the good woman. If she is to serve as an antidote or contrast to Amy, who is the "indictment against New Women," she is ineffectual in that role. Amy's moral depravity is located in her disparaging her husband's efforts to be a respected literary writer. We come to scorn her for abandoning him and share in the suffering she causes him. As the woman who does support a man in all the appropriate ways, Marian gets exploited by him and, despite her loyalty, is further victimized by her subservience and reticence. Significantly, by the novel's end Marian is as victimized as other serious literary men in the story, one of whom kills himself while the other loses his mind. The man she loves, Jasper Milvain, breaks their engagement when he learns that she will not inherit vast amounts of money, and marries Amy Reardon, the widow who has just come into an impressive inheritance. At the novel's conclusion, Marian is a tragic heroine, much as Edward Reardon is. In the last analysis, Marian and Amy personify the stereotypical Victorian dichotomization of female identity, that of virgin and whore, angel in the house and fallen woman, all reductionist and stereotypical definitions of womanhood that were being challenged by both the social and feminist-literary conception of the New Woman.

GEORGE MEREDITH

George Meredith redefined his aesthetics so as to not be caught in the same bind in which Moore found himself. He dissociated himself from Realism, or at least adopted a less militant stance toward literary representation. By far the most popular among male novelists writing about women, Meredith was viewed as a genuine advocate of women's rights. Reflecting popular opinion concerning Meredith's feminist sensibilities both then and now, Edith Slater described Meredith as the exception to the trend in men's essentializing and misreading women. "There is a certain largeness in his conceptions of women," she states, although he "has been accused of depicting and applauding selfishness in women" (576). Adeline Seargant also applauded Meredith's representations of women. The strengths of Meredith's depictions of women, she says, lie in his ability and willingness to let women reveal themselves to him rather than fitting them into preexisting molds:

> George Meredith is one of the few novelists of any age of time who see not only man but woman as she is. Daring actually to draw from the life, and to discard the petty superstitions, and debasing traditions of the past, he presents us with a new type of heroine; not the "veiled, virginal doll" of contemporary fiction, but the woman with blood and brains, the heroine, as he calls her, of reality . . . it is his women who are new. They are not blurred outlines, worn-out types—they are individuals whom we have met, whom we may like or dislike, approve or condemn. (1889, 208)

Meredith's aesthetic philosophy may account, at least in part, for his avoiding literary or even social stereotypes in his own fiction and also for his need to undermine the tendency among novelists to make use of formulaic characters. "Of Dairies and Diarists," the opening chapter of *Diana of the Crossways* ([1885] 1931), argues that there can be many versions of the same story, and that their differences are often based on personal bias, social prejudice, and the inaccuracy of preconceptions. It makes the point that a story can be told variously, while Meredith makes clear his own aesthetics as a novelist. The artistic process, he argues, involves "philosophy," which he defines as the foe of both harsh strict realism and rosy sentimentalism; it bids us to see that we are not so pretty as rose-pink, not so repulsive as dirty drab; and that instead of everlastingly shifting those barren aspects, the sight of ourselves is wholesome, bearable, fructifying, finally a delight. Imagine the celestial refreshment of having a pure decency in the place of sham; real flesh; a soul born active, wind-beaten, but ascending. (13)

Meredith's object in this novel is to save Diana and women like her from the throes of misrepresentation and harsh moral judgment, to reveal her in her truest light because "the multitude of evil reports which [the world] takes for proof are marshalled against her without question of the nature of the victim" (2). In this sense, Meredith's style is appropriate to his task insofar as it allows for a *celebration* of humanity, which he sees as being the main function of fiction. Justifying his willingness to use sentimentalism if necessary, Meredith states that the Realists have not as yet embraced this "Philosophy," and urges his readers to find it, even if only through a purely emotional response. Proposing this compromise between accuracy in representing the human condition and reader engagement, Meredith sets his own aesthetic principles to work, and in the process divests himself from competing aesthetic trends.

What the preface promises and the novel actually delivers are two different things, however, for although Meredith does portray Diana favorably, there are actually two heroines in this novel, neither of whom resembles Caroline Norton very much, the early feminist upon whose life the novel is based. According to Meredith's own proscription that "what a woman thinks of a woman is the test of her nature," Diana has only one substantial female relationship in the novel to vouch for her character (11). Diana's "nature" cannot be appreciated apart from her corollary in the narrative, her friend, Lady Dunstane. Whereas Diana's pitfall is her high social profile and public visibility, her best friend is a social recluse, a cripple who provides Diana with advice and much womanly, conventional wisdom. When Diana escapes from her husband and the impositions of marriage, she attempts to resume her life as a society woman, although she is shunned by that society. Her friend helps her to see the error of her ways and instructs her that true happiness must lie in a new love relationship, this time with a man who is conventionally virtuous. Diana serves as the public persona, minus the insight and wisdom of her friend, and the two women combined would constitute one admirable character, even by feminist standards. Yet set apart in this way, they contradict one another and negate each other's individuality by appeasing their mutual dissatisfactions with social norms and their places in society.[7] At the end of the novel, Emma Dunstane dies after she convinces Diana to marry Tom Redworth. Settling into a promising marriage, Diana no longer needs a conscience, and Emma's place is taken by Diana's future husband. Noting his negotiations with the model of the New Woman and his inability to produce a truly empowering characterization of her, reviews of Meredith's portrayals of women tended to criticize that he "aim[ed] high, but not high enough":

> Meredith shows us women as they too often are—toys, chattels, slaves, by their own consent as well as by the will of men. What hope—what remedy does he suggest? What is his ideal of the future woman? He draws her as she is with almost startling vividness; when we come to what she should be, his portrait loses its life-like hues. Here, in his ideal of woman, George Meredith is to me un-satisfactory. (Seargant, 210)

This observation is still valid today, for if progressive fiction consists not only of criticisms of existing structures but also of an agenda for replacing them with less oppressive ones, Meredith's *Diana of the Crossways* cannot be said to have contributed significantly to the feminist goal of constructing a self-determined, empowered New Woman.

THOMAS HARDY

Hardy has often been applauded as the main liberator of female sexuality in fiction, yet viewed in context, he is remarkable more because of his blunt treatment of sex in general than for his enlightened depictions of female sexuality in particular. Gail Cunningham observes that when *Tess of the Durbevilles* appeared in 1891 (1984) amid objections to its overly realistic representations of immorality, the protest was really against the sexual theme of the novel, especially its attacks on marriage and the intimate knowledge of the protagonists' sexual affairs that Hardy imposed on his readers. It is also suggested that this was an exasperation festered by the previous three years of women's novels, and that Hardy's male-centered *Jude the Obscure* ([1896] 1982) merely complemented the "fierce attacks made through popular fiction on the Victorian concept of the feminine character and the position of women" (1978, 87). The reading public was already antagonized by a series of novels written primarily by women that deliberately set out to attack marriage, to break the bonds of censorship that forbade the treatment of sexuality in fiction, and to argue for the feminist cause. Hardy's main characterization of the New Woman is found in *Jude the Obscure,* where Sue

Brideshead figures as a confusing element in the hero's already troubled existence. Jude's predicament over the conflict between self-satisfaction and society's moral prohibitions is shared by the readers and by Sue herself, but the frustration is greater for Jude, since Sue embodies this conflict and is the object of his desire. Furthermore, she does not know her own mind, so how can her lover know to respect her wishes and what she perceives to be her own best interest? Hardy's treatment of Sue Brideshead reveals that he was familiar with the feminist agenda but less with its underpinnings. The class difference between Jude and his cousin Sue is crucial and is at the core of this problem of desire and its fulfillment. With his wife, Arabella, Jude is able to have satisfactory sexual relationship, although it is morally questionable and possibly objectionable because it lacks emotional substance. Typecast as a typical middle-class woman, Sue is perpetually denying her sexuality, and her relationship with Jude is unconsummated for two years. Hence, Jude's predicament, centered on his class status and the impossibility of his reaching beyond manual labor, is also manifested in Sue. This novel concerns itself with the quest for a happy medium between the potentially self-determined New Woman and the nonpolitical, thoroughly sensual and amoral ways attributed to the working classes. In this battle of the New versus the old, no one wins.

Long discussed in criticism and defined by Hardy as exemplary of the late Victorian "neurotic girl," Sue Brideshead does not exactly qualify as such, because she does not invest in the kinds of soul-searching we see feminists' characters do, such as Caird's Hadria. Hardy apparently approaches Sue Brideshead with some trepidation, since she is puzzled as much by her sexuality as by the reigning morality and by social expectations. She lacks the self-determination that distinguished New Women from other women socially, and recoils from the burden of responsibility such self-command requires. Her final solution to her predicament manifests itself literally as self-renunciation: "I wish my every fearless word and thought could be rooted out of my history. Self-renunciation—that's everything!" she says, while Jude tries to instill courage in her after the death of their children (420). As a woman ready and willing to subordinate her own desire to societal norms, Sue may serve as a model of Hardy's own view of, and puzzlement over, the New Woman. She may know what she wants, but as long as the author is unclear about late Victorian feminist philosophy, she can only be depicted by him as what George Egerton described: "an enigma" bound to be tragic for the author who attempts to represent her ([1893] 1983, 21). Ardis aptly accounts for Hardy's predicament in this and other novels by positing the narrative predicaments he creates as symbolic of his impasse concerning women: "As Hardy releases the New Woman from the trap of society's condemnation of women who are sexually active outside of marriage as 'impure' or 'fallen,' he also . . . silences her, obliterates her. He challenges 'the censorship of prudery,' but refuses to let the New Woman challenge his own monologic discourse" (31). In *Jude the Obscure*, tragedy lies in an unknown that is frightening because its source is beyond human understanding. Tragedy and misery come from an idealized past now made utterly impossible, much as Jude's Ruskinian work ethic is anachronistic in the novel's setting and hence counterproductive; misery also comes from the general disparity between desire and its fulfillment, and in the total absence of control over one's destiny. As Sue Brideshead remains both an "enigma" and a destructive force in this novel, she parallels the many tragic "unknowns" to which Jude falls victim.

While Hardy can still be credited for his frank discussions affirming the existence of female sexuality (as he does in *Tess*) and thereby enhancing the New sexualized female identity promoted by the feminists, Sue Brideshead is sexually impotent. This is a very important missing ingredient in this New Woman, especially when we consider the thrust of the novel: man's quest for fulfillment, rewarding work, love, and intellectual and spiritual stimulation. It is also significant that female sexuality is presented as an important issue here and that Hardy breaks with its traditional Victorian treatment as symbolizing sin and moral depravity. But Sue fails in the capacity of female and/or sexual liberator, and in the novel her inadequacy contributes to Jude's failure to live a meaningful and rewarding life. Hardy does in fact go a long way in terms of validating human sexuality, but he censures the New Woman for failing to meet an essential requirement for being human: She is not sexually or emotionally "pure," but confused and confusing. Hardy was evidently not quite comfortable with the New Woman, and his characterization of Sue Brideshead functions as a criticism of her nonelemental nature, her complexity. This novel makes clear that the New Woman's sexuality is in some ways as problematic as female sexuality had ever been; in this instance it is the New Woman's sexual unavailability and unmalleability that creates problems of tragic proportions. Clearly, Jude would not have been condemned to such tragedy had Sue been less inhibited, and the novel's fatalistic overtones would be ameliorated by, a less "neurotic" Sue. The potential of the fulfillment of Jude's desire is undermined by Sue, and Hardy points an accusatory finger at her as at least partially an agent of Jude's destruction.

In his analysis of Gissing's fiction in *The Political Unconscious,* Jameson works to unravel the discord in some of Realistic fiction's features. According to Jameson, questions such as the problematic treatment of New Women by Realism that I have begun to examine here can be addressed most effectively by examining the relationships between authorial ideology and the mandates of literary production, but especially the author's own "resentment" concerning his subject matter. Presented as distinct from the author's relation to social "resentment" or reality, this activity is best defined as the literalization into the narrative's construction of the author's "attempt to resolve the dilemmas of totality." This process is also dependent on "conceptual conditions of possibility or narrative presuppositions which one must 'believe'" (1981, 194, 201). In other words, the author is compelled to attempt to reconcile his narrative's reality to that of the world outside it, which requires that he accept and, in the process, validate those "real" contexts. The product of this reconciliation can be viewed as the "daydream" in which both author and text engage and are complicitous. Jameson sees the problems in Realist aesthetic ideology as corresponding to the "preconditions which must have been secured in order for the subject successfully to tell itself [a] particular daydream" (201). The "daydream" shared by the authors I have discussed here consists primarily of their aesthetic ideology, the principles of Realism. Situating us within the context of late Victorian class and gender ideologies, Jameson's formulation suggests that the author's attempts to construct an alternative reality is contingent on his ability to reconcile the different components of the ideology that describes the setting or "preconditions" within which he writes as well as the narrative he constructs. In the case of Gissing's *New Grubb Street,* in particular, the "daydream" he attempted to narrativize was incompatible with both his own social position and his presuppositions about his own class identity (Jameson 1981, 182). As a result, Gissing's fiction includes both emancipatory and reactionary attitudes.

While much can be made of this kind of analysis, most important are the possibilities it suggests for understanding the dynamics of writing with a double purpose. For example, the feminist authors I discuss in the previous chapters were aware that their literary project was also a social and political one, and it involved specific ideological revisions. They had to construct a social and political revision of womanhood through their narratives, and were thus always involved in arguing with particular existing patriarchal ideologies and practices. Furthermore, they not only accepted, but articulated and celebrated, what Bhabha calls "the loss of a 'teleologically significant world'," while the Realists insisted on its existence (205). In retrospect, the Realists may be said to have contributed significantly to the feminists' opposition to the marginalized female subjectivity. But there is a crucial difference between them and the feminist authors: The male writers I discuss here have long been cited as "women's advocates" in one sense or another, while their works have been perceived as disinterested and hence more authoritative and reliable than women's narratives of the same period. Realists have been credited with charting new avenues in literature, partly because they were writing under conditions that required formal innovation to court a new readership and to at least partially satisfy the standards established by publishers. In the literary climate of the 1890s, Realism strove primarily to make a place for itself at the forefront of purely aesthetic inquiries. Realist novelists were in a position similar to that of the feminists, and they understood the feminists' predicament as authors with an oppositional agenda. Yet while the feminists wrote with a sociopolitical urgency, for the Realists, concern over the survival of their texts was at the core of fictional uses of women and their changing status in society. This is a fair generalization, even though the 1890s included authors as diverse in style and conviction as H. G. Wells, Rudyard Kipling, Robert Louis Stevenson, Henry James, Joseph Conrad, plus a number of popular writers such as Rider Haggard and Grant Allen. These authors held a variety of positions concerning the social and literary establishment, and some were progressive enough to include women's rights among their concerns. But they came to women's issues as outsiders; that is, they came upon them as themes closely related to their feelings concerning seemingly unrelated issues such as imperialism and their expressed dislike for the repressiveness of traditional Victorian morality.

The contrasts between the feminist and Realist novels are remarkable, but most remarkable of all is the difference in their projects and ultimately in their literary failures and successes, respectively. In the midst of the novel's new popularity, pressing social issues provided Realist authors with an itinerary to guide their stories, rendering narratives in which the contested female subject figured only symptomatically, yet in instrumental ways. In a way Realism resembles other male-dominated aesthetic movements in their appropriation of what feminists and antifeminists alike referred to, as we have seen, as the "eternal feminine" (Gilbert and Gubar 1986, 966). They purport to have an inner knowledge of women and their lots in life. More than this, as in Moore's case, their narrative strategies suggest that they even claim to know women more intimately than women can profess to know themselves, and thus qualify to be women's most precise and insightful spokespersons. That this practice ultimately works to silence women or to at least deprive them of personally motivated initiatives to define their own condition seems to have been a problem that the Realists could overcome stylistically, for they do not appear to be politically problematized by their own power in relation to women. If all of this posturing on the part of the Realists is at all reminiscent of Flaubert's statements concerning what he considered to be his own inherent but repressed femaleness, and if this appears similar to the aesthetes' obscuring gender roles and gender identities, it is hardly accidental.[8] Symons praises Flaubert for revising and beautifying reality. In *Madame Bovary*, for example, Symons sees "what is common in the imagination of Madame Bovary becom[ing] exquisite in Flaubert's rendering of it"; he adds, "Bovary's trivial desires and aspirations give Flaubert all that he wants: the opportunity to create beauty out of reality" (1971, 125-126). Here, again, women represent vulgar reality and men the refiners of it and them. Like aestheticism, Realism did in fact make several worthwhile contributions to the women's cause in a circuitous way, by resisting traditional definitions of women. But posing as the masters of female consciousness in this way, or being privy to it, mainly served as the Realists' literary agenda and appears to have, in the same stroke, reinforced some old oppressive stereotypes.

ENDNOTES

INTRODUCTION:
"Some Preliminary Considerations"

1. An account of the 1890s that is inadequate and typifies the norm in excluding women altogether is G. M. Young's *Portrait of an Age* (1954). In literary history, David Cecil (1965), Richard Levine (1976), and Ernest Baker (1936) either look only at High Culture figures and hence do not consider women, or do so in order to ridicule them.

CHAPTER ONE:
"Identity Crises and Protest"

1. Stone is fairly typical of literary critics who have treated the Realists as revolutionary and radical, both in terms of their place in the literary tradition and in their social views and attitudes. He is willing to concede a sort of selfishness on their part, nonetheless.
2. Jackson's account of the 1890s is particularly important and helpful because he was part of the art scene of the time and writes as a contemporary of the events and people he describes. He serves to give us a clearer sense of the period's view of itself.
3. Lovell also accepts this as true, and adds that philanthropy exposed women to public life and brought them face to face with the men who denied them rights (1987, 103). It seems dubious, however, that it served the same political purpose as the women's activism.
4. There is also a good (if overly harsh) description of the Fabian Society in Raymond Williams's *Culture and Society* (1983). Williams agrees with Barbara Cole's observation that the Society's position on various issues was politically perplexing.
5. Quoted in Janet Murray, *Strong Minded Women and Other Lost Voices from 19th Century England* (1982), 261-262.
6. Philip Dodd, "Englishness and National Culture" in Robert Colls and Dodd, eds, *Englishness: Politics and Culture 1880-1920.* (1986)
7. Dodd elaborates, "[h]ow was a single heritage to accommodate the experiences of the distinct groups? The pattern . . . was that of inclusion, simple exclusion, and transformation" (15).
8. See Hobsbawm's discussion of the national as opposed to the class identity of the working classes (129). Also, Tuchman makes clear the laboring classes' astute understanding of the extent to which they did not benefit from colonialism and of the manipulation late Victorian culture was enacting ensuant to colonialism and colonialist interests: "With the Boer War, the war in the Philippines and the Boxer Rebellion in progress, [communist] delegates found it easy to unite on a resolution. . . . stating that capitalism would collapse as a consequence, not of economic conditions, but of imperialist rivalries" (505).
9. In this analysis, toward the end of the century, the character of the working class is radically transformed by the nearly exclusive economic emphasis on service industries.

10. The one specific issue Phillippa Levine points to as having caused numerous rifts in the women's movement, apart from the suffrage issue, is the Contagious Diseases Act, which was approached differently by various feminists (the older, conservative feminists being more cautious toward it) (1990, 145). Furthermore, she adds that with "protective legislation," "[t]he issue was a sensitive and explosive one for feminists, dividing them . . . less along class lines than along lines of political belief. There was no simple division" (119).
11. Spender, in particular, argues this sense of urgency in her "Great Britain" chapter, as does Roger Fulford (1909; 1958), 81.
12. Also see "Women and Trade Unions" in Rowbotham, *Hidden from History* (1985).
13. Accounts of the evolution of Social Darwinism into a political tool used to fragment and alienate the masses from proper society and vice versa abound in histories of Victorian England. Notions of what might be, and was, considered "natural" are extremely important when investigating the late Victorian cultural economy, because any social problem could be dismissed as unrelated to political structures and situations; class-based elitism did not lend itself to causal relationships between poverty and protest. See, for instance, the argument against feminism based on notions of "nature" in the example of Sydney Grundy's *New Woman*, noted in Chapter 2.

CHAPTER TWO:
"The Idea Is the Fact": Art's Interiority and Literary Production

1. The concept of "aura" comes from Walter Benjamin's essay, "Art in the Age of Mechanical Reproduction" in his *Illuminations* (1968), but I am using it here as it is also used by Andreas Huyssen in *After the Great Divide* (1986). Huyssen sees the destruction of aura as the destruction "of seemingly natural and organic beauty" (10). According to this interpretation, art's aura consists in part of its allusion to a reality that presupposes social wholeness and naturalness; that is, an organic reality in the absence of turmoil and conflict.
2. For an elaborate and informative discussion on Victorian sexuality reforms by feminists, see Jeffries (1985). This is by far the most comprehensive and incisive discussion on the subject.
3. A quotation from Alan Lee's discussion is called for here: "Imperial expansion after the 1870s was ideally suited to exploitation by the 'new journalism.' It provided wars sufficiently distant as not to be too depressing, but successful enough to sustain confidence, with occasional setbacks to maintain tension. It provided opportunity for sometimes vastly imaginative tales of foreign lands, disguised as news. It provided the thrills and passions associated with the possibility of clashes with other great powers." (108)
4. Altick agrees with Lee that new journalism's relation to the public was primarily determined by its profit motive. John Stokes adds, "the journalist is the enemy upon whom the New Woman depends" (1989, 25).
5. N. N. Feltes's study of the impact of mass publishing (1986) also points to a closer relationship between readers and texts that foregrounds mass readers' expectations of texts. Feltes emphasizes the degree to which authors had absolutely no control over their texts, and at the same time the enormous financial profitability in writing for serials.

6. I do not mean to suggest here that satires in general had emancipatory premises or goals. In fact, *Zuleika Dobson, The Green Carnation,* (1894) and the very popular play, *The New Woman,* by Sydney Grundy, mock the New Woman or any woman breaking with convention in one way or another. In the play, for example, there is a drawn-out deliberation concerning woman's "nature," and the dilemma is resolved quite simply: Mr. Sylvester: "In a woman a man wants flesh and blood—frank human nature!" Mrs. Sylvester: "A mere animal!" Mr. Sylvester: "A woman" (88).
7. Truth in relation to the dynamics of social equality are elaborated again in "Culture and Anarchy," where Arnold equates "culture" with "the study of perfection, of harmonious perfection, general perfection, . . . in an inward condition of the mind and spirit." See Trilling, ed., ([1949] 1972), 477.
8. Christina Rosetti is a remarkable exception to my observations here, if she can be considered part of the Brotherhood, which is debatable. Consideration of her critical and oppositional writings in relation to Pre-Raphaelites' idealized depictions of women ("In an Artist's Studio" is a wonderful example) is beyond the scope of my discussion.

CHAPTER THREE
The Politics of Publication: Women In the Literary Marketplace

1. Mona Caird wrote as "G. Noel Hutton," Mary Kingsley as "Lucas Mallet," and "Marie Corelli" was actually Mary Mackay.
2. This essay offers a revision of more conservative estimations of the prominence of journals advocating women's rights than has been available in the past. Cynthia White's "An Industry Is Born," for example, tends to concentrate too much on "domestic" journals and excludes mention of more progressive journals (1970).
3. While each of the aspects of feminist activism is covered in extensive detail, the structure of the "Notes" is otherwise erratic. For example, there is no chronological order at all, and a reference to J. S. Mill may be followed by an archaic definition of women as property. Also, the information is not arranged by subject or genre—fiction is quoted to illustrate a point, beside professional medical and legislative documents.
4. Felski's argument is not as exclusive of the notion of feminist aesthetics as it may appear to be. Her approach is very similar to that suggested by Barrett insofar as it enables a broad-based, comprehensive analysis of oppositional writings as they relate to established literary, social, and political systems.
5. Gaye Tuchman and Nina Fortin say that professional writers' organizations kept women out of the "literary" ranks as well and that the admission into such groups was established with difficulty even for women journalists, who were clearly not as caught in the aesthetic ideology that excluded women novelists from the ranks of socially and professionally validated writing (1989, 188).
6. "The Anti-Marriage League" criticizes authors such as Hardy for threatening the institution of marriage by representing it in unfavorable and critical ways, and makes clear how strongly opposed Oliphant was to feminism.
7. Lovell states that what set "conciliatory" novels apart from other woman-authored novels was their ideological allegiance to the "domestic ideology, wedded to a form of Social Darwinism," used to "account for differences between women, especially differences of class and race" (1987, 123). Feminists, as I have argued in the first chapter, looked for unifying characteristics between women.

8. The plot of *Romance of Two Worlds* ([1886] 1976) is fascinating. The world is depicted as too materialistic a place, in this novel, echoing Arnold and the aesthetes. It features as its hero Heliobas, a Pater-like character who articulates a central truth amounting to "beauty is truth" and "fact is only opinion." In the context of the novel, only a privileged and highly sensitive few may have access to this truth. Another part of the universal TRUTH, and the novel's moral, is that one can only change oneself, but never one's circumstances or surroundings. In the introduction to the 1887 edition, Corelli states: "Materialism does not and can never still the hunger of the Immortal Spirit in Man for those things divine, which are, by right, its heritage" (8).
9. Eliza Lynn Linton stands out among antifeminist writers who looked back to the High Victorian past as a more orderly life and a time of greater naturalness among women. In her popular work titled *The Girl of the Period* (1883) she advocates a woman who "holds to love rather than opposition; to reverence, not defiance; who takes more pride in her husband's fame than in her own...." Quoted from Hollis (1979), 20/1.3.5.

CHAPTER FOUR
Late Victorian Feminist Discursive Aesthetics

1. Jameson argues that one can discern, particularly in the works of late Victorian novelists such as Gissing, a conflict within the narrative that consists of the author's attempts to assert his views, particularly those that may conflict with the dominant social or literary ideology. Such conflicts manifest themselves in what he calls "second-level" or "symbolic narratives," and constitute the author's attempts at a reconciliation between the two that would not compromise the integrity of her text (1981, 183).
2. Elaine Showalter, introduction to *Red Pottage* (1985, viii).
3. Dijkstra locates the source of such depictions in the social evolution of Darwinism and in the misogyny inherent in patriarchal myths and religions, which in turn promoted women's mass identity and their exclusion from social and cultural activity. He concludes that for these reasons late Victorian women occupied a contested but mainly negative place in culture.
4. More specifically, Gayle Rubin's model of gender oppression argues that this is an economy in which women can at best attain the status of "gift" objects to be exchanged among men.
5. Quoted in Stead (1894, 68).
6. This description of Egerton's work appears in the back flap of other novels of the period, as an advertisement.
7. Kristeva defines "jouissance" as the lyrical eruptions within narratives such as James Joyce's, stemming from the authors' resistance toward the status quo of language as a system and of normative social relations. She argues that such disruptions in social discourse can be traced to the pre-Oedipal and hence non-symbolic stage of development, in which the unformed "self" merges and identifies with "selves" (not yet "Others") apart from it. It is an appealing and useful concept, particularly as it applies to many of George Egerton's writings that clearly do not manifest any of aestheticism's reactionary elements.

CHAPTER FIVE
Defining the Political: The 'Realistic' Appropriation

1. Bhabha's analysis suggests a parallel between the "facts" of appropriation, which serve as significant subtexts for marginalized peoples to read just as notions and subsequent interpretations of "facts" serve to inform the activities of imperialists.
2. H. D. Trail's contemporary account of Realism illustrates Realists' growing defensiveness (1897, 1). See also, Paul Bourget (1893).
3. Examples of rampant antifeminist literature include: Anonymous, "The Cult of Cant" (1891) and Hogarth (1897); an article that is directed specifically against men who support women's rights is Linton's "The Partisans of the Wild Women" (1892).
4. As I mention in Chapter 1, women and the working classes were seen to pose a threat in late Victorian culture, precisely, as Huyssen suggests, because they were viewed as entirely elemental. The irony is that this entirely "external" existence was ensured by the upper classes. These distinctions between "exterior" versus "interior" states of being and their attendant prejudices persist today.
5. Some examples of directives from women on how one might read fiction are "Ouida" (1899), "Vernon Lee" (1891), and "Vernon Lee" (1894).
6. Since Oliphant was not a feminist, Mudie's censure of her books hints at the more general gender prejudice against women, which has been alluded to by cultural historians of the period.
7. There is much in Meredith's novel to suggest that the two "types" are combined rather than serving some more subversive function: Emma dies at the novel's end, clearly because Diana no longer needs a conscience and is on the "right" path since her decision to marry; Emma is entirely asexual, while Diana is far too passionate; Emma represents the martyrdom typically assigned to nineteenth-century virtuous women. Also, the language Meredith uses makes it appear as if Diana and Emma were soul sisters. Emma, however, is far too traditional and verges on being reactionary, for her credo is, "there is nothing the body suffers that the soul may not profit by," sentimentally suggesting that there is honor to suffering (Meredith 396).
8. Pater also praises Flaubert for seeking to promote "the world's adjustment to [his words'] meaning[s]" rather than vice versa (1908, 28).

Works Cited

Adelman, Paul. *The Rise of the Labour Party, 1880-1945,* 2nd ed. London: Longman Group Ltd., 1986.
Althusser, Louis. *Lenin and Philosophy and Other Essays.* New York: Monthly Review Press, 1971.
Altick, Richard. *The English Common Reader.* Chicago: Chicago University Press, 1957.
Anderson, Bonnie, and Judith Zinsser. *A History of Their Own: Women in Europe.* New York: Harper & Row, 1988.
Anonymous. "The Cult of Cant." *Temple Bar* 93 (Oct. 1891): 189-198).
Ardis, Ann. *New Women, New Novels: Feminism and Early Modernism.* New Brunswick, NJ: Rutgers University Press, 1990.
Arnold, Matthew. *Essays In Criticism: First Series.* 1865. London: The Macmillan Co., 1932.
———. Four Essays on Life and Letters, ed. E. K. Brown. New York: Appleton-Century-Crofts, 1947.
Baker, Ernest A. *The History of the English Novel, Vol. 10: Yesterday.* New York: Barnes and Noble, 1936.
Barrett, Michele. *Women's Oppression Today: Problems in Marxist Feminist Analysis.* London: Verso, 1986.
Beerbohm, Max. *Zuleika Dobson.* 1911. London: Penguin, 1988.
Benjamin, Walter. *Illuminations: Essays and Reflections.* New York: Schocken Books, 1968.
Bhabha, Homi. "Articulating the Archaic." In Peter Collier and Helga Geyer-Ryan, eds., *Literary Theory Today.* Ithaca, NY: Cornell University Press, 1990.
Bourget, Paul. "The Limits of Realism in Fiction." *The New Review* 8 (Feb. 1893): 201-205.
Buckler, William E. *Walter Pater: Three Major Texts.* New York: New York University Press, 1986.
Butler, Josephine. "The Ladies' Appeal and Protest Against the Contagious Diseases Acts." In Janet Murray, ed., *Strong Minded Women and Other Lost Voices from Nineteenth Century England.* New York: Pantheon Books, 1982.
Caird, Mona. *The Daughters of Danaus.* 1894. New York: The Feminist Press, 1989.
———. "The Evolution of Compassion." *Westminster Review* 145 (May 1896): 635-643.
———. *The Morality of Marriage and Other Essays on the Status of Women.* London: George Redway, 1897.
Cameron, Laura. "How We Marry." *Contemporary Review* (May 1896): 690-694.
Carlyle, Thomas. *Sartor Resartus: The Life and Opinions of Herr Teufelsdrockh.* Baltimore: R.H. Woodward & Company, 1838.
Cecil, David. *Victorian Novelists: Essays in Revaluation.* Chicago: Chicago University Press, 1965.
Cholmondeley, Mary. *Red Pottage.* 1899. New York: Penguin-Virago Press, 1985.
Cobbe, Frances Power. "Wife Torture in England." In Janet Murray, ed., *Strong Minded Women and Other Lost Voices.* New York: Pantheon Books, 1982.
Cole, Margaret. *The Story of Fabian Socialism.* Stanford, CA: Stanford University Press, 1961.
Colls, Robert. "Englishness and the Political Culture." In Robert Colls and Philip Dodd, eds., *Englishness: Politics and Culture 1880-1920.* London: Croom Helm, 1986.

Corelli, Marie. *A Romance of Two Worlds.* 1886. New York: Garland Publishers, 1976.
———. *Free Opinions, Freely Expressed on Certain Phases of Modern Social Life and Conduct.* London: Archibald Constable, 1905.
Cunningham, A. R. "The 'New Fiction' of the 90s." *Victorian Studies* 17 (1973): 177-186.
Cunningham, Gail. *The New Woman and the Victorian Novel.* New York: Harper & Row, 1978.
DeVere White, Terence, ed. *A Leaf from the Yellow Book: The Correspondence of George Egerton.* London: The Pichards Press, 1958.
Dijkstra, Bram. *Idols of Perversity: Fantasies of Female Evil in Fin-De-Siecle Culture.* New York: Oxford University Press, 1986.
Dodd, Philip. "Englishness and National Culture." In Robert Colls and Philip Dodd, eds., *Englishness: Politics and Culture 1880-1920.* London: Croom Helm, 1986.
Doughan, David. "British Women's Serials." In J. Donn Vann and Rosemary T. Van Arsdel, eds., *Victorian Periodicals: A Guide to Research.* New York: Modern Language Association, 1989.
Eagleton, Terry. *Criticism and Ideology: A Study in Marxist Literary Theory.* London: Verso, 1978.
———. *Literary Theory: An Introduction.* Minneapolis: University of Minnesota Press, 1983.
"Egerton, George" (Mary Chavelitta Dunne). *Keynotes and Discords.* 1893, 1894. London: Modern Virago Classics, 1983.
Engels, Friedrich. *The Condition of the Working Class in England.* 1892. Stanford, CA: Stanford University Press, 1968.
"Ethelmer, Ellis" (Mrs. Wostenholme Elmy). *Woman Free.* London: Women's Emancipation Union, 1893.
———. "A Woman Emancipator: A Biographical Sketch." *The Westminster Review* 145 (May 1896): 424-428.
Felski, Rita. *Beyond Feminist Aesthetics: Feminist Literature and Social Change.* Cambridge, MA: Harvard University Press, 1989.
Feltes, N. N. *Modes of Production of Victorian Novels.* Chicago: University of Chicago Press, 1986.
Fernando, Lloyd. *"New Women" in the Late Victorian Novel.* University Park, PA: Pennsylvania State University, 1977.
Fulford, Roger. *Votes for Women: The Story of a Struggle.* 1909. London: Faber and Faber, 1958.
Gilbert, Sandra, and Susan Gubar. *The Norton Anthology of Women's Literature in English.* New York: Norton, 1986.
Gissing, George. *The Emancipated.* 1890. London: The Hogarth Press, 1985.
———. *New Grubb Street.* 1891. New York: Modern Library, 1985.
———. *The Odd Women.* 1893. New York: Dutton, 1983.
Grand, Sarah. *The Beth Book.* 1897. New York: Dial Press, 1980.
———. *Ideala.* London: E.W. Allen, 1888.
———. "Janey, A Humble Administrator: A Study from Life." *Temple Bar* 93 (Oct. 1891): 199-218.
———. *Heavenly Twins.* London: W. Heinemann, 1893.
Griest, Gueneviere. *Mudie's Circulating Library and the Victorian Novel.* Bloomington: Indiana University Press, 1970.
Grundy, Sydney. *The New Woman.* London: Chiswick Press, 1894.

Hardy, Thomas. "The Science of Fiction." *The New Review* (April 1891): 304-319.
——. *Tess of the Durbevilles*. 1891. New York: Bantam, 1984.
——. *Jude the Obscure*. 1896. Harmondsworth: Penguin, 1982.
Hitchens, Robert S. *The Green Carnation*. London: Unicorn, 1949.
Hobsbawm, Eric. *The Age of Empire: 1875-1914*. New York: Pantheon Books, 1987.
Hogarth, Janet. "The Monstrous Regiment of Women." *Fortnightly Review* 68 (December 1897): 926-936.
Hollis, Patricia. *Women in Public: The Women's Movement, 1850-1900*. London: George Allen & Unwin, 1979.
Homans, Margaret. *Bearing the Word: Language and Female Experience in Nineteenth-Century Women's Writing*. Chicago: University of Chicago Press, 1986.
Huyssen, Andreas. *After the Great Divide: Modernism, Mass Culture, Postmodernism*. Bloomington: Indiana University Press, 1986.
"Ignota." "The Part of Women in Local Administration." *The Westminster Review* 150 (September 1898): 248-260.
Jackson, Holbrook. *The Eighteen Nineties: A Review of Art and Ideas at the Close of the Nineteenth Century*. 1913. Harmondsworth: Penguin Books, 1950.
James, Henry. *The Bostonians*. 1886. Oxford: Oxford University Press, 1985.
——. *"The Aspern Papers"* with *"The Turn of the Screw"*. 1888. New York: Viking Penguin, 1984.
Jameson, Fredric. *Aesthetics and Politics*. London: Verso, 1980.
——. *The Political Unconscious: Narrative as Socially Symbolic Act*. Ithaca, NY: Cornell University Press, 1981.
Jeffries, Sheila. *The Spinster and Her Enemies: Feminism and Sexuality, 1880-1930*. London: Pandora Press, 1985.
Kahler-Marshall, Alice. *Pen Names of Women Writers from 1600 to the Present: A Compendium of the Literary Identities of 2650 Women*. Camp Hill, PA: The Alice Marshall Collection, 1985.
Knox-Little, W. J. "Marriage and Divorce: The Doctrine of the Church of England." *The Contemporary Review* (August 1895): 690-694.
Kristeva, Julia. *Desire in Language*. New York: Columbia University Press, 1980.
Lang, Andrew, ed. *The Pre-Raphaelites and Their Circle,* 2nd ed. Chicago: University of Chicago Press, 1975.
Lee, Alan J. *The Origins of the Popular Press in England, 1855-1914*. London: Croom Helm, 1976.
Lee, Gerard. "The Sex-Conscious School in Fiction." *The New World: A Quarterly Review* (March 1900): 77-84.
"Lee, Vernon." (Viola Piaget) "Of Readers and Writers." *The New Review* 5 (December 1891): 528-536.
——. "The Craft of Words." *The New Review* vol. 11 (December 1894): 528-580.
Levine, Philippa. *Victorian Feminism: 1850-1900*. London: Hutchinson, 1987.
——. *Feminist Lives in Victorian England: Private Roles and Public Commitment*. London: Basil Blackwell, 1990.
Levine, Richard. *The Victorian Experience: The Novelists*. Ohio: Ohio University Press, 1976.
Linton, Eliza Lynn. "The Partisans of the Wild Women." *Nineteenth Century* 31 (March 1892): 455-464.
——. "The Girl of the Period." In Patricia Hollis, *Women in Public: 1850-1900*. London: George Allen & Unwin, 1979.

Lovell, Terry. *Consuming Fiction*. London: Verso, 1987.
Macherey, Pierre. *A Theory of Literary Production*. London: Routledge, 1989.
"Malet, Lucas" (Mary Kingsley). "The Threatened Re-Subjection of Woman." *The Fortnightly Review* (1905): 806-819.
Masters, Brian. *New Barabbas Was a Rotter: The Extraordinary Life of Marie Corelli*. London: Hamish Hamilton, 1978.
Meredith, George. *Diana of the Crossways*. 1885. New York: Modern Library, 1931.
Mix, Katherine Lyon. *A Study in Yellow: The Yellow Book and Its Contributors*. New York: Greenwood Press, 1969.
Moers, Ellen. *The Dandy: Brummell to Beerbohm*. Lincoln: University of Nebraska Press, 1960.
Moore, George. *Literature at Nurse: Or, Circulating Morals*. London: Vizatelli and Company, 1885.
———. "The Dramatic Censorship." *The New Review* 3 (Oct. 1890): 354-362.
———. *Esther Waters*. 1894. London: Oxford University Press, 1964.
Mumby, F. A. *Publishing and Bookselling: A History from the Earliest Times to the Present Day*. London: Cape, 1956.
Murray, Janet. *Strong Minded Women and Other Lost Voices from Nineteenth Century England*. New York: Pantheon Books, 1982.
Noble, James Ashcroft. "The Fiction of Sexuality." *The Contemporary Review* (April 1895):493-4.
"Ouida." "Unwritten Literary Laws." *Fortnightly Review* 66 (December 1899): 803-814.
Oliphant, Margaret. *Hester*. 1884. New York: Penguin-Virago Press, 1984.
———. "The Anti-Marriage League." *Blackwood's* 159 (1896): 135-149.
———. *Autobiography*. 1899. Chicago: University of Chicago Press, 1988.
Pater, Walter. *Appreciations, With an Essay On Style*. 1887. New York: Macmillan and Company, 1908.
Reed, John R. *Decadent Style*. Athens: Ohio University Press, 1985.
Rowbotham, Sheila. *Hidden from History*. London: Pluto Press, 1985.
Rubin, Gayle. "The Traffic in Women: Notes on the 'Political Economy' of Sex." In Karen Hansen and Ilene J. Philipson, eds. *Women, Class and the Feminist Imagination: A Socialist-Feminist Reader*. Philadelphia: Temple University Press, 1990.
Schreiner, Olive. *Story of an African Farm*. 1883. New York: Viking, 1983.
———. *Dream Life and Real Life*. 1893. Chicago: Academy Chicago, 1981.
———. *Woman and Labour*. Leipzig: B. Tauchnitz, 1911.
Seargant, Adeline. "George Meredith's Views of Women—By a Woman." *Temple Bar* (June 1889): 411-425.
Sedgwick, Eve Kosofsky. *Between Men: English Literature and Male Homosocial Desire*. New York: Columbia University Press, 1985.
Showalter, Elaine. *A Literature of Their Own: British Women Novelists from Brontë to Lessing*. Princeton, NJ: Princeton University Press, 1977.
———. *Sexual Anarchy: Gender and Culture at the Fin de Siecle*. New York: Viking, 1990.
Slater, Edith. "Men's Women in Fiction." *Westminster Review* (May 1898): 571-577.
Somerville, Edith and "Martin Ross." *The Real Charlotte*. 1894. New Brunswick, NJ: Rutgers University Press, 1986.
Spender, Dale. *Women of Ideas (And What Men Have Done to Them)*. London: Ark Paperbacks, 1982.

Stead, W. T. "Some Books of the Month: 'The Heavenly Twins." *The Review of Reviews* 7 (1893): 543-547.

———. "The Novel of the Modern Woman." *The Review of Reviews* 10 (1894): 64-74.

Stokes, John. *In the Nineties*. Chicago: University of Chicago Press, 1989.

Stone, David. *Novelists in a Changing World: Meredith, James, and the Transformation of English Fiction in the 1880s*. Cambridge: Cambridge University Press, 1972.

Stonyk, Margaret. *Nineteenth-Century English Literature*. New York: Schocken Books, 1983.

Strachey, Ray. *The Cause: A Short History of the Women's Movement in Great Britain*. London: Virago, 1978.

Stubbs, Patricia. *Women and Fiction: Feminism and the Novel, 1880-1920*. New York: Barnes and Noble, 1979.

Stutfield, Hugh. "The Psychology of Feminism." *Blackwood's Edinburgh Magazine* (January 1897): 104-117.

Sutherland, J. A. *Victorian Novelists and Publishers*. Chicago: University of Chicago Press, 1976.

Symons, Arthur. *The Symbolist Movement in Literature*. 1908. New York: Haskell House Ltd., 1971.

Trail, H. D. *The New Fiction and Other Essays on Literary Subjects*. London: Kennikat Press, 1897.

Tuchman, Barbara W. *The Proud Tower: A Portrait of the World Before the War, 1890-1914*. New York: Macmillan, 1962.

Tuchman, Gaye, and Nina Fortin. *Edging Women Out: Victorian Novelists, Publishers, and Social Change*. New Haven, CT: Yale University Press, 1989.

Ward, Mrs. Humphrey. *Marcella*. 1894. New York: Penguin-Virago, 1984.

———. *Helbeck of Bannisdale*. 1898. Harmondsworth: Penguin Books, 1983.

Wells, H. G. *The Time Machine/The Invisible Man*. 1895. New York: Signet Classics, 1984.

———. *The Outline of History: A Plain History of Life and Mankind*, vol. 2. 1920. New York: Garden City Books, 1961.

White, Cynthia L. *Women's Magazines, 1693-1968*. London: Michael Joseph Ltd., 1970.

Williams, Raymond. *Problems In Materialism and Culture*. London: Verso, 1980.

———. *Culture and Society: 1780-1950*. New York: Columbia University Press, 1983.

Williamson, Judith. "Woman Is An Island." In Tania Modleski, ed., *Studies in Entertainment: Critical Approaches to Mass Culture*. Bloomington, IN.: Indiana University Press, 1986.

Young, G. M. *Victorian England: Portrait of an Age*. New York: Doubleday, 1954.

Index

A
Adelman, Paul, 7, 12, 19
Aesthetes, 2, 24, 29, 34, 36, 39, 44, 48, 53, 78, 81, 82, 101, 103, 128
Aestheticism, ix, xv, xvi, 25, 28, 34, 38, 39, 42, 78, 81, 83, 85, 111, 119, 128, 132n
Althusser, Louis, x, 11
Altick, Richard, 2, 31, 75, 130n
Ardis, Ann, 61, 62, 103, 104, 111, 124
Arnold, Matthew, 25-29, 37, 38, 40, 42, 51, 130n, 131n

B
Baker, Ernest, 2, 65, 88, 129n
Barrett, Michele, xi, xii, xiii, 131n
Beardsley, Aubrey, 28, 39
Beerbohm, Max, 34, 29
Benjamin, Walter, ix, x, 130n
Bhabha, Homi, 71, 105, 108, 126, 129n, 132n

C
Caird, Mona, xiii, xiv, 48, 52, 54, 57, 63, 79–81, 87, 91, 92, 96, 97, 99, 100, 124, 130n
  Daughters of Danaus, 79, 91
  Morality of Marriage, The, 62, 81
Carlyle, Thomas, xv, 4, 25, 37, 40, 44, 72
Cholmondeley, Mary, xiii, 51, 77, 81–84, 87, 90, 91, 96
  Diana Tempest, 50
  Red Pottage, 51, 81, 83, 84, 90, 131n
Circulating Libraries, xiv, 33, 36, 41, 48

Cobbe, Frances Power, 9, 17, 91
Cole, Margaret, 4, 7
Colls, Robert and Philip Dodd, 24, 129n
Colonialism, 4, 5, 42, 129n
Contagious Diseases Acts, 15, 17, 29, 77, 87, 94, 96, 129n
Corelli, Marie (Mary Mackay), 59, 67, 68, 130n, 131n
  Free Opinions, 67
  Romance of Two Worlds, 67
Cunningham, A. R., 62–63
Cunningham, Gail, x, 62, 72, 123

D
Decadence, ix, 2, 24, 39, 49
Dijkstra, Bram, 88, 96, 131n

E
Eagleton, Terry, xi, 24
"Egerton, George" (Mary Chavelitta Dunn), xv, 53, 63, 88, 101–104, 124, 132n
  Discords, 53, 103
  Keynotes, 53, 101, 102
Eliot, George, 69, 84
Engels, Friedrich, 4
  Condition of the Working Class in England, 18
"Ethelmer, Ellis," see Mrs. Wostenholme Elmy

F
Fabian Society, 7, 129
Fawcett, Millicent Garrett, 15, 104

Felski, Rita, 61, 131n
Feltes, N. N., 35, 50, 51, 130n
Fulford, Roger, 16, 129n

G

Gilbert and Gubar, 11, 127
Gissing, George, 110, 118–121, 126, 131n
  The Emancipated, 118
  New Grubb Street, 119, 120, 126
  The Odd Women, 120
"Grand, Sarah" (Frances McFall), xiii, 48, 63, 71, 77, 81, 84–89, 91, 93–95, 100
  The Beth Book, 51, 71, 84, 86, 93, 95, 98
  Heavenly Twins, 51, 77–79
  Ideala, 51, 89, 90, 94, 95, 98
Griest, Gueneviere, 48, 73, 116

H

Hardy, Thomas, 50, 115, 116, 131n
  Jude the Obscure, 123–125
  Tess of the Durbevilles, 115, 123
Hobsbawm, Eric, 2, 3, 5, 8, 10, 13, 20, 21, 66, 82, 129n
Huyssen, Andreas, 12, 21, 38, 103, 114, 130n, 132n

J

Jackson, Holbrook, ix, x, 2, 3, 25, 27, 37, 88, 101, 129n
James, Henry, 35, 110, 127
Jameson, Fredric, xii, 41, 79, 111, 126, 131n

L

Labor Movement, 6–9, 13, 15, 18–21, 50, 54
Lane, John, 53, 102
Lee, Alan J., ix, 30, 32, 130n
Lee, Gerard Stanley, 52–53
"Lee, Vernon" (Viola Piaget), 55–56, 76, 78, 132n
Levine, Philippa, 7, 13, 14, 32, 74, 129n
Linton, Eliza Lynn, 49, 69, 73, 114, 131n, 132n
Lovell, Terri, 27, 41, 66, 72, 103, 110, 129n, 131n

M

Macherey, Pierre, 70, 89, 108–109
Marx, Karl, 4, 13
Meredith, George, xiii, 27, 110, 113, 132n
  Diana of the Crossways, 121–123
Moore, George, xiii, 27, 41, 42, 56, 58, 72, 86, 103, 107, 110, 113–118, 121, 127
  Esther Waters, 107, 113, 114, 116–118
  Literature at Nurse, Or Circulating Morals, 41, 56
Mudie, Charles, xiv, 33, 36, 41, 42, 48, 51, 78, 116, 132n
Murray, Janet, 16, 17, 129n

N

New Journalism, xiv, 29–31, 33, 35, 48, 50, 56, 58, 101, 130n
New Woman, xiv, xvi, 13, 15, 34, 52, 62–64, 66–67, 88–90, 95, 97, 104, 107–109, 112–114, 118, 120, 121, 123–125
Noble, James Ashcroft, 52, 78

O

Oliphant, Margaret, 51, 59, 64–65, 74, 92, 93, 131n, 132n
  Autobiography, 64, 65
  Hester, 65, 74, 92, 93

P

Pater, Walter, xv, 25, 36–38, 40, 42, 43, 72, 76, 111, 131n, 132n
  Appreciations, 37, 40
Philanthropy, 6, 7, 16, 91, 92, 94

R

Realism, xii, xvi, 2, 27, 29, 33, 45, 59, 62, 88, 107, 108–113, 115, 116, 122, 126–128, 129n, 132n
Rossetti, Christina, 44, 130n
Rossetti, Gabriel Dante, 44, 83
Rowbotham, Sheila, 4, 13, 129n
Rubin, Gayle, 44, 100, 132n
Ruskin, John, xv, 4, 25, 36, 37, 40, 44, 72, 116, 125

S

Salisbury, Lord, xiii, 4, 5, 21, 49
Sedgwick, Eve K., 29, 44
Schreiner, Olive, xiii, 17, 43, 48, 50, 53–54, 60, 61, 62, 99
Seargant, Adeline, 121, 123
Showalter, Elaine, x, 59, 62, 63, 93, 105, 131n
Slater, Edith, 115, 121
Social Darwinism, 6, 22, 96, 97, 129n, 131n
Socialism, 6, 8, 10, 18, 19, 21, 24, 30, 79
Stokes, John, 31, 35
Stone, Donald, 1, 6
Strachey, Ray, 16, 21
Stubbs, Patricia, x, 73, 74, 103, 120
Stutfield, Hugh, 62, 67, 73
Suffrage, 66, 67, 129n
Symons, Arthur, 23, 39, 40, 103, 128

T

Tuchman and Fortin, 4, 5, 13, 62, 64, 65, 70, 76, 110–112, 129n, 131n

W

Ward, Mrs. Humphrey, 59, 66, 69, 73, 116
    Marcella, 66, 69
Wells, H. G., 11, 34, 127
Wilde, Oscar, 28, 29, 34, 39
Williams, Raymond, 6, 22, 129n
Williamson, Judith, 5, 6, 10, 39, 43
Women's Emancipation Union, 56–58
Wostenholme Elmy, Mrs., 47, 52, 57
    Woman Free, 47, 56–58, 62

Y

Yellow Book, The, 66, 103
Young, G. M., 25, 129n
"Young Girl Standard," xiv, 33, 36